Helen Bailey

knowing me
knowing you

h

Hodder
Children's
Books

A division of Hachette Children's Books

Typeset in Berkeley by Avon DataSet Ltd,
Bidford-on-Avon, Warwickshire

Printed and bound by CPI Group (UK) Ltd, Croydon, CR0 4YY

The paper and board used in this paperback by Hodder Children's Books
are natural reyclable products made from wood grown in
sustainable forests. The manufacturing processes conform to the
environmental regulations of the country of origin.

Hodder Children's Books
a division of Hachette Children's Books
338 Euston Road, London NW1 3BH
An Hachette UK company
www.hachette.co.uk

For Hat and Classy Pam:

friends who I met on the Net, with love and thanks

Sometimes the idea for a book begins with a character, as it did with Electra Brown, and other books are inspired by an event, such as the fraud trial in *Running in Heels*.

Knowing Me, Knowing You began when I noticed a teenage girl hanging around a bandstand in a seaside town in East Kent one summer. She was wearing a black net tutu, a pair of red Converse trainers, black knee-high socks and a silver jacket. As I watched her holding hands with one of the skater boys while the others practised their flips and spins, she looked bored and sullen, but there was an air of vulnerability about her, as if there was some deep sadness in her life. From the moment I saw her, I knew I *had* to write about her.

The girl at the bandstand with the lanky skateboarding boyfriend became Channy Allen in *Knowing Me, Knowing You*, a girl who in trying to find out who she is and where she fits in, puts herself in terrible danger.

I have become very fond of Channy. I hope you will take her and her story to your hearts, too.

With love,

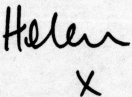

Chapter One

The shock wasn't that Aunty Julie was getting married again – after all, she made a habit of it – or even that after three divorces from unsuitable foreign men she'd decided to *bat for the other team* as Mum put it, and marry Rosemary Bunyan, the slightly odd woman who runs the local garden centre and breeds championship pugs. No, surprise numero uno was that having chosen Turkey (Omar), Greece (Giorgos), and the Elvis Chapel in Las Vegas (a nightclub singer called Bud who turned out to already have a wife, four children and a criminal record in Texas) for her previously unsuccessful marital unions, Aunty J decided to break with the holiday romance theme and hold her fourth wedding in a dreary registry office on the East Kent coast in front of about a hundred family and close friends. But the unusual choice of venue was eclipsed by the second and biggest wedding-related shock: Aunty Julie chose *moi* to be her bridesmaid.

I've never been a bridesmaid. At one point when my cousins on my dad's side seemed to be forever pouring themselves into candy-coloured dresses and smiling sweetly for the camera, I even began to suspect I was being bridesmaid blacklisted.

Other than yours truly, all the Allen girls are blonde, leggy beauties; glossy foxes with delicate features and skin that turns golden at the mere hint of a good spray tan, whereas my hair (according to the box) is Smashed Plum, I'm squat, pale-skinned and have a *seriously* flat nose. I honestly look as if the moment I was born someone took one look at me and either punched me in the face, or tried to stuff me back in. So not a good look in bridal photos.

Anyway, as a kid, not being a bridesmaid became a bit of a thing for me, and clearly Aunty J had remembered my childish sobs of disappointment when she returned home with sunburn, a bag of Duty Free booze, and yet another dodgy husband. But probably because she's been too busy getting married and divorced, my mother's only and older sister obviously forgot how old I am. Carrying a basket of flowers whilst dressed in billowing layers of neon pink satin and scratchy white lace, my naturally straight shoulder-length hair curled into ringlets, piled on to my head with sixty-eight hair grips and topped with a sparkly plastic tiara is something I craved when I was five, ten at the most. But looking like a raspberry gateau is no fun at fifteen-years one-month and four-days old, and instead of carrying a basket of sweet-smelling blooms, I'm holding two wheezing black pugs, straining on their diamante leads.

These are the bridesdogs: Puglicious Kylie and Puglicious Dannii, two of Ros's favourite hounds, dressed up in outfits identical to mine, only designed to make going to the loo easier, as demonstrated by Kylie who squatted just as the official said: *Please sit* in the registry office. When the bridal procession moved away I was relieved to see there wasn't a wet patch on the red carpet, probably because as I discovered in the car on the way to the reception (a silver stretch Hummer complete with pink and white ribbons; I nearly died when I saw it), my white petticoat had been turned into an enormous piece of kitchen roll, sucking up the pee and staining the lace trim bright yellow.

It's The Frocky Horror Show on so many levels.

I glance down at the dogs in their pink and white frills, a couple of flat bug-eyed faces looking up at me beneath their sooty black ears, and realize with horror that I'm the spitting image of a pug in a party dress.

I've set up camp right by the buffet table, leaning against it as though I'm guarding the platters of pastry-wrapped snacks with my life.

I'm leaning because I daren't sit down. Moments ago, exhausted from standing upright for more than an hour, my back breaking under the weight of hairspray and tiara, the pins in my up-do viciously stabbing my scalp, I attempted to lower my shiny satin-covered butt on to a gold plastic chair.

Bad move.

I shot straight off the seat like a scud missile, landing on the carpet in an undignified heap, pugs licking zit cover-up off a particularly vicious crop of chin spots. Dog breath and naked zits were bad enough, but my accident revealed to Mum that I wasn't wearing the crystal-encrusted high-heeled silver sandals she'd bought me, plumping instead for my favourite pair of battered red Converse Hi-Tops, something that didn't go down well and was accompanied by threats that I'd have to pay for the metallic trotters out of my own money. I don't know what Mum's worrying about: you can't see my feet, though as the sneakers are three inches lower than the sandals, to avoid tripping over the hem of the dress I've had to march up and down the aisle with ramrod-straight legs. I'll look as if I'm impersonating a Nazi solider in the wedding video.

'I need a drink,' I snap at Crab. He's beside me, filling his mouth with mini Scotch eggs. He's got a five-pound bet with my dad that he can't fit twenty in at once. 'See if you can get a rum and coke. Flash someone else's ID if you have to.' I bark this as an order, *not* a suggestion.

Crab stares at me, his cheeks puffed out like some crazed hamster. Then he holds out a single orange orb, forces it into his bulging gob and then punches the air, spitting Scotch eggs back on to the plate as if they're balls in a pinball machine.

'Back of the net!' he yells, wiping his mouth with the back of his hand. 'Get in! Pay up, Trevor Allen!'

'Er, a drink?' I remind him.

'It's a cash bar,' Crab points out. 'It's not free.'

'So pay!'

Crab dutifully scuttles off.

I shouldn't really have a drink, given how long it took me to go to the loo last time. The cubicle was so full of dress, despite furious rummaging in the appropriate area it took me ages to find my knickers, and *then* I had to ask some stranger in a pale pink suit to stand guard outside the door because it wouldn't lock. But I'm in a *seriously* bad mood. It didn't help when Crab saw me in my horror-frock and said I reminded him of the bog-roll cover in his nan's loo; Crab's nan is a *seriously* chavy coffin-dodger, the sort of woman who's always pestering people in the street for fags, even picking up half-smoked ones thrown down outside the entrance to Lidl.

Anyway, Crab can talk about fashion fiascos, the lad who's wearing an Arsenal football shirt to a wedding! I mean, I know I've bent the rules with my footwear, but at least no one can see them unless I hitch my skirt up, and even if they do, these Hi-Tops are classics. But a replica strip! I've seen footballer and WAG wedding pictures in *Hello!* Even Premier League footballers don't wear footie shirts to weddings, not that a seventies karaoke disco and cold buffet on a Saturday night in the Seashell Suite at The Pavilion-on-the-Sands function rooms in Broadgate-on Sea is likely to feature in a gossip magazine, but still. To be fair, Crab was at the ceremony in a proper white shirt, and even a black tie borrowed from his dad, but once he got to the reception, he peeled them off, revealing the chav-wear underneath. And because he's got his nickname plastered across his shoulders, he's spent most of the time explaining the name Crab Stix came about because he fell asleep on the beach as a kid and got sunburnt on one side of his body, whilst remaining lily-white on the other.

I didn't invite Crab, Mum did. I'd rather have brought best friend Taryn as my plus one, but Mum being *completely* out of touch with the state of my love life just sort of assumed that Crab would be coming, and then he just sort of assumed he was coming, and then Mum met Crab's Mum in Tesco Extra and Mrs Snittersley mentioned that she'd bought Crab new grey trousers for the wedding from a place online that specializes in clothes for skinny giants, but even then she'd had to turn down the hems, so by then it was too late, because as Mum pointed out, you can't send back trousers that have already been altered.

I watch as Crab patiently waits at the back of the crowd at the bar, towering over the other guests, his spotty neck bent forward. He's got short bright-yellow hair and a sort of square head, like a giant pineapple chunk perched on a cocktail stick.

It's a bit sad really. The things that I used to love about him: his dodgy nickname; his height; his unusual hair; his encyclopaedic knowledge of Abba lyrics which *totally* impressed my parents – all now irritate me to death. Why did I ever fancy him in the first place? Actually, amazing as it is to believe now, once, I really *really* fancied Crab. It was during my skater-rat groupie phase when I used to hang around the bandstand and watch lads like Snorbs, Tubs and Bucket perfect their skateboard moves, even though a sign warned them that they'd be prosecuted for skateboarding, something that added to the excitement. Out of all the skate-rats, Crab was the best at flips and spins, putting together really complicated routines, hardly ever falling off, everyone clapping in admiration at his silky skills. Then we started going out, and he spent more time with me than his skateboard; when he tried to do a simple kickflip a few weeks ago, he fell off, burst into tears, and ended up in A&E with a badly bruised hip.

Not cool.

So, the thought of school breaking up next month and him hanging around me like some lanky parasite for the entire summer holidays is horrific. I really don't know if I can stand it. Taryn is trekking around Patagonia because her dad is writing a textbook on South American glacier formation, so during my holiday on Planet Boredom I'll either be home alone, out alone, home with Crab or out with Crab. It's enough to make me try to slash my wrists with the tiara.

If only I could be like everyone else and go away, preferably for the whole six weeks. Perhaps I could just clear out my savings account, grab my passport from the kitchen drawer, pack a rucksack (which I'd have to buy) and disappear to somewhere exotic, like Peru. I doubt Mum and Dad would even notice I'd gone. Summer is a busy time for them, what with weddings and festivals and summer fêtes. They'd probably just think I was asleep, or reading, or roaming the streets looking for skateboarders to date. I'd arrive for breakfast in my school uniform on the first day of term in September and they'd look up from their Coco Pops and say, *Oh! Hi Channy! Ready for school?* having absolutely no idea that I've been hanging out with Incas and alpacas, rather than down the seafront watching boys tombstoning from the pier in their undercrackers.

I seriously consider my Peru plan, then remember that my cash situation is dire because of several major purchases (new iPod, ticket to a music festival, straw Stetson bought to wear to said festival), and wonder whether disappearing to Dover on the bus for six weeks would be more exciting than staying here.

I grab two sausage rolls from the buffet table, ram both into my mouth and am just leaning over pile of mushroom vol-au-vents for a lamb samosa when—

'Oh. My. God! Don't you look super gorge?'

I'm not sure whether it's Stacie Allen or Tracie Allen squealing in a high-pitched *I've just snorted helium* voice. My cousins are such identical twins, they claim they've even gone on dates with the same boy and he never noticed. Either he was a lame brain, or their snogging styles are identical too. I wish they'd at least wear different coloured watches or have a prominent birthmark, just to help me tell them apart.

'Soooo cute!'

'Thanks.' I take one look at the twins' perfectly flat tums and lob the samosa at the pugs, who leap on it with doggy delight. 'I'd have preferred something in black.'

'Oh, Channy, you are *so* funny,' unidentified Twin One giggles. 'I meant those two.' She points at the pugs. '*You* look like a gothy Little Bo Peep, but with dogs, not sheep.'

Goth! How *dare* she? My preferred look is Kentish boho rocker! I could kick her, whoever she is, but I'm consoled when she pops a Scotch egg in her mouth, oblivious to the fact that it's laced with a light drizzle of Crab's saliva.

Twin One bends down and starts fussing over the dogs, who, having devoured the curried triangle in record time, jump up and lick her face which is Clearasil clear of spots, and therefore in no danger of having heavy-duty spackle dislodged by grainy canine tongues.

'They look as if their heads have been run over,'

10

Twin Two says, her pert nose wrinkling in disgust. 'Like twitchy roadkill.'

'Trace!' Stace gasps, thereby solving the riddle of who is who, but only as long as they don't move. 'That's gross.' She looks up at her twin. 'Shall we ask Mum for a dog? Something cute that will fit in a handbag?'

If I am an ugly pug, my slightly younger cousins are definitely a pair of privately-educated glamorous salukis, real-life Barbie dolls wearing matching fuchsia-pink strappy dresses, Tiffany silver charm bracelets, and shed-loads of mascara and lip-gloss.

I've always been jealous of them, not because I want to look plastic fantastic or talk in that silly gas-snort voice, but because, like Taryn and her sisters Seren and Carys, Stacie and Tracie have each other. Despite scraps over make-up, boyfriends, and who's the best looking in *Twilight*, they're great friends.

I'd have loved a sister. When I was a kid, I wanted a sister so much I had an imaginary one: Donna. Donna went everywhere (except the loo) with me, and there were major tantrums if anyone inadvertently squashed Donna by sitting on a chair which *appeared* to be empty, but which I knew Donna was using, or if the parentals thoughtlessly failed to set a place for Donna at tea. In the end, Mum and Dad got so fed up of Donna they

11

pretended they'd sent her to stage school in London, and because she was having such a great time (without me!) she never came back, even for holidays. I was heartbroken. To be rejected by an imaginary sister felt very real at the time.

So now Donna's gone I'm an only child, and with Mum and Dad often out, if Taryn or Crab aren't around, I'm usually home alone.

I used to be sent to a variety of childminders, until I complained I was fed up of trying to do my homework surrounded by kids singing Igglepiggle songs and trying to stuff Stickle Bricks up my nose. *It was putting me off my homework* I said. *It was harming my chances of decent GCSEs*. Faced with my possible educational meltdown, when I was thirteen, Mum and Dad agreed that I could be left home alone, on the proviso that I didn't have any wild parties involving drugs, alcohol and rampant teenage boys, and that I wouldn't answer the door to strangers, even ones from the gas board who poked their ID through the letterbox.

At first, after the chaos of the childminder's, it was fabulous to have the house to myself. I felt incredibly grown up doing my homework, ordering a takeaway, and then lounging on the sofa watching soaps or reading. And then when I started going out with boys they'd come round and we'd eat takeaways and snog, though I usually kept my eyes open so I could watch the soaps or read behind their back at the same time.

But after two years of being home alone I don't feel grown up, just fed up. There's no one to talk to about what's on telly or what I've just read. I'm bored with microwaveable meals for one, and I'm fed up of ordering takeaways. Trust me, being home alone stinks, but if I tell the parentals how I feel, they'll ship me back to the land of songs and Stickle Bricks. It's a no win situation.

I haven't even got a pet since Twiggy, my stick insect, fell off her branch and died. I can't say Twigs and me ever had deep conversations about the meaning of life or literature, and to be honest, *she* could have been a *he* because I never really bothered looking, but at least Twigs was something to talk to. Perhaps I should get a new pet, not a stick insect, but maybe a rat. That's it! I'll get a pet rat, a black one.

'I'm getting a pet,' I say, briefly cheered by my loneliness-busting plan. 'A black rat called Kurt, after Kurt Cobain.'

'You are *well* weird, Channy,' Stacie says, pulling a face. 'You know that, don't you?'

'It's been said before,' I say drily.

'Smile!' Tracie orders, pointing her moby towards me

13

and taking a picture.

I don't smile, I scowl, my natural reflex when I'm anywhere near a camera.

'Was the plakky thingy your idea, Channy?' Tracie trills, fiddling with her phone. 'It's very you.'

What the *hell* is she on about?

'The black flower in your boob crack,' Stacie explains, pointing a French nail at my cleavage.

I look down to see a mass of black plastic spewing from my boobs, as if they've turned into a couple of erupting volcanoes, lava spewing over the satin ruffle.

Bridesmaid dresses don't have pockets, and as no one thought to make me a little bag I could swing from my wrist, I had to stuff the pugs' pooper-scooper bags somewhere. Rushing to get into the stretch Hummer, my chest seemed as good a storage place as anywhere.

OMG! Did I walk down the aisle with doggy-bag boobage? There was a lot of rustling, but I thought it was the dress. Can today get any worse?

'I've just Facebooked some wedding snaps and tagged you,' Cousin T says, as I ram the escaping bags back down.

Clearly, it can. A photo on Facebook means half of East Kent's teenagers will see me looking a total nerdette, holding a couple of mutts, whilst sporting poo bags as an accessory. And since when was wearing plastic bags *very me*? I'll kill Crab for not telling me my chest was exploding.

'How many friends have you on Facebook?' Tracie asks me.

'Um, I dunno,' I shrug, knowing that I only have a paltry fifty-four. I refuse to be 'friends' with anyone I don't actually know, so my friend list is made up of people in my class, a few of Crab's skateboarding mates and my cousins. I'd like to lie and say five hundred, but one of the twins might look me up and expose me as a Facebook fraud. 'Enough.'

Cousin T is still fiddling with her phone. 'I've got . . . yay!' She jumps up and down with excitement, flapping her arms and squealing like a hungry seal. 'Paige Preston has friended me; I've got one thousand and fourteen!'

'No!' Stacie looks miffed. 'You cow! I'm still on one thousand and thirteen. I'll never get to two thousand by Christmas at this rate.' Her pale brows knit together. 'Who the heck is Paige Preston anyway?'

'No idea,' her sister shrugs, tossing her buttery blonde locks over her skinny shoulders. 'She just came up as a friend suggestion so I clicked her.'

Crab arrives holding the drinks. 'Just Coke,' he moans. 'No rum.'

'Why didn't you tell me I had poo bags in my boobs?' I hiss at him. 'I looked a freak!'

'I thought you'd stuffed them down there to make your baps look bigger.' He shrugs. 'You've done it before.'

During one of our early sofa and snogging sessions, Crab made a daring (and unwanted) assault on the contents of my bra, resulting in a handful of Superdrug cotton wool rounds and a slapped face. I've never lived the padding episode down, and he's never let me forget it.

'Crab,' Stacie says coyly. 'Can we be Facebook friends?'

Crab looks as if he might drop the drinks with delight.

Stacie's profile picture is rather racy for a not-quite fifteen-year-old: she could easily pass for eighteen, wearing that silver bikini and those high heels, and clearly Crab being friends with a girl who looks straight out of *Nuts* magazine would go down well with his mates. I'm not sporting a bikini in my profile picture; I'm wearing a book burqa, a copy of Jane Austen's *Pride and Prejudice* held in front of my face, just my heavily black-lined peepers showing above the cover. It's meant to signify that I am mysterious, intelligent *and* sexy, though the latter might not be quite so obvious if I removed the book to reveal my pale spotty pug-face.

'God, yeah!' Crab says, his tongue practically hanging

out. 'That would be, like, awesome.'

'Are you down as Crab Stix or your proper name?' my cousin asks, her fingers poised over her phone. 'What is your proper name?'

'I'm down as Gordon Snittersley,' Crab says. 'Mum said I had to use my real name so as not to attract freaks and weirdoes. She says I'm already a weirdo magnet.'

He grins at me, and just to underline the point he's calling me a weirdo, nudges me in the ribs.

It's impossible; Crab and I are *totally* incompatible. I spend days searching charity shops and jumble sales for interesting vintage clothing and read books about tormented minds. He wears football shirts and reads *Nuts*.

Poor Crab. He doesn't know it yet, but he's heading rapidly towards Dumpsville.

Chapter Two

'Speech! Speech!' the crowd yells out, as Aunty Nicola (dressed in a white wedding meringue and looking like a galleon in full sail) and New Aunty Ros (a small skinny dark-haired woman in a shiny grey suit and pink tie) climb hand-in-hand on to the small stage at one end of the room. I say stage, someone has bolted together a selection of wooden crates, so it's more of a small rickety plinth with a few fairy lights strung along the front, the sort Aunty Nicola and Uncle Kevin have around their home bar, a corner unit in the living room complete with full-sized drinks optics, beer mats and a giant whisky bottle containing twenty pence pieces which will be donated to the local hospice when it's full. Uncle Trevor (who made his money from fitting double glazing and conservatories) even rings a bell and calls out: 'Time!' when he wants people to go home.

'I'm not one for speeches,' New Aunty Ros mumbles into a microphone, 'but I'd just like to thank everyone for coming today, for witnessing Jules and me getting married!'

'It's a civil partnership, not a wedding,' a woman next to me in a blue flower-sprigged tent hisses under her breath, as she piles bite-sized pork pies on to a paper plate. 'It's against the laws of nature.'

I'm jostled as people abandon the buffet table to get a closer look at the newlyweds standing beneath a gold and white banner proclaiming: *Mrs* ♥ *Mrs*.

As good as her word, New Aunty Ros decides not to say anything else, and hands a beaming Aunty Julie the microphone.

'I'd just like to say that Ros has made me the happiest woman in the world today.' Aunty J smiles at Ros, who flushes crimson. 'Just think, I went to the garden centre for Busy Lizzies, and came away with a wife and a new life!'

The crowd laughs.

The dogs bark.

I want to gag.

'Thanks also to my lovely niece Chantelle for not only being a beautiful bridesmaid,' Aunty J continues, 'but for looking after Kylie and Dannii. A big round of applause for our Hound Handmaiden! Channy, where are you?'

They can't miss me: Crab is helpfully pointing me out. The crowd clap and whoop. My face burns. I start to stress that a red face and neck next to a pink strapless dress will make me look like one humungous throbbing zit. Various people slap me on the back and nudge me in the sides whilst Aunty Julie runs through a list of others she has to thank, everyone from Michelle the hairdresser who blow-dried her dark bob and touched up her grey roots, to the woman in the bakery who gave Ros a deal on the cupcake tower in exchange for ten bags of rotted chicken-manure compost.

'But I know it's not just me and Ros you want to see!' Aunty Julie shrieks. 'Tonight they could have played Folkestone! They could have played Gravesend! But they didn't, because they're here, at our wedding, please welcome Kent's premier Abba tribute band featuring my sister, Sandy, and my brother-in-law, Trevor: Bjorn At The Beach!'

From under the safety of my side-fringe, I glance around the room. Clearly I'm the only person who isn't practically passing out with hysteria as two men and two women bound on to the stage to the opening bars of *Dancing Queen*. The women are wearing teeny-weeny white silk dresses and silver thigh-high platform boots, the men matching sparkly catsuits, which as well as being slashed to the waist, leave nothing, and I mean *nothing*, to the imagination in the family tackle department.

'*Oh Ooh! You can dance,*' the blonde and the red-haired woman belt out, whilst a weedy looking man with a fringe strums an electric guitar and the other, sporting a beard and longish hair, whacks the hell out of a keyboard.

I'm dying from embarrassment, not because Aunty Julie and New Aunty Ros are right now doing their first dance, shaking their butts and their boobs, Aunty J practically dislocating New Aunty R's shoulder as she hurls her around the floor, but because two of the silk and sequin-clad figures on the stage are my mum and dad.

Yes, whereas Taryn's father, Dr Dermot Griffiths PhD, is an internationally renowned geologist, and her mum, Pippa, is a Ceramic Artist famed for her biologically realistic sculptures of naked people, my parents make their living by pretending to be one half of Seventies super-group Abba, the other half being a couple called Sue and Bob Myers who Mum and Dad knew at school.

It's Dad's group and he's Benny, the sandy-haired beardy-weirdy on the keyboard, so really they should be called Benny At The Beach, but everyone agreed that sounded more like one of the children's entertainers on Broadgate sands every summer than a Swedish rock act. Mum plays Frida, the dark-haired one; Sue is Agnetha, the blonde with the big bum, and Sue's hubby, Bob, is Bjorn, all weak-chinned and pudding-bowl haircut.

'I don't suppose you want to dance?' Crab asks.

'Too right I don't,' I sneer.

He knows I don't dance to this type of music, or any music if there are others around. I'm not the dancing in public type, though I will admit to doing a particularly fantastic Lady Gaga-esque Poker Face strut in the privacy of my own room.

'You go.'

I was sure that Crab would hear the undertone of *Don't you dare leave me* in my voice, but if he does, he ignores it, and launches himself on to the dance floor, leaving me stranded with the dogs who are yip-yapping along to the music.

You can dance! You can jive! Having the time of your life!

Not me, I think bleakly, grabbing a handful of crisps and stuffing them in my mouth, cheese and onion crumbs spattering my cleavage. Seeing other people having a good time always makes me gut-wrenchingly miserable, even when I'm not impersonating a loo-roll cover.

Stacie and Tracie are dancing with their dad; Aunty Nicola is dancing with Crab who's not really dancing, just scuttling from left to right and back again, waving his pincers in the air; Nana Allen is flinging herself around, probably not a good idea only a month after she had her left hip replaced after breaking it jet skiing at Palm Bay. At the front of the stage, a group of small children dressed in their best clothes are bopping along, becoming ridiculously hysterical, a state of over-excitement that can only end in tears and tantrums.

I feel the corners of my eyes sting with tears, as a wave of desolation engulfs me.

With or without the shocking frock, I find family gatherings excruciating.

My relatives are always the first up to dance or do karaoke, or to suggest charades, whereas I would rather die than go through that whole: *It's a book! It's a film! It's a play!* routine.

Watching them together on the dance floor, singing, bumping bums and waving arms, they all seem to fit together like a jigsaw, whereas I feel the odd piece, the bit people turn over and over again, looking at it from all angles thinking: *Now where does this fit in?* before they put it to one side and conclude that it must be from a totally different puzzle.

They used to try to include me, drag me to the floor and force me to sing YMCA complete with hand movements. *Once you're up, you'll enjoy it!* they'd promise.

But I never did.

I hated it.

And now they don't bother to include me, which I thought would be fine, but isn't, because it just underlines what a lonely misfit I always feel.

I wish I'd stuffed a book in my knickers so I could slope off and read it. I *love* books; teen-lit, chick-lit, classic-lit, even at a pinch, sh*t-lit, you name it, I'll read it.

If *only* Pippa and Dermot would adopt me, I could live in Taryn's rambling old house in Granston Avenue and spend all day reading.

Granston Avenue is one side of the Broadgate roundabout, the side with elegant houses slotted alongside chocolate-box pretty cottages and tiny winding streets. Our house, Number Seven Lea Crescent, is on the other side of the Broadgate roundabout, the side with Asda and the KFC drive-thru, full of estates made up of clutches of identical, bland, semi-detached boxes built by the same developer. Forget about coming from the wrong side of the tracks; I come from the wrong side of the roundabout.

At Taryn's, room after room is stuffed with bookcases: paperbacks and hardbacks rammed one against the other on the shelves, books pushed in wherever there's a space. At ours, other than in my bedroom, the one bookcase in the living room is full of DVD's. It's the same at Stacie and Tracie's place, except all their DVDs are stored in boxes which are meant to look like leather bound books, a totally weird concept as you think you're picking up Charles Dickens' *Great Expectations*, and find yourself clutching a copy of the director's cut of *Gladiator*.

Next to me, a big girl with a dark bob, more of a pit bull in thick glasses than a pug in frills, nudges me in the ribs just as I'm about to put a cupcake in my mouth, sending vanilla icing and rainbow sprinkles up my nose.

It's Slow Jo, a distant relation on Mum's side, and a total Fruit Loop. She must be pushing forty, but she's dressed in a weird little girl/grandma hybrid get-up of a brown tweed skirt and cream twinset, sparkly hair accessories, pink T-bar shoes and frilly white ankle socks.

'It must be great having famous parents like yours,' she shouts above the noise, swaying and bumping her hips with my hips. 'Like, every day must be a *Mamma*

Mia day for you!'

I glare at her as I pick buttercream out of my nostrils.

'Do they sing all the time at home?' Slow Jo yells. 'Do they just burst into song over breakfast? Is it like, *The Winner Takes it All* when you play Boggle?'

'Nutter,' I mutter, wondering when we last played anything as a family.

'It must be great having Benny as your dad!' Slow Jo gushes as Dad/Benny gives the keyboard another battering. 'I like Benny the best.' She gives a coy smile. 'I'd marry him if he wasn't married to the other lady.'

Oh, this is just great! A minging frock, snorting dogs, and now I'm stuck with the only mentalist at the party.

'Why don't you go and dance?' I suggest. 'You know, go down the front and see Benny close up.'

'My doctor says I'm not to get too excited,' Slow Jo says seriously.

Despite trying to ignore her, Slow Jo keeps trying to talk to me about Benny. Every time I move away from her mega hips, dragging the poor pugs with me, she shuffles towards us, clearly having zero idea of the concept of personal space.

'Do you speak the Sweden language at home?' she yells in my ear as the group start to sing *Chiquitita*. I feel her spit splatter my cheek. ''Cos your dad's from Sweden?'

26

'You do know that Benny isn't really my dad, don't you?' I yell back, somewhat more cruelly than I intended. 'I'm not really related to Benny.'

Slow Jo's pudgy face, a moment ago full of smiles and adoration, crumples.

'The man on the stage in the porno-catsuit? He's nothing to do with me,' I add, putting the knife into Slow Jo's fantasy of being distantly related to a Swedish billionaire popstar. 'He's not my real dad.'

'No?' Slow Jo's bottom lip quivers as she stares at Dad/Benny who's now headbanging over his keyboard.

'Er, like no!' I say sarcastically. 'I thought everyone knew that!'

Kylie starts sniffing Dannii's bottom, and I start freaking that the spicy samosa I gave them earlier will have me reaching for the poo bags inside the Seashell Suite.

Time to go.

Chapter Three

I stand in the street outside The Pavilion as Kylie and Danni do a lot of sniffing and squatting, but thankfully nothing more solid.

A group of lads saunter by. Judging by the smell of their aftershave and the look of their new shirts and over-gelled hair, they're out on a Saturday night pulling spree. When they see me, they shriek and nudge each other.

'Oi! Bo Peep! You got a licence to drive that dress?' one of them yells.

I flick him the finger, and they all shout, 'Ooooh!' and collapse with sneery laughter.

Years of being desperate to be a bridesmaid, and now that I am one, it stinks. And on top of my usual feelings of being a party misfit, of feeling different to everyone else and being irritated by Crab, I feel ashamed that I

28

snapped at Slow Jo. As I left with the dogs, she rushed past me towards the toilets in floods of tears carrying an entire plate of cupcakes. I shouldn't have been so mean to her. I should have let her have her little fantasy that Abba really are playing in Broadgate tonight. She's probably right now sobbing in the bogs, binging on carbs and stabbing a sparkly hair slide into her thighs. It could put her therapy programme back years.

I turn the corner and drag the dogs along the esplanade until I find a bench to plonk myself on. I'm under a streetlight, thereby attracting attention to my pink monstrosity, and I've probably sat in seagull poop, but I don't care. When I get home, I'm going to dump this minging dress and stuff it under my bed to rot. It's not like I'm ever going to need it again, though when Mum, Aunty Julie and I went for the final fitting in Miss Haversham's Bridal Boutique, there was lots of talk of being able to shorten it to use again for *summer balls and parties*. Yeah. Right. Like, even if I went to those sorts of dos I'd wear this crazy thing, butchered or not.

'There you are!'

Crab's found me.

'What are you doing out here?'

He sits next to me and puts an arm around my bare shoulders.

'I took the dogs out,' I say, looking out to sea where lights from ships in the English Channel are twinkling in the dark. On a clear day, you can actually see the French coast. Sometimes it looks so close I feel I could almost swim across to France, not that I want to. Taryn's mum says they flush the toilets from the ferries straight into the sea. 'They needed a pee.'

Crab lifts one buttock off the seat and fiddles around in his trouser pocket. 'This'll cheer you up,' he says. 'I was keeping it for later, but if you want it . . .'

He unfurls a pink napkin and offers me a flattened sausage roll.

Just because he's brought me a squashed meat snack, doesn't change how I feel deep down.

'Crab,' I say gently. 'I'm really sorry, but I think we should break up.'

'OK,' he shrugs, picking up the sausage roll and eating it.

'Is that all you have to say?' I gasp, watching the crumbs fall from his mouth and land on his new trousers. 'I've just broken up with you and all you can say is, *OK*, and stuff your chops?'

Crab licks his lips. 'Well, it's not like you meant it,' he says. 'This is the . . .' he counts on his greasy fingers, 'eleventh time we've broken up since we started going out, and the third this month. We'll be back together by school on Monday. We always are.'

It's true. In the eight months since Crab and I have been seeing each other we've always been breaking up and making up, because however much he annoys me, underneath he is still the same Skateboarding Stud who was so fanciable I wrote *Crab 4 Channy 4 Ever* up my left arm and all over both thighs in indelible black marker pen. So then we make up again, which involves lots of snogging and him buying me chocolate. But this time feels different, though I admit I've never binned him whilst dressed as Little Bo Peep.

'Breaking up is never easy I know, but this time we're through,' I say.

'Knowing Me Knowing You, Ah Hah,' Crab chants back. Sometimes I think he only asked me out because, like Slow Jo, he's a bit of a Bjorn At The Beach groupie.

'Crab!' I yell. 'I mean it, this time we really are through!'

Damn! I'd meant to remain calm and composed, not get all stroppy and start reciting Abba lyrics.

'Have you got PMT?' Crab asks. 'Are you due on? Maybe that's why you're so crabby. Get it? Crab, crabby.'

He guffaws, and for about the millionth time today I'm nudged in the ribs.

'I do mean it!' I shout, jumping up, dragging the poor dogs up by their necks with me. 'I'm really sorry, but I don't want to go out with you any longer. End of.'

Crab doesn't look quite so confident that we'll be back together any time soon.

'Is it my zits?' he asks, running a hand down his lumpy face. 'The doc says the antibiotics will take six weeks to kick in. And I know you're narked about the shirt. It *is* clean.'

'It's not your spots, or the shirt, or anything you've done!' I say. It's taking every ounce of self-control not to blub like a baby, which would be a disaster as it would mean Crab coming all over caring and us having a sympathy snog and nothing in my life *ever* changing. 'It's just - I don't know!' I look up at the starry sky. Something bright is moving at speed across the sky. It could be a shooting star, or a plane on its way to Heathrow airport. 'Up there are whole undiscovered galaxies, and down here there's just crap!'

'Yeah, one of the pugs is pooing,' Crab says, as an unwelcome smell slams into my nostrils. 'A runny one too.'

I can't stand it any longer. I dig a poo bag out of my boobs and throw Kylie and Danni's leads at Crab. 'Don't call me or text me,' I sniff. 'Just leave me alone!'

Avoiding the steaming pile, I stomp off to phone Taryn to tell her that I've broken up with Crab, *again*. But I've only done a few stomps when I realize that because of the whole lack-of-pockets problem, Crab has my phone.

I head back towards the Pavilion, past the little wooden smoking shelter that's been built in the beer garden.

'And you're absolutely sure that Josephine got it right?' A woman's voice cuts through the night air. 'It was definitely Chantelle, the girl in the pink bridesmaid's dress?'

I stop, my heart pounding, wondering if I'm going to hear her slagging me off for being sarky to Slow Jo.

'Totally. Josephine's not, you know, the full ticket like, but she can remember the smallest of details. And Chantelle definitely said it, though of course poor Jo had no idea of the significance when I found her slumped in a cubicle with the cake plate.' This is another woman, a woman with a broad cockney accent.

'I wonder why they decided to tell her now?' says Voice One. 'After all these years.'

'I didn't fink they was ever going to tell her,' Cockney Woman adds. 'Unless she needed a new kidney or somefink.'

'Maybe the poor kid *does* need a new kidney,' a man says. 'Or a liver transplant. I'd heard Sandra has something hidden in her knicker drawer in case they were mashed up on the M2 by a foreign lorry.'

'It was always going to come out at some point,' Cockney Woman says. 'You can't keep somefink like that secret for years. Look at *EastEnders*! Don't matter whether it's ten episodes or ten years, the truth will always out.'

I stand stock still as I hear them sucking on their fags, inhaling, breathing out slowly, drenching the air with nicotine. Then the man says, 'Poor kid. No wonder she always looks so bloody miserable. Finding out your parents aren't really your flesh and blood must have been one hell of a shock.'

Chapter Four

The morning after the night before, a number of things are worrying me:

1. Will I need a new kidney or liver, i.e. are the family keeping it from me that my organs are likely to expire before I do?
2. What if I inadvertently fall in love with my unknown half-brother, we get married, have children, and all our kids turn out to be aliens with two spines and rampant body hair?
3. How many people will see the bridesmaid snap Cousin Tracie posted on Facebook and leave rude comments about my similarity to a roadkill-faced hound?
4. When I next see Crab, will he assume we're back together, just because we always are?

Weirdly, the one thing that isn't stressing me is the fact that I overheard the startling revelation that Mum and Dad aren't my biological parents, because, as Taryn pointed out when I rang her at one in the morning and woke her up with the news, I always half-expected to discover at some point in my life that I was switched at birth; that despite wrist tags and security systems and the whole idea that you're supposed to instantly bond with your baby and recognize its cry across a crowded room, I was taken home and brought up by the wrong set of parents.

Dressed in five shades of black, slumped in a chair with a book, scowling at Mum and Dad as they worked on their cheesy dance routines in the living room with Sue and Bob, I often fantasized that somewhere out there was a totally cool set of parents, parents sitting at their kitchen table trying to discuss Baudelaire's poems with their perkily blonde slightly dim daughter, a girl who loves disco moves and pleads with them to send her to stage school. So, instead of being freaked, I'm thrilled that my gut instinct was right all along.

I didn't say anything on the way home, not because I was shocked at what I'd heard, but because Crab was sitting in the back of the Abbamobile, perched on an amplifier, still chuffed that he'd won a fiver from Dad. We hadn't got back together (as if!), but Mum had promised Mrs Snittersley we would run Crab home, and felt that just because I'd binned him wasn't a good enough reason to leave him roaming the streets on his own at midnight. And then by the time we got back to Lea Crescent and unloaded the van, it was too late to casually detonate the sort of genetic bomb that would have everyone up all night. So I dumped the dress under my bed, extracted sixty-seven hairpins, rang Taryn, went to sleep, had a nightmare that I was the secret love child of Susan Boyle and Simon Cowell, and woke up with the sixty-eighth hairpin wedged in my ear. I did plan to casually mention the gossiping guests at breakfast, but by the time I emerged from my pit around eleven, the parentals had left a note on top of the Sunday papers on the kitchen table reminding me they're playing at the Pig & Whistle's Hog Roast at lunchtime, and won't be back until four.

It's now midday, and Taryn's round for a wedding post-mortem.

She's lying on my bed, slowly twirling one of the two bright red bows of nylon hair pinned on either side of her head, whilst I paint each of her ten toenails a different colour.

The wacky hair is Taryn's latest thing. She thinks coordinating her hair to her outfit makes her look edgy and alternative; coupled with the short red-and-white polka dot ruffled skirt and white bow-fronted peep-toes she's wearing today, *I* think the overall effect is more mental Minnie Mouse than edgy teen.

Taryn is always changing her look. Before Mental Minnie, it was Emo with Electric, a phase during which she poured herself into tight black jeans, wore electric flex around her wrist and carried an old silver kettle instead of a handbag. The use of household appliances would have been fine, except you can't fit much in a kettle, so my bag (an ex-army canvas satchel with a military eagle crest on the flap) was always acting as Taryn's overflow bag. I love her to bits, but in the kettle stage, whilst she was sauntering along swinging her stainless steel, I'd be staggering next to her, weighed down with Taryn's emergency Lil-lets and panty liners; all the make-up she owns; her diary; a camera; a big pair of earphones to go with her iPod Nano, and a selection of the little notebooks she uses to sketch things she finds appealing: pebbles on the beach; the cliffs at Louisa Bay; the cute lad with the tattoos who works at the chippy. Unlike me, Taryn knows *exactly* what she wants to do with her life. She's going to take a gap year and travel round Australia and then to go to art school, where I expect kettle handbags look normal. Anyway, her bag *de jour* is a large shoulder bag she crocheted from strips of supermarket plastic bags. I'm just hoping it doesn't biodegrade *too* quickly, and the tampons make a break for freedom at some embarrassing moment.

I know most girls say that they've known their bezzies since they started primary school together, bonding over handmade Mother's Day cards or a hatred of the egg-and-spoon race, but I've only known Taryn since I was eleven when we both started at Haine Court, standing like a couple of lonely lemons in the school playground, everyone else having formed cliques the moment the register was called out.

To be honest, I was desperate for a friend. Before we all changed schools, I went to Homewood Middle and was bezzies with a girl called Leanne Curtis, whose parents owned a pub, The Snout and Truffle. Leanne and I didn't do much: we just used to sit in each other's bedrooms and listen to music or read magazines, or sneak downstairs and pinch packets of Pork Scratchings from behind the bar. Sometimes she'd get stuck on her homework and I'd do it for her and she'd give me bags of crisps in return.

Then in Year 6, we had to take the 11+ exam.

Friendships were ripped apart, there were tears and tantrums, and that was just the parents, and whereas I got into Haine, a grammar school, Leanne got shunted to Newdon Road, a school that always comes bottom of some lists (GCSEs, A Levels, university places), and top of others (truancy, pregnancy, most likely to end up in prison). After a bit of meeting up after school and texting each other, things fizzled out, and then her parents sold the pub and moved to Gillingham to run a care home.

Thank goodness I met Taryn, though I miss Leanne's regular supply of bar snacks.

'If you were swapped, what do you think your real parents are like?' Taryn muses now.

'Into books, art, probably a bit boho,' I say, painting one of Taryn's little toes silver, and the other, gold. 'Like your parents.'

'You can have mine,' Taryn snorts. 'I came downstairs last week to find a row of clay willies lined up on the kitchen table. You don't know how lucky you are to have your parents.'

'My adopted parents,' I primly correct her. '*Not* my bio parents.'

'You make them sound like some sort of washing powder,' Taryn giggles. 'Anyway, how come the parents of the stage school brat don't know? Odds are *someone* realized they'd got the wrong rugrat.'

'Dunno,' I shrug. 'Maybe they preferred the other baby.'

A knot forms in my gut. OMG! Not only don't I belong here, I wasn't wanted there either! What a terrible start I've had in life! No wonder I constantly feel miserable.

'*I* know!' Taryn's hair twirling becomes manic. 'Maybe you weren't swapped; maybe you were adopted because your dad fires blanks or your mum's ovaries packed up.'

Ugh. I really don't want to think about my parents' reproductive systems on a Sunday morning. It's even worse than finding a pottery todger on the breakfast table.

'Whatever it is has to be kept a secret unless I need a new organ.' I look down at my stomach, and for the first time, instead of worrying about its size, fret about what's going on inside. It's impossible to tell from the outside, and you hear stories about people thinking they've just had one éclair too many and then find out they've got a tumour the size of a grapefruit in their gut. And until I know the truth, I can never have children, not if I don't want to sprog a double-spined hirsute alien.

'You could steal your parents' spit,' Taryn suggests. 'Then send it off for a DNA test. I saw that once on Jeremy Kyle. This bloke did it to prove the baby belonged to his father, not him. Like, it was his half-brother, not his son.'

My head spins at all the possible parental scenarios. 'My folks don't go around randomly gobbing,' I point out. 'I can't secretly collect saliva unless I pinch their toothbrush or something.'

It might be difficult to explain away why the electric toothbrush has suddenly lost its entire collection of detachable colour-coded heads. I'm not sure they'd believe me if I said that evolution had turned the Tooth Fairy into the Toothbrush Fairy.

'He got her to lick a stamp,' Taryn says.

'But stamps are already sticky,' I point out.

Taryn waggles her freshly painted toes as she assesses the situation. 'It seems a bit weird this Slow Jo broad knew about the babe swap but you didn't,' she muses. 'Like, why would they tell someone who hasn't got all the dots on her dice, but not you?'

'Oh, keep up!' I reply, irritated that Taryn doesn't seem to be on top of the DNA deception. 'It was just a coincidence. She was rabbiting on about Benny being my dad, really narking me, so to shut her up I told her that he wasn't, meaning Dad was only *pretending* to be Benny. She must have told one of the rellies who thought I knew.'

Taryn sits bolt upright.

'So you never mentioned your mum?' she asks. 'You never said: "Frida's not my mum" or anything.'

'Frida was never mentioned,' I say. 'What are you getting at?'

Taryn rocks back and forwards on her butt, hugging her knees. 'I def think you sort of look like your mum, especially when she had long dark hair, you know, when she was Cher.'

Before Mum and Dad were Benny and Frida, they were Sixties singing duo Sonny and Cher. They ditched the act when the real life Cher started having so much plastic surgery Mum couldn't keep up, but before that, they toured pubs and clubs warbling *I Got You Babe* and *If I Could Turn Back Time*.

'But even if your dad shaved his beard off and cut his hair, I don't think you'd look anything like him.'

Oh. My. God! Taryn's right! The beard! The hair! It's all starting to make sense. All these years Dad's kept the Neanderthal Man look, not just to resemble Benny Andersson, internationally famous pop star, but to put people off realizing that we're not related. Even when he was Sonny, he had some gross handlebar mouche. Clearly, he's always used facial hair to disguise the fact there's nothing pug-like about his appearance.

I scramble off the bed and rush to my desk. I tip out the contents of my brown furry pencil case and hold it over my mouth.

'What do you think when you see this?' I say through a mouthful of nylon fuzz, a rough approximation of Dad's beard. 'What's your first thought?'

'That your hormones are dodgy and you need to wax or shave,' Taryn giggles.

'Taryn! I'm serious!' I shriek. 'Do you think I look like Dad? Am I Dad in a black net tutu?'

I'd like to point out that I'm also wearing a grey hoodie together with the red Hi-Tops and black knee-high socks. I'm not painting Taryn's nails practically naked. And the tutu was an amazing find: two pounds in the local hospice charity shop, *and* it has an elasticated waist. I can wear it for years!

'If your Dad came in dressed like a slutty ballerina I'd wet myself with laughter,' Taryn hoots. 'And suggest he gets transgender counselling.'

'Taryn, I'm really serious!' I yell, flinging the damp fur at her. 'What's been going on? I don't know who I am any more! What am I going to do?'

Suddenly I don't feel excited about the whole baby-switch thing; I feel terrified, and upset when I think of Dad trying (and failing) to help me with my maths homework, or driving miles because I had to get the latest Harry Potter and everywhere round here had sold out. I can't pretend I like my parents jumping around on stage dressed in body-skimming silk and stacked shoes, but the thought of Dad not being my father shakes me. I know the date my parents got married (1st June), and I know my birthday (9th May), and they're about two years apart. If Dad isn't my real dad, then Mum must have had an affair with someone *after* they got married.

Has Mum been duping Dad for fifteen years too?

Is he unaware that someone else is my Sperm Daddy?

Could it be still going on behind our backs?

I slump against the edge of the desk and start to cry.

'Oh, Chan, don't!' Taryn gets off the bed. She comes over and puts her arms around me. 'Listen, hon,' she says. 'There's only one way to find out what's gone on. You'll have to ask your mum.'

Chapter Five

Taryn's right of course.

Except, I can't.

I mean, just when is a good time to tell your parents you overheard some alcohol-soaked nicotine-drenched rellies gossiping about the fact you're the biological black sheep in the family?

Before breakfast and ruin the day?

At tea and spoil everyone's appetite?

'Yes please, Mum! More Shepherd's Pie. Oh, and who did you sleep with nine months before my birthday?'

I don't think so. And anyway, Dad *is* my real dad. He's always been there for me even when he hasn't wanted to be: the unfortunate incident with Red Bull and the cops by the clock tower which I still maintain wasn't my fault (someone must have spiked the can with vodka), or taking me and Taryn to the Picasso exhibition in London,

46

even though he could barely stand up for flu. Dad said later he wasn't sure whether he was looking at a weird impressionist painting, or had overdosed on Night Nurse and was hallucinating.

At some point, I'll find out what's been going on, but not yet. I'm going to put it out of my mind until after I've finished university, assuming I go to uni.

But wait!

What if I take a gap year?

What if my gap year involves visiting places with dodgy hospitals and no dialysis machines, and I do need a new kidney after all?

Clearly, I'm going to have to get any medical implications of my discovery sorted out *before* I volunteer to build houses in Malawi.

I sit on the green brushed-velvet sofa, drumming my feet on the green carpet, looking out of the window lined with green velvet curtains, wondering what to do next. Mum's very into matchy-matchy home accessories, but she's gone too far with the green theme this time, especially with the floor-to-ceiling wall-to-wall mirror that runs along one side of the room (so the group can practice), making everything appear doubly green; it's like sitting in a field.

So far, I've printed off some photos of Dad, Tippexing

out his beard to see if we're alike under all the fuzz, but I just make him look as if he's been attacked with a can of whipped cream.

I found a photo of me and drew a beard in, but I didn't look like Dad, just a freak exhibit in a fairground: The World's Hairiest Teenage Girl.

I've drunk loads of water to keep my kidneys flushed, just in case there is something terminally wrong with one of them.

I've gone to the loo, like, a million times because of all the water I've drunk.

I've flicked through the Sunday newspapers and tried to read a book, but can't concentrate long enough to read.

I've changed my Facebook relationship status, deleting Gordon Snittersley as my boyfriend and updating it to: Single.

And now I'm at a loose end.

I gaze upwards, not for a sign from the heavens or even to study the yellowy-brown stain on the living room ceiling (from when the shower in the en suite leaked), but because above me is Mum and Dad's room, or more specifically, Mum's knicker drawer. I can't forget what the smoking rellie said: there's something in Mum's scanty drawer in case my parents die in a motorway pile-up, though quite how finding out I've been duped for fifteen years is going to help my grief isn't clear.

A couple of times I've got up, walked slowly up the stairs and then, scared of even looking at the drawer and what it might contain, bolted back down again.

Distraction. I need distracting from my mother's underwear.

I grab my phone from the arm of the sofa.

No grovelling texts from Crab, which is mega-annoying.

Last time we split up (two weeks ago after he narked me by ogling a blonde minx in the high street, actually swivelling his bony neck almost one hundred and eighty degrees to catch every glimpse of her) he sent me twenty-eight grovelling texts (which also annoyed me) and pushed a five-bar pack of Flakes through the letterbox. Perhaps he's taken me at my word that we're finished. I've burnt my boats now. Maybe I shouldn't have binned him until I had someone else lined up. But who? Other than swoony Daniel Delbridge, I can't think of anyone I'd even consider going out with, but as Dan the Man is in the sixth form and seeing Michaela Wright (strawberry blonde curls, a smattering of freckles, totally modelly gorge, you get the gutting picture), he's out of my league, except in my dreams.

My stomach rumbles.

Taryn will be at home eating Sunday lunch: beef, roasties, Yorkie puds, carrots, peas, gravy, the works; my mouth waters at the thought of it. I imagine the Griffiths sitting round the rectangular pine table in their kitchen, bickering over who gets the last Aunt Bessie, nattering about their plans for Patagonia. To be fair, Taryn said I could go back with her, that there would be loads of food, but despite the bleak alternative, I declined her offer. Weirdly, being with the Griffiths sometimes makes me feel even lonelier than I already am; it sort of underlines the isolation, especially when I come home from their lively house and find ours graveyard quiet. I'm not so bad when there's just Taryn and me, or even Pippa, Dermot, Taryn and me, but when Taryn is with Seren and Carys and her parents, I feel awkward. I don't get all the family in-jokes; I can't join in with their tales of tents collapsing in storms when they went on holiday, or how funny it was when Pippa forgot to put the oven on for the turkey on Christmas Day, so they ate beans on toast with a sprig of holly on top.

Mum and Dad were performing at a top London hotel last Christmas, so we had breakfast together, and then they dropped me at Aunty Nicola and Uncle Kevin's and I watched as The Helium Twins unwrapped gift after gift, including some seriously expensive bling from Tiffany's. I did get a present from that branch of the Allen family tree: a leather bookmark with my name stamped on it in gold. They've obviously spent fifteen years thinking I'm called Chontel.

I potter into the kitchen, peer in to the fridge, take some stuff out and, still wondering what's upstairs, make a saddo cheese and pickle sarnie. Then I take the plate through to the other room, plonk myself on the sofa and take a bite.

I don't believe it!

I've missed out the Utterly Butterly! Even with the pickle, it's too dry.

If I was so busy thinking about what's hidden in Mum's knickers that I couldn't make a measly sandwich, how on earth am I going to be able to sit in my room and study for exams with only the bathroom separating me and THE drawer? It's mission impossible.

I jump up – not a good move if you've still got a cheddar and Branston sarnie on your lap – and rush upstairs.

My lunch might be on the carpet, but my heart is in my mouth.

Three o'clock. An hour until Mum and Dad get back, plenty of time to root through bras and knickers and find my birth certificate, confessional letter or whatever it is I'm looking for. Quite what I'm going to do if I find incriminating evidence, I'm not sure.

There's a false start when I choose Dad's drawer and get a handful of disgusting *performance pouches* as he calls them, but I quickly find Mum's and start rootling through a frankly horrific selection of shapeless big pants, thongs that have lost their elastic and several pairs of knickers with holes in the gusset, chucking them over my shoulder on the bed as I go.

'Channy?'

I scream, and toss a pair of humungous red lace pants in the air in fright.

They land on my head, draping themselves across my face, which burns hot with panic.

Squinting through one leg hole I can make out my mother standing at the bedroom door, dressed as Frida.

'I didn't expect you back!' I gasp, pulling the pants off my head, practically yanking a silver hoop earring out at the same time.

'Obviously,' Mum says coolly. 'What are you doing?'

I hold up exhibit A. 'Borrowing some knickers?' I try.

'Channy?' Mum's voice has a warning tone. Clearly, she knows that never in a million years would I wear *any* of her underwear for fear of having a road accident and someone seeing it. I'd *have* to die, just because I couldn't live knowing people had seen me lying in the street in big pants.

I feel cornered. Trapped between a pine chest of drawers and the reproduction Victorian bedstead by a woman with dyed dark hair, false eyelashes and scarily bright-green glittery eye shadow. Courtesy of the silver platform boots, she's also towering above me. There's nothing for it but to come quietly, and reveal the real reason for having my mitts in her knicks.

'Where's Dad?' I ask.

'Unloading the van,' she says. 'I needed a wee, so I came in. Come on, Channy, what's going on? I'm bursting here.'

I take a deep breath, swallow hard and brace myself.

'Mum,' I croak, my throat sandpaper dry, my legs buckling with nerves. 'I know . . . I know . . .'

'Know what?' she asks, taking her pants out of my sweaty hands.

'Where babies come from.'

NO! I've bottled it! I was all fired up to confess what I'd heard and what I was looking for, but at the very last moment I pulled out, swerved the issue, dodged the bullet, acted the wimp.

'I know you do,' Mum says, puzzled. 'We had that chat when you were eight, and again when you started seeing boys.'

'So we did!' I say brightly, pretending I've only just remembered the humiliation of our Facts of Life talk. 'I completely forgot you knew I knew.'

I'm not fooling anyone, not least Mum. She pushes the pile of pants to one side and sits down on the bed, patting the cream and beige satin duvet cover.

'Channy, are you going to tell me what's going on, or am I going to have to torture you until you confess?'

She's smiling, but I know she means business. Previous parental tortures have included sewing hundreds of scratchy sequins on to their stage costumes, or putting promotional leaflets through the letterboxes of people I know whilst dressed in a pink T-shirt with Bjorn At The Beach plastered over my boobage in silver letters. *Totally* humiliating.

'Mum,' I say close to tears, flopping down beside her. 'I overheard some of the rellies talking at the wedding. They said something about me needing a new kidney.'

Mum swivels her head and stares at me as if I'm nuttier than Slow Jo. Then she bursts into fits of giggles. 'Were they plastered?' she roars. 'Overdone the sparkling wine?'

'Maybe, I don't know. The thing is, after I was talking to Slow Jo . . .'

'Oh you can't believe anything Josephine says.' Mum rolls her eyes. 'She's definitely missing a few buttons on her remote control. Remember when she dressed up in tennis whites and walked up and down the queue at Wimbledon pretending she was seeded in the women's tournament? She even signed autographs!'

'No, it was me that was doing the talking.' I can hear my voice flutter. I'm just thankful I'm sitting on the bed or I might slide on to the floor with jelly legs. 'You know Slow Jo thinks Dad is really Benny? Anyway, I told her he wasn't, but she got the wrong end of the stick . . .'

'Which is why we call her Slow Jo,' Mum says. 'We shouldn't really. It's cruel. Her grandmother was known as Barmy Brenda you know. Wouldn't wear shoes, *ever*. Used to say they made her feet feel claustrophobic. Poor woman was always ending up in A&E with cuts or frostbite.'

'Mum!' I can't stand this wittering about loopy rellies any longer. 'It wasn't Slow Jo that said you and Dad weren't my real mum and dad. It was the others. They said you had hidden something in your knicker drawer, in case you died in an accident.'

I sit there, shell-shocked. I wanted to get all this out in

the open, but now that I have, I'm terrified of what lies ahead. Why didn't I stick to my original plan of saying nothing until I was ready, until I had more facts; at least until I'd done my A Levels?

I glance sideways at Mum. Her hands are clasped in her lap, her neck slightly bent, her face completely blank, emotionless, like a living death mask with mega-false eyelashes.

I don't know what to do next. I sort of thought that Mum would break down in sobs and tell me the truth. I hadn't reckoned on the silent poker-face treatment. That's the sort of method *I* use when I'm annoyed with *her*, not the other way round. This turning of the tables has totally thrown me.

'I think you're my real mum because Taryn says I look like you, well, you did when you were Cher, but even when I put a furry pencil case over my face I don't look like Dad.'

'Your father is a slightly overweight, hairy forty-year-old,' Mum says sharply, getting up and clomping towards the window. 'As a fifteen-year-old girl, I should jolly well hope you *don't* look like him.'

She stands with her back to me, the word *Frida* picked out across her shoulders in blue sequins. Unless she's fascinated by the Crawfords' campervan parked on the opposite driveway, I'd say she's avoiding my eyes. I can also tell she's in a right old state as the white satin of her Abba dress is quivering.

'You should know better than to listen to drunken wedding gossip,' she adds crisply.

'So why did they say it?' I press. 'Did they just make it all up, cos if they did, you should sue them for slander or libel or something.'

For a moment, nothing happens; no one says anything. Then Mum turns from the window and quietly shuts the bedroom door.

My blood runs cold and my stomach hurtles towards my feet. The very fact that Mum's closing the bedroom door is a sign that the gossip is true. She never closes the door on our conversations, not even the one we had in my bedroom when I was seven about periods and feminine hygiene products. Dad had been outside painting the landing, chipping in with the odd fact that he remembered from his biology lessons, sounding all pleased that he could remember the oestrogen and progesterone cycle and knew the term: *fallopian tubes*.

'It's true, isn't it?' I whisper, not because I'm trying to keep my voice down, but because I can't summon up anything stronger to rise above the whooshing sound in my ears. 'When were you going to tell me? When I was sixteen? Eighteen? When?' My voice rises along with a feeling of hysteria. 'Were you hoping I'd never need a new kidney and have to be told? That I wouldn't have alien babies?'

'Of course you don't need a new kidney.' Mum sounds tense and irritated, and although my brain is in shock, a tiny part of me is thinking: *Phew!*

'Does Dad know?' I ask. 'Does he know I'm not his daughter?'

'You *are* his daughter,' Mum snaps. 'He's done everything parents do, from changing nappies to sitting with you in A&E when you tried to pierce your own belly-button with a safety pin.'

'But there's no bio bond, is there?' I say, wincing at the memory of that painful (and unsuccessful) episode. 'We don't share a double helix, do we?'

Mum bites her lip and looks shifty. 'Who cares about biology? A bit of . . .' she wrinkles her nose, '*stuff* doesn't make a dad!'

Stuff. She means sperm. Fifty-percent of my DNA. My genetic blueprint.

All the bones vanish from my body and I struggle to catch my breath.

So, it really is true. Right up until this moment, I thought that Mum was going to be able to successfully explain away my fears, that in years to come we would laugh about the time I thought I didn't belong to Dad. But I know now that day is never going to come, because whilst he'll always be my dad, Trevor Allen isn't genetically speaking, my father.

Even though I thought I was ready for this, that I'd known all my life that something wasn't quite right, that one day I'd find different parents, parents who liked reading not dancing and had books rather than mirrors lining their sitting room walls, now it's happened, I feel shivery with shock.

'Does *he* know about me?' I whisper. 'Does my bio father know I exist?'

'No,' Mum admits. 'He doesn't, and I want it to stay that way, Chantelle. OK?' She jabs an index finger at me, flicking it as if flames are shooting from its tip.

She's angry. It's Chantelle, not Channy. I'm only ever Chantelle when she's angry. I've done nothing wrong but she's mad with me. Hypocrite! Shouldn't she be comforting me, telling me everything is going to be fine, apologizing for deceiving me?

'No, it's not OK!' I yell. 'What about me? What about what I want?'

Nothing.

'So who is he?' I demand. I'm off the bed, standing in

the room with my arms folded across my chest. 'Come on! I need answers. You can't just drop this bombshell on me and ignore it!'

'*You* dropped the bombshell, not me!' Mum points out.

'I need something!' I cry. 'A name, details of how you met, anything! If you don't, I could fail my GCSEs for stressing about it.'

Still silence.

'So you'd rather I flunked school than told me the truth?' I strop. 'Fine! I'll just pinch Dad's toothbrush and send it off to a DNA lab and find out the truth!'

'You will not,' Mum rounds on me, her eyes blazing under her sparkly lids. 'Replacement heads are very expensive.'

I'm shocked by the tone of her voice. As a rule, she's a pretty laid back type of parent, unlike Gaia Taylor's mum who once hurled a burnt pizza at Gaia like some sort of foodie Frisbee because Gaia forgot to tell her mum she wouldn't be back for tea because she was coming to the seafront with us for fish and chips. Hot cheese in the face is practically child abuse. It took ages for the burn to heal.

'Then I'll ask Dad.' I hate to threaten Mum, but I've got no choice. 'I'll ask him who my real dad is!'

'Chantelle Elizabeth Allen, don't you dare!' Her voice is venomous. 'This is all in the past and it needs to stay that way, do you hear me?' And then she marches to the en suite bathroom and hurls the door shut.

Wow! *Full* use of my name. She must be nuclear angry.

'I'll stay here until you come out!' I yell, tying myself to the bedhead with one of Mum's grey/white bras, a sort of modern day suffragette, only demanding genetic information for illegitimate daughters, rather than votes for women.

'If you don't fess up I'll throw myself in front of a moving vehicle!' Nothing too fast obviously: a milk float or one of those weird mobility scooters coffin dodgers use to beetle around town.

Clearly Mum would rather I became teen roadkill than divulge DNA details, as my threat of suicide is met with the sound of her blowing her nose, the loo flushing, but no movement on the door front.

'Everything OK?' Dad puts his head around the bedroom door. 'I heard yelling from the drive.'

Like a ferret up a trouser leg, Mum's out of the bathroom.

'It's nothing!' she says brightly. 'Channy's just upset over splitting up with Crab, aren't you?'

I look at Dad, still dressed as Benny, my heart breaking that he's not my real dad, despite years of wishing he wasn't.

'And that requires unusual use of underwear?' He grins and nods at my wrist.

'Oh, you know what teenage girls are like,' Mum says, yanking her bra from me, practically giving me a Chinese burn with the lacy elastic. 'Drama queens, the lot of them. But you're fine now, aren't you, Channy?'

I turn my gaze to Mum. Every cell in her body is screaming at me to agree with her, not to rock the boat, to keep up the pretence that this furry-faced man standing in the room with us is my real father.

Then I slide my eyes back to Dad, his face etched with concern that I'm upset over the lad who snaffled a fiver from him by cramming his mouth with Scotch eggs.

Right now I don't care about hurting Mum, but I can't hurt Dad.

'I'm fine,' I growl, stomping out and slamming my bedroom door.

Chapter Six

'God you look rough!' Taryn pulls a face when she sees me leaning against a road sign at the life-dividing roundabout, our rendezvous before walking to school. 'Bad night?'

'You can say that again,' I mutter. My brain was so buzzing I hardly slept, and when I did I dreamt that giant cartoon sperm were bombarding me yelling: 'I'm the Daddy! I'm the Daddy!'

'What was it like this morning?' Taryn asks, as we start ambling arm-in-arm down the road. 'Tense?'

'Grim,' I say. 'Monday mornings are bad enough without my mother's eyes glowing over the Coco Pops.'

'And she's not going to fess up who your father is?'

I shake my head. 'She's gone into total shutdown mode.'

'So what's the plan?' Taryn squeezes my arm. 'Let

sleeping sperm lie or become a DNA detective?'

'I have no plan,' I admit. 'I've nothing to go on.'

The problem is, you can't search for someone if you don't even have a name. Is it any wonder that kids who don't know anything about their birth parents pretend they're descended from African Kings or Premiership footballers?

When I was at Homewood Middle, there was this girl called Brogan Hickey who was adopted. She used to go round telling everyone that her real parents lived in Florida and were minted. Instead of being impressed, we all felt gutted for her that she'd ended up living in a terraced house in Margate rather than a Miami mansion, but at least she had a dream, even if turned out that her bio mum was a crack addict holed up in a squat in South East London.

So after my dramatic exit from the parental bedroom yesterday afternoon, I rang Taryn to update her and then festered on my bed thinking back to Brogan Hickey and wondering who my father really is.

At first I fantasized he was a titled bigwig: Sir Algernon Double-Barrel, a toffee nose living in a stately home stuffed with first editions of famous books, and children called Petronella and Theodore. Then, feeling gloomy over the whole thing, I decided The Sperm Daddy is more likely to be someone called Barry Bristow who runs a mobile disco and has his own set of decks and flashing coloured lights, in which case my sibs are probably called Cindee-Barb and Bubba-Wayne.

I spent *hours* searching the Internet for stories just like mine, and although sitting next to a pile of thongs in my parents' bedroom I felt totally alone, I was gobsmacked to find out the world is full of people being kept in the dark about their family tree: a boy in Denmark who really does need a new kidney, his birth father being his last chance of a tissue match; a couple in Indiana who'd got married not realizing they were twins separated at birth; and a girl from Rochdale who'd been told her parents had died in a car crash when she was a baby, when in reality her father was in prison for murdering her mother.

I would never have believed so many families were keeping such guilty secrets.

Until now.

And as if my brain isn't stressed enough, Crab is waiting for me by the bus stop on Broadgate Road, black trousers grazing his ankles, wrists sticking way beyond the black cuffs of his school blazer, his tie knotted at his skinny neck, protruding like a grey and red striped Adam's apple.

'Don't tell Crab about the dad thing,' I hiss at Taryn as we walk towards him. 'I don't want him coming over all sympo. Anyway, him and me are finally over. I promise.'

'All right?' Crab mumbles through his chewing gum, falling into line with us, even though it means he has to walk in the road, so risks being clipped by a car's wing mirror. 'You feeling less stressy now?'

He tries to hand me a giant bar of Cadbury's Fruit and Nut, and I have to practically gnaw my hands off to stop myself taking it. Accepting chocolate from an ex-boyfriend would be a signal he's no longer an ex.

'What's it to do you with you?' I sneer. 'You're history, remember?'

'Still?' Crab says. 'I thought you'd have changed your mind by now.'

I stop, pulling Taryn to a halt with me. Crab keeps walking and talking and waving the chocolate slab in the air until he realizes he's ahead of us, so double backs.

'I mean, you usually have,' he shrugs, standing in front of us, his right shoulder dipped from the weight of his rucksack. 'Why not now?'

'You knew I was upset on Saturday night,' I snap, as we start walking again. 'But you never bothered to phone me or text me. Like, I'm really going to go back with you after you treated me like that!' I toss my hair around in a suitably diva-ish manner, and assume what I hope is an angry-yet-hurt face.

'But you told me not to contact you!' Crab protests, looking bewildered. 'I did what you said. I wanted to come round, but I thought you might slap me!'

Taryn gives a dismissive snort. 'God, Crab, you are *such* a loser!' She makes an L shape with her right hand and waves it at him. 'Everyone knows girls never say what they really mean.'

'Though I really meant it when I told you not to put your hand up my skirt,' I quickly add.

Crab looks confused. I feel sorry for him and not just because his uniform doesn't fit and his zits seem to be on double throb mode this morning. I don't want to go out with him any more, but he doesn't deserve to be humiliated outside the school gates.

'I'll see you inside,' I say to Taryn, throwing her a beat-it look.

She raises her eyebrows at me and stays put. She probably thinks that if I'm alone with Crab I'll change my mind and end up agreeing to get engaged or something, after all, she's had to deal with the whole break-up and make-up scene zillions of times before.

'Have I taken the chocolate?' I point out, pushing her away. 'Go!'

'Look, Crab,' I start, once Taryn has headed off, scowling over her shoulder still waving an L sign in the air. 'I really think we should cool it.' Then just in case I change my mind later add, 'For now, at least.'

Crab looks crestfallen and starts anxiously tugging at the collar of his white shirt. 'Was it cos I said you looked like a bog roll cover?' he asks. 'Cos I meant it in a nice way. Or the shirt? I shouldn't have worn the footie shirt, should I? Mum went ape when I came home in it. And now Dad's gone nuts cos I left his tie at The Pavilion and it's his funeral tie. Went back to get it yesterday. Totally gone! He needs it on Thursday cos some bloke he knows fell off his scooter and slid under a cement mixer. I'm in major league shit with everyone, especially you.'

I've known Crab long enough to know he's gabbling because he's nervous, and for one moment I seriously consider taking him back, confessing that I was being stroppier than a stroppy cow with a major strop on, and that it was only a temporary bin. Despite his spots he's good looking *and* he's thoughtful: how many other lads would bring you a squashed sausage snack and confectionery to cheer you up? But this time, even chocolate covered nuts won't change my mind.

'It's nothing to do with what you've said or what you've worn or anything,' I say heavily. 'There's just a lot of stuff going on in my head at the moment.'

I'd make room in my brain for thoughts about him, I think to myself as Dan the Man strides through the gates holding hands with perky Michaela.

'What stuff?' Crab asks suspiciously. 'Have you met someone else?'

I hope I don't have a letchy look on my face when Delish Dan sauntered by.

'Cos I'd be well narked if you'd been unfaithful.' Crab's fingers start to scratch his neck, ripping the tops off zits, blood seeping into his collar. 'Gutted.'

'Of course not!' I assure him, wondering if mentally snogging sixth formers counts, as if so, I've been unfaithful to Crab every day for at least the last three months. 'Just stuff that's stressing me.'

'If it's about that monster on your chin,' Crab suggests, 'just squeeze the hell out of it in the bogs and bung some TCP on.'

'Actually,' I snap, furious that having already murdered the ruddy zit, it seems to be rising from the dead and filling up again with gunk, 'it's major parent stuff.'

'Like what?' Then Crab's mouth drops open. 'Holy shit!' he gasps. 'Your folks are splitting up!' He starts chewing rapidly, his jaws chomping up and down. 'Look, Chan, don't stress. The real couples in Abba divorced and they still kept the group together. It doesn't have to be the end of Bjorn At The Beach.'

I really, really want to slap him. 'God, Crab, Taryn's right!' I explode. 'You are such a loser! Do you think I'd be stressed over the stupid group splitting up? Get real! I've just found out my dad's not my real dad. I don't know who he is and Mum won't tell me.'

I just couldn't help myself, could I? I've told Taryn and now I've told Crab, and by the looks of several kids staring at me, quite a few pupils at Haine Court too.

But instead of Crab looking shocked, he just nods his head like that annoying bulldog in the insurance ads. 'Oh, yes,' he says gravely. 'It's *Mamma Mia* all over again. You're just like Sophie trying to find out who her father is.'

'What are you on?' I snap, furious that he doesn't seem to be taking this life-changing news seriously. 'This has nothing to do with Abba!'

'It does.' Crab looks smug, as if he's just got a correct answer on University Challenge. 'I knew though, I always had an inkling, I just never said anything cos I didn't want to freak you out, and you freak out dead easy.'

'You knew?' I gasp, trying not to freak out and thereby proving Crab right. 'How come?'

'Just by looking at him.'

'Looking at who?'

'Bjorn Bob.'

'Bjorn Bob?' I squeak. 'What's he got to do with anything?'

Crab looks around as if he's being spied on. Then he bends his legs slightly and using the slab of chocolate as a shield whispers, 'My mum said your mum had a fling with Bob Myers before she married your dad.'

This is news to me, but it doesn't explain anything.

'Get real!' I snap. 'I was born *after* Mum and Dad got married. So you're well wrong there.'

'Am I?' Crab says, straightening up. 'Maybe they carried on where they left off.' And then he winks; either that or he's got some grit in his eye.

'Mum and that little scroat face?' I gasp, as visions of Bjorn and Frida getting it on leap into my brain. 'You cannot be serious!'

'Just look at him, Channy,' Crab says, deadly serious. 'Weak chin, squat nose, weird little face, the total spit of you. Isn't it obvious? Bob Myers is your real dad.'

Chapter Seven

'Mum! Mum!'

I storm through the front door, screaming at the top of my voice.

'Mum! Where are you?'

'She's gone to Asda.' Dad appears in the hall dressed in jeans and a T-shirt, a blue-and-white tea towel in his hand. When he sees me his face falls. 'Channy! Whatever's happened? Has there been an accident?'

The sight of him looking so concerned reduces me to floods of tears, though to be honest, I've been ready for a mega blub from the moment Crab described me as a weak-chinned, squat-nosed weirdo. I belted him in the nuts with my school bag and ran straight home, so now we really *are* over; bruised brussel sprouts don't exactly make a boy want you back.

But now I'm not crying over how I look. I'm crying

because I so want this man with his arm round my shoulders to be my real dad. I don't want it to be Bjorn Bob.

Bob and Sue have a daughter, Claire, who's in Year 7 at Haine Court, a piglet in specs and an absolute pain. I hardly ever see her, but when I do, she follows me around whining that she likes my clothes, or pestering me about whether I have a boyfriend. I don't want whiny Claire as my half-sister; I want someone achingly cool with whom I can discuss books and music and soaps; someone with a wardrobe comprised of stunningly original vintage pieces sourced from charity shops and flea markets. Saddo Claire thinks fashion is a High School Musical T-shirt studded with pink rhinestones. And Bob Myers as The Sperm Daddy! This is truly terrible news! I'd hoped my real dad would love literature, maybe even be a writer. How come I've ended up with two dads, *both* Abba wannabes?

Still with his arm around me, Dad ushers me into the living room and gently guides me to the sofa.

'Is this still about Crab?' he asks softly, sitting next to me. 'You'll get back together again, you always do, and if you don't, well, there are plenty more shellfish in the sea.' He laughs at his own joke, slapping the tea towel on his thigh.

73

'It's not about Crab,' I sob. 'Crab's history.'

'Have you and Taryn had words then?' Dad tries. 'Or one of the other girls?'

'No.' I shake my head and keep sobbing.

'So what is it?'

I need to come up with a good excuse for bunking off school first thing on a Monday morning.

My eyes flick around the living room hoping for fib inspiration: standard lamp with green tasselled shade; glass clown ornament; scented candle in the shape of a prickly cactus; a seriously naff picture of sheep huddled under stick-like trees as they shelter from a snowstorm . . .

'I'm missing Twiggy,' is the only thing my mashed brain can come up with. 'I saw this little stick lying in the gutter on the way to school, and it brought it all flooding back.'

'Your stick insect?' Dad replies. I can tell that already he's casting doubt on my story, especially since he was with me when I tossed Twig's corpse in the recycling bin along with a pile of old *heat* magazines.

'She wasn't just a stick insect,' I wail. 'She was the perfect stick insect: a princess among stick insects.'

I'm really bawling now, not for Twiggy, but for Dad and me, for Mum and Dad, for what all this means for our little family.

'Channy, Twiggy has been dead for weeks, maybe even months as you never cleaned out the tank and didn't realize.' Dad's tone is one of sarcasm mixed with disbelief. 'Now come on, what's really going on to get you so upset?'

He takes my hand to show he's feeling sympathetic, even though he knows I've tried to bluff him with a false tale of stick insect grief. Looking at my pudgy fingers next to his slender digits underlines the biological difference between us, though of course Dad hasn't got a couple of coats of Rimmel Oyster Pink on his nails. I prefer something darker, but Chanel's Rouge Noir (a birthday present from Taryn) would have Mrs Connelly, our form tutor, reaching into her drawer to get out the nail varnish remover. She's a total witch when it comes to make-up, and is in possession of a whole range of removers. Once, slightly slutty mean girl Kourtney Elliot thought she'd got one over on Mrs C by claiming she couldn't remove her make-up with the wet wipes usually doled out, because if she did, she'd have a severe allergic reaction, her eyes would swell to the size of golf balls, and her parents would sue the school for millions of pounds. Undeterred and looking sickenly smug, Mrs Connelly whipped out a packet of *hypoallergenic* wipes and we all sniggered as a humiliated Kourtney rubbed away her slap, revealing a face like an uncooked current bun: pale and spotty.

'Channy?' Dad prompts, as beside me my phone vibrates in my bag.

I reach for it. Four missed calls, all from Taryn. She'll be wondering what's happened at the school gates.

'Ignore the phone,' Dad orders. 'Come on, talk to me.' He gives me a steely glare. 'You're not pregnant are you?'

'No!' I shriek. 'As if!'

'So?'

I don't say anything. I *can't* say anything.

'Well, we can stay here until you tell me,' Dad says, sitting back and folding his arms. 'At least until Thursday evening; we've got a gig in Dartford.'

I contemplate spending four days and three nights in our sitting room. I could watch telly all day and sleep on the sofa, but there's not a pot plant to pee into, and what would I do about food? I should have whipped that chocolate from Crab.

'Channy?'

I take a deep breath. I feel as if I'm standing on Broadgate pier, about to plunge into the cold water below, not knowing if I'm going to smash my head on a rock, or bob to the surface, spluttering but alive.

'Did you know Mum went out with Bob Myers before she met you?' Nervously I toss my phone from one hand to another, as if I'm juggling a hot potato.

'Bob? Yes, when they were at school,' Dad replies. 'Or maybe just after they left.'

'And you never thought to *mention* it?' I say accusingly. 'You didn't think it might be *relevant*?'

'Not really.' Dad sounds puzzled. 'It was a teen romance, you know, like you and Crab. This is such a small town, everyone's been out with everyone else at some point. Before she married Bob, I took Sue to see Dirty Dancing at the little cinema by the harbour.'

OMG! My head swims at this parental dating merry go round. My boring little life seems to have suddenly descended into a strange Channel 4 play, the sort of play where everyone swap wives and husbands.

'Channy.' Dad takes my mobile phone off me and squeezes my hand. 'Come on, what is it? You can tell your old dad anything, you know that.'

This isn't strictly true. I'm pretty sure if I told him I'd been caught shoplifting bottles of voddy from the local Londis, or had decided to ditch school to become an exotic pole dancer, he'd go completely ape.

'I've found stuff out,' I whisper, the tears falling again. I wipe my runny nose with my arm, smearing snot over my blazer. The slimy trail looks as if a slug has crawled over me. 'Important stuff.'

'Like what?' Dad asks cautiously.

This time I'm not going to dodge the issue or wimp out. I know Mum doesn't want Dad to know I know, and I'm truly terrified of the consequences of him knowing, but if I don't discover the truth, it will eat away at my brain like some sinister tumour. Also, I really don't want to spend four days marooned on a green velvet sofa.

I take a deep breath and plunge in, feet first.

'Like, that after you were married, Mum carried on seeing Bjorn Bob and that Bjorn Bob is my real dad!' I jump up, hysterical, as if I've been scalded. 'Dad, I'm so sorry! I didn't want to be the one to tell you. Crab told me.'

I brace myself for some sort of shocked reaction, perhaps a bit of room pacing and groans of *Oh no!* or even bolting from the house and heading to Asda to confront Mum over her infidelity in the fresh fruit aisle, but instead, Dad dissolves into fits of laughter, his entire body vibrating with amusement.

So not the reaction I was expecting.

'Oh, Channy! Bob Myers isn't your father,' he laughs. 'I can promise you that.'

For a moment, my whole body floods with relief, and I sink back on to the sofa next to him. Then I hear myself whispering, 'But you can't promise me you're my real dad, can you?'

I keep my head down, unable to look at him, tears dropping off the end of my nose. My throat feels tight with tension, and my insides are flopping around like washing in a tumble dryer.

'Of course I can promise you that I'm your real dad,' he replies quietly, still clutching my hand. 'A father isn't necessarily a dad; he may be there at the start, but a dad is around for the duration.'

'You knew?' I gasp. I feel as if I've been slapped in the face with a big wet fish: perhaps a halibut.

Dad swivels towards me and clutches both my hands in a clammy vice-like grip, shaking them. 'Channy, you've got to believe me when I tell you from the moment you were born, I've never thought of you as anyone other than my own flesh and blood, my real daughter.'

'You knew all along?'

'Of course,' Dad says. 'Your mum and I don't have secrets.'

'And you never thought to say anything?' I rip my hands from his, shocked to find out that both Mum and

Dad have been deceiving me, spinning this web of lies together.

'I wanted to tell you years ago, but your Mum was keen to keep things in the past, not stir up old hurts.' Dad sounds desperate. 'Then you had exams and then it never seemed the right time, and then it never seemed important and life just went on.' He clamps his hand on his forehead and looks up to the ceiling. 'Channy, I'm so sorry.' Then he covers his face with his hands, rests his elbows on his knees and grinds his palms into his eyes. 'We should have told you before, before you heard it from someone else. How did you find out?'

'I overheard stuff at the wedding and asked Mum. She's pretty much admitted it, but she won't tell me anything.' I can hear my voice: surly, snappy, accusing.

'Is that what all that fuss was about yesterday?' Dad asks. 'The stuff in the bedroom?'

'Yes.' I start crying again.

I glance under my hair to look at Dad in the mirror opposite. He's crying too, tears running down his face, mingling with his beard, plopping on to his lap. He tries to wipe them away with the tea towel, but they keep falling.

'I'm sorry if we've hurt you Channy,' he says. 'We didn't mean to. We just wanted the best for you, you do know that, don't you? And we've been OK, haven't we, just the three of us? I mean, we wanted more, wanted you to be part of a family, but it never happened. And you're fine about that, aren't you?'

I know Dad wants me to tell him that it's OK, that we can just go on as before. But I can't. The genie is out of the bottle and I can't stuff it back in.

'I'm sorry, Dad,' I sob. 'I don't want a new dad, but I do need to know the truth.'

Chapter Eight

I write the name of The Sperm Daddy in the sand with my finger, staring at the damp letters as the wind coming off the grey English Channel whips strands of hair around my face, pinging my skin like an elastic band.

JOHN SMITH

That's what my biological father is called: John Smith.

John Smith, who, during a blip in the early days of my parents' marriage, went out with my mother and did 'something in the City', a phrase that could cover anything from selling newspapers on a street corner to billion-dollar share deals.

Quite frankly, I'm gutted that he isn't called something more interesting. Even Barry Bristow sounds better than dreary *John Smith*.

I suppose it could have been worse; I could be like Brogan Hickey and find out my missing parent was a deranged druggie, though at least Brogan's background sounds like something you might read about in a gritty young adult novel. John Smith, man in the City, is hardly the stuff of gripping fiction, is it?

I trace a line underneath John Smith's name, and decide it might look less boring if I drew a sort of squiggly box around it and added a few ornamental twirls at each corner.

Then I sit back and look at my sandywork.

Nope. Now it just looks like a boring name in a psycho frame.

Grinding my heels into the sand, I look out to sea, watching the ferries and the tankers glide by on the horizon in a vain attempt to put the brakes on my racing thoughts. I can practically feel the synapses short-circuiting in my brain, one after another, fizzing and sparking and giving me the sort of headache that no amount of paracetamol will cure.

I shouldn't be sitting on the beach at eleven o'clock on Monday morning of course; I should be in double Latin, listening to Mr Walker drone on about Ablative Absolutes. That's where Taryn will be now, stressing that Crab (so not a Latin boy) has abducted me and is keeping me hostage in a cave until I change my mind and agree to go back out with him.

I fish my moby out of my bag and stab out a short text assuring her I'm fine and will explain everything later when I'm in a better headspace, *if* I'm ever in a better headspace.

The weird thing is, when I left Lea Crescent I thought I was totally cool with the John Smith revelation. I even assured Dad that I was fine, that there was no need to wait for Mum to bring the Abbamobile back from Asda so he could run me to school, and no, I didn't need chaperoning to the gates. Because an hour ago, I *was* fine.

Just before going back to school and in need of a quick face and hair repair, I stood in front of the mirror in my bedroom and stared at myself, and as well as a rather blotchy pug-faced girl with pale-lips and a monster zit on her chin staring back, I also saw the face of the daughter of a man called John Smith and a woman called Sandra Allen, and not only was I OK with it, I was *very* OK with it: I was delighted. John Smith's genes explained so many things about my appearance: my flat nose; my punched-in face; the lank hair, all the rubbish bits about me. I no longer felt like some sort of alien Allen, a gargoyle amongst the glam, the proverbial black sheep in the family, because it turns out I'm not really in the Allen flock at all. I'm a Smith, and Smiths aren't leggy blonde beauties, they're as bog-standard ordinary as their bog-standard surname. Standing looking at myself, for the first time in my life I felt my genetic jigsaw was finally beginning to fit together, pieces of John Smith DNA slotting comfortably alongside Mum's.

So when I promised Dad I'd go straight back to school, I meant it.

But moments after I hugged him on the doorstep and sauntered out of the cul-de-sac clutching a note to Mrs Connelly explaining I was late this morning because of a family emergency, it was as if someone blew a hole in my head, random thoughts rushing in to fill the space: Who is he? Where does he live? What does he do? Do I have any half-sisters or brothers? Is his wife a witch or a honey? Is he rich? Does he carry a genetic disease which will require me having a new kidney before I'm twenty-one? On and on the questions came as my brain went into overdrive, its neurons firing at warp speed, my thoughts going into orbit and rattling around my skull. So by the time I arrived at the gates of Haine Court, the chances of me being able to sit meekly in class and concentrate on lessons were roughly the same as the odds of my becoming an international teenage supermodel: zero.

So I carried on walking down the road, past the

building site that is to be our new school, down the high street lined with kebab shops and estate agents towards the sea, which is where I am now, sitting bang in the middle of the beach in my school uniform, the tide going out, my legs spread-eagled, my black pleated skirt tucked under my thighs to prevent an inadvertent display of a purple Top Shop lacy thong, mulling over the John Smith issue, grabbing handfuls of yellowy-brown sand, letting the grains slip through my fingers.

The 'blip' in my parents' marriage wasn't some *coup de foudre*, a thunderbolt of love when Mum met John Smith. Like the real Sonny and Cher, a year after they got married, Mum and Dad started having arguments over silly things: Dad peeing on the loo seat; Mum having a mountain of clothes on a chair in the bedroom; no one doing the washing up. So after one argument too many, Mum left Dad to live with Aunty Julie and first hubby Omar and carried on as Cher, whilst Dad ditched Sonny and tried his hand at being an Elvis impersonator. But Dad missed Mum and the clothes on the chair, and Mum found Omar dripped on the loo seat too, so after three months apart they decided a few pee stains on white enamel or a pile of bras was neither here nor there in the big scheme of things and made up, *after* which Mum discovered she was preggers with me. Dad accepted it, I was born, they started Bjorn At The Beach with Sue and Bob, and the blip was never mentioned again.

So, as far as Mum and Dad are concerned, their little plan has worked out beautifully: everyone now knows the truth and everyone is fine with it. Dad even said that he'd talk to Mum about helping me look for John Smith after my GCSEs next year, *if* I'm still curious.

Except everything's not quite as neat as they think it is, because they're forgetting one person in all this: John Smith, a man who doesn't know he has a daughter because Mum and Dad decided not to tell him.

How dare they deny him the right to know me? Who do they think they are – choosing who my father is, putting Trevor Allen on my birth certificate, knowing it was a barefaced lie – God? What if John Smith would have liked to know me, to have included me in his family, to have me as part of his life? The poor man never stood a chance with those two plotting against him.

Fizzing with fury, I toss a handful of sand angrily towards the sea, a bad move as a gust of wind blows it back in my face. I spit salty grains out of my mouth and rub my eyes, an exfoliation too far as they're already sore from all the morning sobbing. And when my eyes have stopped watering, suddenly everything comes into focus and I'm staring at two slim brown feet standing right over The Sperm Daddy's framed name. Feet aren't the most elegant part of any lad's body, Crab's being particularly odd, like a couple of skate wings strapped to his ankles, but these feet are beautiful: nicely shaped nails, straight hairless toes and no horrid purple veins bulging through the surface.

I follow the feet of beauty up bronzed bare calves that disappear into beige knee-skimming cut-offs, to see a lad of about sixteen in front of me, brandishing a white pole and a black net. He's wearing a football shirt, but whereas Crab looks like some chavy fan in his, the blue top coupled with sheeny olive skin, dark curly hair and a pair of electric blue retro Ray-Bans perched on his nose, makes this lad look like something straight out of a glossy mags' style section, the sort of photo that accompanies an article about footballing hunks under the headline: *Who Would YOU Score With?*

Ray-Ban Boy would be perfect but for two major flaws.

Firstly, by the look of the emblem on his footie shirt he's French.

I hate the French, particularly French girls and the way they manage to look all pouty and sultry, even if they're just paying for a can of Red Bull in Tesco, or the fact that they can wear head to toe black without resembling a stick of liquorice. I particularly hate how they look so judgemental all the time, as if they pity us for not being born French.

But the biggest obstacle to Ray-Ban Boy being voted Hunk of the Day is that he's clearly one of the despised Broadgate Language Academy students, foreign kids sent here to learn English.

Don't get me started on language students! Everyone round here who doesn't make money out of their visit loathes them. With matching rucksacks on their backs and wearing tacky I ♥ London T-shirts, they descend on the town in the summer like aliens from outer space, roaming the streets in giant packs, blocking pavements, screeching with excitement, flooding shops and cafés as they wave their discount vouchers, gabbling in foreign accents and getting shirty over why they can't pay in Euros.

So even though he's seriously hot, this lad stands no chance being French *and* from the language school: a double whammy of despise.

'You've stomped on my father!' I snarl at him. 'His name is the only thing I've got left and you've sabotaged it!' I stab a finger at the letters which are buried somewhere between this foreigner's (cute) ankles. 'You idiot!'

He might not understand the word *sabotaged*, but *idiot* is a pretty universal term.

All around me, volleyball nets are being erected.

Every Monday and Friday, the college organises a beach volleyball tournament, supposedly to bring all the countries together in perfect harmony. The Italians play against the Spanish, the Dutch challenge the Swiss, and the Germans face the Greeks, but from what I can gather, no one wants to mix with the French so they usually have to play with themselves. And now this speccy French boy wants me to move, just so he can put his volleyball net where I'm sitting. Like, no way!

'Get lost,' I sneer. 'Preferably over there.' I point across the water to the French coastline. 'Là-bas!'

I'm just feeling smug that I've put Johnny Foreigner in his place (almost) in his mother tongue, when he starts setting up his volleyball net – right across me.

'Don't you dare!' I shriek, reaching up and grabbing the net, getting a handful of something lumpy. Ray-Ban Boy yells a very English sounding expletive, but with a French accent, and does a bit of hopping around, like he's been dropped in a pan of boiling water.

'Antoine! Antoine! Is there a problem?' A woman with vast boobage bouncing under her yellow polo shirt comes running up. It's one of the Yellow Perils, our nickname for the language school's staff: men and women who follow the foreign kids around town to stop them sneaking into pubs and rolling joints by the clock tower when they should be in lessons.

'Er . . . zur gurl, she will not . . .'

I eyeball him in what I hope is such an aggressive manner he is unable to remember the most basic English, plus, by glaring at him, I can study him for longer.

'Moove.'

And then if I was in any doubt that he indeed is French, he runs his hands through his oily raven-black curls and gives a deliciously moody shrug.

'*I'm* not moving,' I say defiantly, letting go of the netting and lying on the sand, my arms and legs outstretched. 'This sand belongs to everyone, *including* me. Anyway, I was here first. Bog off.'

'I see you're from Haine Court,' the woman says snootily, looking down her nose at me and nodding at my uniform. It's not just the tie that gives me away, it's the slightly odd school crest on my blazer pocket; it's supposed to be a unicorn, but looks more like a donkey with a plunger stuck on its forehead.

The Yellow Peril is called Pam and she speaks French, German and Italian. I know this not because I have met her before, or because my current brain meltdown has given me extraordinary mind-reading powers, but because Pam has a name badge dotted with foreign flags stuck right over her left nipple, and as both Pam's boobs are dangling over me like bags of quivering lemon blancmange, I can't help but get an eyeful of nip name badge.

'Shouldn't you be in school?' Blancmange Boobs demands.

'What's it to you?' I mutter. 'You're not even a proper teacher.'

She flips open her mobile phone. 'Then perhaps I should tell the proper teachers at Haine you're here, on the beach, stranded like a dead starfish. Who's your form tutor?'

This is all I need, being dobbed in it by this witch who has likened me to rotting marine life.

'OK,' I say, scrambling to my feet in a rather undignified way, flashing far too much pasty porky thigh.

In all honesty, I'm glad for the get-out. My beach protest has gathered quite a crowd, barely-dressed volleyballers staring at me, sniggering and whispering behind their hands. And not just boys, girls too, girls with long legs, long hair and real tans are looking down their snotty continental noses at me.

I start trudging across the beach, brushing sand from my clothes, muttering to myself about how unfair my life is and how much easier it would be if I lived abroad, or even on the other side of the Broadgate roundabout.

Stomping up the set of steps that run from the beach to the esplanade, I notice Antoine jogging across the sand. The sun has come out and he's stripped off his top. Most of the foreign kids round here are pretty weedy: all bum fluff and spotty backs, but this guy looks ripped: fab bronzed abs and pecs to die for.

He waves a perfect arm and I look around to see who he's waving at, which foreign fox with Rapunzel hair cascading over her shoulders he's trying to attract.

And then I realize. It's me. Pug Girl.

OMG! OMG! Keep calm. Remind yourself that even though he's drop dead gorgeous and racing towards you, he's still a snail-munching verb-learner.

'What?' I shout out, keeping a slightly cool sneer to my voice as Antoine bounds up the stairs.

My mind is racing ahead with thoughts of steamy dates over garlic bread, day trips to Paris on the Eurostar, and of course, authentic French kissing. And don't they say that the best way to really learn a language is to take a foreign lover? Well, clearly at only fifteen I'm talking sub-lover status here, more serious boyfriend, but if it helps me get an A* French GCSE, that would be a bonus.

Antoine is now level with me, fifty per cent naked, all long limbed and golden like a beautiful freshly baked baguette instead of the sort of lad I'm used to: a pink and white crab stick. The vintage Ray-Bans have been pushed back through his dark curls and he's studying my face with puppy-brown eyes fringed by long lashes.

I hadn't realized how tall he was: given that I was flat on my back and he was standing over me it was hard to tell, but close up I can see he really is a fantastic specimen of French manhood, moody and brooding, stylish in that casual way that only foreigners manage to achieve. Truly, a fabulous frog, or should I say, *une grenouille fabuleuse*.

Then without saying anything, he thrusts a long brown arm towards me, and just when I think he's going to be very proper and shake my hand, he gives me my mobile phone. I must have left it on the beach when I was doing my dead starfish impression.

'*Merci*,' I say, in what I hope is a breathily sexy French accent, pretending to polish sand off the phone when in fact I'm using the silver case as a mirror to perform a speedy nostril and gnasher check. A stray Coco Pop in the gums or a bogey in the nose would crush the 0.000001 per cent chance I have of The Fabulous Frog finding me attractive.

And then safe in the knowledge I'm clean in all visible orifices, I look up with a smile that I hope makes me appear coolly coy rather than mentally deranged.

Antoine? He's vanished into thin air, like he's been vaporized. I even look at the ground to check there's not a smouldering pile of ash at my feet.

As I lean over the stair rail I see his dark curls bob down the steps. Then he stops, looks up at me, sees me looking down at him, our eyes lock and for a brief moment I think he's going to bound back up the stairs, where clearly he will take me in his arms and smother me in hot French kisses.

'Antoine! Antoine!' One of the French foxes is calling him from the beach.

He looks down at her.

He looks up at me.

'Antoine! Rapide!'

Stay with me! I silently beg him. *Don't go to her! You've given me The Look, I know you have. Not just any old look, but a Loaded Look, a look if not of love and lust, at least of interest.*

But he does. With a smile he shrugs, lopes down the last few steps, races across the beach, picks up a white ball and slams it over the net towards a bronzed minx in a white bikini top.

Chapter Nine

'What next?' Taryn asks as, along with over a thousand other kids, we leave Haine Court at the end of a very draining day, the sort of day that's impossible to get through without serious chocolate consumption and two doses of Nurofen.

After my encounter with The Fabulous Frog, I ambled back to school via the newsagents for medically required chocolate supplies because:

A. I couldn't think of anything else to do.

B. Staying away would have meant asking Dad to write me another note, thereby alerting him to the fact that I bunked off.

C. I wanted to see Taryn to update her on everything.

'I dunno,' I sigh. 'I just can't get him out of my head.'

'Well, like your dad says, just wait until after your

GCSEs and then start looking for him,' Taryn suggests. 'I'll help you.'

'I'm talking about The Fabulous Frog, you idiot!' I giggle, keeping an eye out for Crab who's been stalking me between lessons, even though I've made it quite clear he was wrong about Bjorn Bob and that no, we're never ever getting back together, even if he bulk buys me posh Green and Blacks chocolate.

'Oh, now I know you're talking about foreign-lad totty rather than The Sperm Daddy, let's put on loads of slap and hang around the seafront,' Taryn suggests.

'You're on!' I say, grateful for the chance to delay going home, worried about facing Mum over the fact I've confronted Dad.

'Channy?' A woman with long blonde hair, a blunt fringe and bug-eyed sunnies ambushes me in the street. 'There you are.'

It's Sue Myers. I hardly recognized her because I usually only see her dressed as Agnetha Faltskog, and without make-up and sequins, she looks rather plain.

'Claire's already in the car; we're just waiting for you,' she says briskly, as if it's every day she stands outside the gates of Haine Court waiting to take me home in a pea green Nissan Micra with the Bjorn At The Beach logo plastered on each door.

'Me?' I say, looking over the road to where the car is parked. Claire's in the back seat, peering out of the window. 'Why?'

Sue looks puzzled. 'Didn't Sandy or Trevor ring you?' she asks. 'Tell you what's been decided?'

'What's been decided?' I don't like the way this conversation is going. Whatever has been decided has obviously been decided without me, and those sorts of decisions usually stink: witness the green living room which appeared whilst I was on a school geography trip to Romney Marsh.

Sue purses her lips so tightly they're sucked into her face. 'Me and Bob went round to yours this lunchtime to run through the new choreography for *Chiquitita* because I'm finding it a bit, well, challenging, and we walked slap bang straight into the middle of an atmosphere.'

'An atmosphere?' I repeat. 'What sort of atmosphere?'

Sue looks embarrassed. 'Arctic. Icy. Your dad was a bit cagey, but it's obvious your parents are having a few difficulties.' She mouths *difficulties* as if it's a rude word. 'Well, on the way home Bob and I agreed they needed some time and space on their own, so I rang Trevor, and he said that would be good, just for a night or two.'

'*They* need some time and space?' I snap. 'What about me?'

'What about you?' Sue asks. 'You're not part of Kent's premier Abba tribute band, Channy. The atmosphere meant we couldn't practise the step changes. I'm in danger of getting my ankles mixed up and falling off my platforms!'

'What did Mum say?' I ask. I can't believe, even if she is angry with me for confronting Dad, she'd punish me by sending me to the Kent equivalent of Siberia: the Myers' house. It's worse than our place: full of DVDs and feather and crystal dream catchers, not to mention whiny Claire.

'That's the point,' Sue says gravely. 'I didn't see her. Your father said she was in her room with a migraine, but she doesn't get migraines. Heavy periods? Yes. Headaches? No.' Her angular face softens. 'Claire would love to have you stay for a couple of nights. I thought we'd swing by yours so you can pick some stuff up, you know, clean underwear, deodorant.'

I am horrified. I don't want time and space in Sue and Bob's terraced house in Southdown Road whilst World War Three is breaking out at Number Seven. I want to forget about The Sperm Daddy and go to back to the beach with Taryn (via Superdrug to use their make-up samples) and see if we can spot the Totty *de Jour*, stripped to his waist, playing volleyball, the ball slapping against his taut brown arms as he digs it over the net. Other than chocolate, the smouldering looks between us have been the only thing that's been keeping me going all day, as long as I forget that he chose French Minx over *moi*.

'Thanks, but no thanks,' I say. 'I'll be fine.'

Sue's whips off her sunglasses and glares at me with flinty eyes. 'Let's put it another way, Channy. Your parents need some time-out for the good of the group. If Bjorn At The Beach split up, we're *all* out of work. I'll have to go back to serving behind the bar at The Snout and Truffle, and your mum hasn't had enough plastic surgery to pass off as Cher nowadays. We'll just be another set of casualties on the showbiz scrapheap.'

'I don't care about the ruddy group!' I growl. 'I hate the group!'

Taryn puts her hand on my arm. 'Chill out, Chan,' she says. 'If they want you out of the way, come and stay at mine.'

It's a toss up whether I stay at Sue and Bob's and run the risk of murdering their daughter for being such a whiny pain, or killing myself by sleeping on the top bunk in Taryn's room. Last time I stayed, I turned over in bed in the night and rolled straight on to the floor, saved only by the pile of clothes we'd spent the previous evening trying on.

But I'm tired. Tired of having arguments all day in my brain; rowing with Mum and Dad about The Sperm Daddy; reliving the bust up with Crab; wishing I'd thought of something cutting and clever to say to Blancmange Boobs and taken on all those snotty French vixens just because even the thought of them annoys me. I don't have enough energy left to be stroppy with Sue. I don't want to talk to drippy Claire, but I do need a night's sleep, and if I'm going to lie awake worrying about breaking my neck from one false bunk-move, the Myers are a better bet.

'I'll see you tomorrow,' I say wearily to Taryn.

There's a faint knocking at the door of the spare bedroom.

I ignore it and keep reading, lying back on one of the two single beds.

The knocking continues. It's driving me crazy. I can't finish this page whilst it carries on: it's too distracting.

I get up, stomp over to the door and throw it open.

'What?' I say to the podgy child standing before me in a bright pink T-shirt and grey baggy-kneed leggings. 'What do you want?'

'Um, nothing,' Claire says shyly, pushing her thick

lenses up her nose. 'I just wondered how you were?'

'I'm just the same as when you asked me when I arrived, when we had tea, and when I left you after *EastEnders* to come up here,' I snap. 'In other words, I'm fine.'

This is far from the truth; I'm constantly veering between Antoine lust and parent-directed anger. When I went back to Lea Crescent to pick up my things there was no sign of Mum, just Dad, sitting on the end of the stairs, bleak-faced. When I asked him what was going on he just said: 'I'm sorry, love. Just give us a day or two, eh?' and moved out of the way to let me go upstairs. And by the time I came back down, Sue was in the hall being all perky and pushing me back out on to the drive.

'What are you reading?' Claire asks, her round shiny face peering at the book I'm holding.

'It's about Sylvia Plath,' I mutter.

'Is she on telly?' Claire asks. 'Or in a girl band?'

I hear myself let out a derisory snort. 'As if!' I sneer. 'She's dead! She sealed up the kitchen and stuck her head in a gas oven, but she wrote loads of stuff before she did it.'

Then I close the door and fling myself back on the bed.

Oh, God. I've been mean to an unfortunate female.

It's Slow Jo all over again, and look what happened after that! Being mean to people creates bad karma – other than to Crab, Blancmange Boobs and French girls, *obviously*.

I haul my tired bod off the bed and open the door.

Claire's still there, a piglet in a training bra.

'Come on in,' I say.

'I like having you here,' Claire says, sitting on the edge of one pink and white flowery duvet-covered single bed, whilst I sit crossed legged on the other, powering up my laptop, having abandoned Sylvia because it was just too depressing, even for me who likes a bit of misery in my books. 'How long are you staying?'

'Dunno,' I say.

I log on to the Myers' wireless network, which Bjorn Bob has helpfully told me has a highly secure and impossible to guess password: *Abba1221*. I have absolutely no intention of doing any homework tonight – I'm much too stressed by the whole situation to even consider doing anything vaguely academic – but having invited Claire into her own spare bedroom, I realize I've nothing to say to an eleven-year-old who can't take her speccy eyes off me.

'Why are you staying?' Claire asks.

'Parent stuff,' I mutter, Googling John Smith. Over five million hits and that's not counting the fact that he might really be called Jonathon or Jon or Johnnie or even Smyth. My head spins at the number of ways The Sperm Daddy could spell his name.

I give up and load Facebook.

'I heard Mum talking to Dad in the kitchen. She seemed to think Bjorn At The Beach might break up. Do you think they will?' Claire asks.

'Dunno,' I shrug, peering at the screen. Cousin Tracie has posted the bridesmaid photo of me that, whilst rank, isn't as bad as I thought it might be, the dressed up dogs distracting from the dire dress and the black bags.

'I wish it would,' Claire says glumly, as I type in the comments box that I look like a pug in a frock, mainly to run myself down before anyone else does. 'I hate the group.'

I'm surprised. Whiny Claire looks exactly the sort of girl who would love to bop around to Abba tunes and drool over sequins. She'd have made a much better daughter for Mum and Dad than I do.

'Me too,' I say, looking up from the screen. 'I'm more of a Nirvana type of girl. I'm going to get a rat called Kurt, you know, after Kurt Cobain?'

Claire looks blank.

'The pioneers of grunge rock from Seattle?' Clearly this girl has no musical education.

'It's not the music.' Claire hugs her knees and pulls a face. 'I'm fed up of them being out performing all the time. I get shipped over to Mrs Wallen's, the childminder. It's dead boring over there, full of stinky little kids. I just watch telly and eat crisps and sweets.'

Obviously, I think rather unkindly.

'Well, you are only eleven,' I say. 'You can't be left home alone at eleven. It's illegal.'

Claire looks as if she might explode. 'I'm twelve!' she squeaks. 'I was twelve at the end of April! And *you* stay home alone.'

'Not until I was a teenager,' I point out primly. '*That's* different.'

I turn back to Facebook and update my status to: *Channy Allen: has been kidnapped.*

'What are you doing?' Claire asks.

'Updating my Facebook status,' I say, noticing that almost instantly Cousin Tracie has come back with a: *WHAAAAAT?*

I'm being held against my will in a terraced house with a bra-wearing piglet, I type back.

Taryn's clearly on Facebook rather than doing her homework, as she comments: *Not going so well at Aggie*

Sue's house then? To which Cousin Stacie replies: *Hahaha hahahahahahaha!!!!! Luv Ya!* Which would be nice if she didn't put *Luv Ya!* on the end of every single Facebook comment.

'Can I look?' Whiny Claire asks, leaving her bed and hovering by my side.

I can't have her seeing my piglet comment, so I pull the screen protectively towards me. 'Don't you have your own Facebook page?' I ask.

'I'm not allowed until I'm thirteen,' she pouts, still hovering, clearly furious at the injustice of not being allowed to social network. 'Mum won't let me. This girl in my class, Bethany, she's the same age as me, but *her* mum lets her have a page. That's how she met her boyfriend, Elliot. Well, she hasn't actually met him, but they email each other all the time. Do you have a boyfriend?'

This puts me in a difficult position. I am clearly some kind of hero to this kid. *No* isn't the type of answer she's expecting.

'Of course,' I say, as if this is the most ridiculous question in the world.

'What's he called?'

I could lie and pretend I'm still seeing Crab, but if I'm going to fib, I might as well go the whole way and make the lie a really juicy one. And pretending you have a foreign boyfriend isn't that much different from pretending you have a sister called Donna, is it?

'Antoine,' I say. 'He's French.'

'Oh!' Claire looks all dreamy-eyed, as if she's just been plonked in front of a mountain of Walnut Whips. 'French! That is *so* cool. How did you meet him?'

'Well,' I say, feeling much better now that I'm talking about Antoine rather than stressing about what's going on in Lea Crescent without me. 'He's a student at The Broadgate Language Academy, here to learn English. I met him on the beach when he was playing volleyball.' At least this bit is true.

'How long have you been seeing him?' Claire's tongue is hanging out and I swear there's steam on her glasses. 'Is it serious?'

I fold my arms across my chest. 'Only about four weeks,' I say gravely, but yes, it's *very serious*.' I lower my voice to almost a whisper. 'Don't tell anyone, but I'm thinking of visiting him in France when he goes back at the end of his course.' Antoine is so gorgeous, if we were really going out, I'd be prepared to swim across the Channel, even if I did come head-to-turd with sewage.

'What does he look like?' Claire is practically hyperventilating, and I must admit, just thinking about

Antoine is setting my pulse racing. 'Is he super-gorge?'

'Mega super-gorge,' I assure her. 'The body of a Love God: dark hair, really ripped pecs, buffed to bits, the total package. I call him The Fabulous Frog.'

'Can I see him on Facebook?'

Ah. This has rather thrown me. Claire is now standing next to me, her tummy sticking through her T-shirt, a roll of fat spilling over her waistband. Whilst she's been cross-examining me over my fake boyfriend, Stacie has sent a message demanding a picture of a pig in underwear.

'He's not on Facebook,' I say, clicking on Tracie's snap of me in my bridesmaid dress so that Claire won't see the piglet comment. 'But look at me here!'

I swivel the laptop round.

'You and the dogs look sooo pretty,' Claire coos, though I'd rather she hadn't mentioned me in the same adoring breath as the pugs. 'I've never been a bridesmaid.'

'It's overrated,' I tell her. 'Believe me.'

'If you marry Antoine, can I be your bridesmaid?'

'Umm,' I say, not having progressed the Antoine fantasy to going beyond serious snogging under the clock tower on the seafront. 'Maybe one day.'

'Are you sure he's not on Facebook?' Now Claire's

heard about Antoine, she's not giving up. 'Have you tried searching for him, looking for his picture?'

'I think I'd know if my boyfriend was on Facebook,' I snap. 'And he's not, OK?'

I pull the laptop back towards me, and Claire retreats, wounded, to the spare bed, hugging her knees for comfort.

I've been a bitch. Again. Bad things will happen to me as revenge.

'Look, Claire, I'm sorry,' I say. 'I'm just a bit of a stress-head with all the stuff going on at home. Ignore me.'

'S'OK,' Claire says, unconvincingly, clearly hurt that me, her new, older best friend with a hot foreign guy in tow has shot her down. 'I just thought searching for him wouldn't do any harm.'

Claire's dad comes in, and then knocks on the inside of the door. Looking at him I'm mega relieved that he's not The Sperm Daddy. I *so* wouldn't want those genes.

'It's gone nine, Claire,' Bjorn Bob smiles, tapping his watch. 'Time you were getting washed and ready for bed.'

Claire sits sullenly on the bed, refusing to move.

'Claire?' Her dad's voice has that tone parents use in front of visitors, trying to be both stern and yet friendly.

'Look,' I say to Claire. 'Do as your dad says and if you

ever come round to ours, I'll let you try on that bridesmaid's dress. OK?' I've honestly not crossed to the dark side, the side of parents and rules and sticking up for Bjorn Bob, it's just there's something Claire has said which means I have to get her out of this room ASAP. I don't intend her ever to set foot inside *my* bedroom, so there's no need to worry about playing dress-up.

'Coo-ul!' Claire beams, scrambling off the bed. She hovers by the door. 'And the tiara? You'll let me try on the tiara?'

'*And* the tiara,' I promise her. 'Now scoot!'

Chapter Ten

'You bloody idiot,' Taryn screeches. 'I can't believe you've done what you've done. Pretending to the kid that you have a foreign boyfriend is one thing, but sending all those messages! You're one pickle short of a jar!'

We're lying in the sun on the grassy bank just inside the school gates, making the most of our pitiful half-hour lunch-break before being herded back into pens and force-fed GCSE maths. I've just been updating Taryn on what happened at Sue and Bob's last night, and to say my news hasn't gone down well is somewhat of an understatement.

'Thanks for your support,' I say sourly, shoving my hand into a packet of Quavers and shortly afterwards biting down hard on a light and cheesy curl. 'If I'd known you were going to be all arsy about it, I'd never have told you.'

'Well, you have, and now you're going to be inundated with weirdos and paedos and all sorts of freak balls. That's the sort of dumb-ass thing I'd do, not you!' She pelts me with one of the salted cashew nuts she's eating. 'How many did you fire off?'

'One thousand three hundred and thirty-seven,' I admit, thinking back to how I spent pretty much all last night and most of the early hours of the morning on the laptop: choosing, cutting, pasting and clicking. It could have been more (there are over seventy-five thousand John Smith's on Facebook), but I became so tired I fell asleep mid-click, and only woke-up when Sue brought me a cup of tea in the morning and found me still in my school uniform, my head resting on my kaput laptop, the battery having drained down in the night.

Yes, I've started searching for The Sperm Daddy.

The thing is, I can honestly say that I never intended to look for him on Facebook. When Claire left to go and snuggle under a mountain of cuddly toys, dreaming about my fictional boyfriend, I meant to search for Antoine, to find out a bit more about The Fabulous Frog, especially since I'm supposed to be going out with him. But when despite rapidly scrolling through more than six thousand pictures I couldn't find anyone called Antoine who looked even remotely like the buff boy on the beach, more from boredom than anything else I typed: *John Smith* into the name search, and saw all these potential Sperm Daddies pop up, and although no one looked like me, out of curiosity I randomly picked one man (glasses, bald, clearly an accountant) and composed a message saying I was Chantelle 'Channy' Allen, and I was looking for my father John Smith, a man who fifteen years ago did something in the City and knew mother, Sandra Allen, also known as Cher. I apologized if I'd got the wrong John Smith, and said that if he was the right John Smith I didn't want to cause any hassle with his new family or stir things up, and I wasn't going to demand money (I might review this if I find he's loaded), but I'd like to know what he looks like, whether I have any half-brothers and sisters (particularly brothers because of the whole alien-baby scenario) and where he lives, just in case I have to contact him not for cash, but for one of his organs.

And then I pressed Send, and it didn't feel too bad. I didn't freak out or have a panic attack at what I'd done, and I knew that my privacy settings were Colditz tight and he can't see what I look like because of the Book Burqa, so I started all over again with the next John Smith, being careful not to choose anyone who looked too young from their photos to be the father of a fifteen-year-old. But then I became gripped with Sperm Daddy fever, and started setting myself targets like: *I'll just do ten; I'll stop at fifty; make it a hundred*, until the hundreds mounted up and then I had to try for a thousand and beyond. My ambition before I fell asleep was to contact one thousand five hundred John Smiths.

'I didn't send a message to anyone who had weird photos,' I assure Taryn, omitting the fact that I'd sent one to a John Smith who'd used a picture of Herbage Dappledawn (one of the little brown rabbits from Sylvanian Families) as his profile shot, just because when I was a kid I used to love Sylvanian Families and I thought it was such a cute picture to use.

'Well, that's all right then, isn't it?' Taryn snaps. 'You can obviously tell a Warp Head just by looking at his picture.'

'I hoped you'd understand,' I mutter through another mouthful of fried corn strips, spitting Quaver shards into the air. 'I thought you might even help me track him down.' I angrily brush crumbs off my lap. 'You're being totally neg about the whole thing. Some friend you are!'

'Look,' Taryn says, her tone softening. 'I just think this whole thing will end in tears. You've only known about The Sperm Daddy for a few days, and so far it's ended up with a row at home, you moving out . . .'

'I was pushed out,' I grumble. 'I didn't move out.'

'Chan, give it up!' Taryn pleads. 'For now, anyway. Promise me?'

Just to shut her up I mumble something non-committal as Ameena, Emily and Gaia amble up. I quite like Ameena and Emily, but Gaia's a gossip.

'We could hear you two arguing from round by the science block,' Gaia says. 'Having a lovers tiff?'

'Hah! Hah!' Taryn sneers, as the three of them sit down and pull their skirts over their thighs.

'What's up?' Emily asks, tipping her freckle-face towards the sun.

I throw Taryn a look to let her know that if she tells anyone what I've done and why I've done it, she's as good as dead on the grass.

'Nothing,' I say as convincingly as I can.

'How come Taryn was walking to school on her own this morning then?' Gaia starts her interrogation. 'You weren't on the roundabout. I looked down from the bus. You was nowhere.'

'I spent the night at Bjorn Bob and Aggie Sue's,' I say.

'Kinky!' Gaia giggles. 'Does Crab know?'

'Oh get lost,' I snort. She knows fine well they're part of the group. 'We're having some work done at home, building stuff, so I'm staying in Southdown Road for a bit. And I've binned Crab, remember?'

'Don't look now,' Ameena whispers. 'But I think a kiddiewink has a lezzer crush on one of us.'

She nods at a girl hovering at the edge of the grass, staring at us with a soppy smile on her face. When she sees us looking at her, she gives a shy wave. It's Claire Myers.

'It's OK,' I say. 'She's just the kid of the people I'm staying with.'

I give a sort of half-wave back, more of a hand of acknowledgment than a friendly wagging of the mitt. Unfortunately, Claire takes this as a sign to come over, her bulk bobbing up and down as she hurries towards us.

'Hi,' she says breathlessly, looking down at her feet, her white socks spilling over the edge of her black ballet flats.

'Yeah?' I say, trying to let Claire know that whatever happened in the spare bedroom last night, Year 7's and Year 10's don't mix during break-time leg-tanning sessions.

'I – I just wondered,' Claire stutters nervously, red faced, 'whether you were coming home with me and Mum, or, or, whether you were seeing your boyfriend after school.'

'You just said you and him were over,' Emily points out. 'Binned.'

'You've broken up with Antoine?' Claire's face falls. 'Oh, poor you! And you were so in love!'

'Who the heck is Antoine?' Gaia asks, as several sets of eyes fix on me.

'Channy's boyfriend! The Fabulous Frog!' Whiny Claire seems thrilled that she has info my friends don't. 'He's a fit French boy she met on the beach. They've been going out for four weeks, he's got the body of a love god and it's *very* serious. You're going to go back to France with him, aren't you?'

If the kid thinks she's going to try on my bridesmaid's dress now, she can think again. If I had the tiara on me, I'd ram it down her throat.

'It's complicated,' I mumble.

'Obviously,' Taryn says sarkily, though I can tell she's trying not to wet herself laughing.

'So what does Crab think about the fact that you've been two-timing him?' Gaia asks. 'Does he even know?'

'Who's Crab?' Claire's wide-eyed.

'Channy's other boyfriend,' Ameena explains.

'You've got two boyfriends?' Any pedestal Claire put me on has just been cranked up to an even higher level. 'Wow! So you haven't really broken up with Antoine?'

She stares at me and I mutter 'No' under my breath, which of course is the truth. I haven't broken up with him because I didn't go out with him in the first place.

'So shall I wait for you or not?' Claire asks.

'I'll make my own way back to yours,' I snap irritably, as the bell goes for afternoon lessons.

Never I have I been so grateful to be forced back inside.

Chapter Eleven

After two nights camped out in the Myers' spare room, I'll be back in my own bed tonight.

Mum left a message on my moby whilst I was belting a shuttlecock around a badminton court this afternoon, to say that it was about time I came home and she was cooking my favourite meal. Clearly, the arctic atmosphere has thawed, and the white flag of surrender has gone up, or rather the Shepherd's Pie of Peace.

Sue Myers turns the pea on wheels into Lea Crescent and pulls up to the curb outside Number Seven.

'Thank you for having me!' I say cheerfully, scrambling out as Sue opens the boot of the car.

'Any time!' Sue trills with cheerful insincerity, thrusting my bags at me.

The only person in the car who isn't cheery is Claire. She's in the back seat looking heartbroken, stuffing her face with pastel-coloured Flying Saucers. The poor kid actually had tears in her eyes when she saw me packing my bag and stripping the bed, though my warbling of James Brown's *I Feel Good* perhaps wasn't the most tactful exit.

I wave as Claire and Sue drive away, gather up my stuff, and head towards the front door, shuffling sideways to get past the Abbamobile, difficult with four bags: overnight stuff, laptop, school and gym.

A darkly dressed figure darts out from behind the van and ambushes me on the drive, grabbing my wrist. Given that I was expecting to be hugged rather than mugged, I scream and start battering my attacker with the full might of my baggage, swinging everything I've got at this evil assailant until he loosens his grip.

'Ow! Stop it! You're hurting me!' the attacker wails.

It's Crab, still in his school uniform.

'You bloody idiot!' I scream. 'You could have given me a heart attack.'

'How could you?' Crab yells. His eyes are puffy, wet and red-rimmed. He's been crying. 'Gaia told me that you've been seeing some other lad! That's why you binned me!'

'It's not like that,' I mutter, trying to dodge past him. 'You've got it all wrong.'

'Have I?' Crab body blocks me. 'So you never told Gaia that you've been seeing some foreigner for the last four weeks?' he asks accusingly. 'Some greasy frog called Anton.'

'It's *Antoine*, actually,' I say in my best French accent, 'and, well, yes I did but . . .' I let my voice fade away. Perhaps if he thinks I'm seeing someone else he might realize we're never going to get back together. 'I'm sorry Crab, I didn't want to hurt you.'

'I asked you whether there was someone else and you said no!' Crab is winding himself up. 'You lied to me! All this stuff about your head being filled with family crap was lies, wasn't it?' He's flinging his arms around. They're long, there's not much room and I'm concerned that he might inadvertently give me a black eye.

'No, it really is,' I say, flattening myself against the Abbamobile. 'Look, don't say anything to anyone. My Sperm Daddy wasn't Bjorn Bob, it's a man called John Smith. I've started looking for him. It's caused a bit of trouble in there.' I nod towards the house. 'Honestly.'

'Honest?' Crab snipes. 'You don't know the meaning of the word!'

'Channy?' It's Dad. If he's come to rescue me from my mugger, he's a bit slow off the mark; I could be slumped on the tarmac by now. 'Everything OK?' He looks at me, and then to a damp-eyed Crab. 'What's going on?'

'Ask her!' Crab snaps. 'The two-faced lying cow!'

'Crab!' Dad snaps. 'Don't speak to my daughter like that!'

My ex-boyfriend stares at Dad. 'But she isn't your daughter, is she?' he sniffs. 'She's someone else's daughter. She's got her two-faced genes from The Sperm Daddy!'

Dad slides his eyes across to me. I slide my eyes to my feet.

'She's been looking for him too, haven't you?'

This isn't the Crab I know, the kind caring Crab. But he's hurt, lashing out, trying to get at me, wounding Dad in the crossfire.

'Right!' Dad yells. 'That's it, Crab! I want you to go and I want you to go *now*!'

For a moment, Crab stands his ground, jutting his chin out. Then he bursts into tears.

'Ask her!' he sobs, scuttling off into the street, jabbing a bony hand in my direction. 'Ask her what she's done!'

Dad heaves my bags off the drive and makes towards the front door.

'What did you do?' he asks over his shoulder.

'I sent a few messages to men called John Smith on Facebook,' I admit.

Dad drops the bags and swivels to face me. 'No, I meant to Crab. But now you've mentioned it, did you find anything out?' His voice is wobbly and wary, like he's just asked the doctor: *How long have I got to live?*

'Yeah, that there are millions of John Smiths, so I couldn't be bothered. If I thought he was rich I might have tried a bit harder though,' I say, laughing with nerves. I don't tell him that so far I've had twelve messages back, some polite saying: *Sorry, I can't be your father, but good luck in your search*, others along the lines of a quick: *Not me!* or: *Damn! I've been discovered!* One made me feel sick just reading it as it said chillingly: *I can be anyone you want me to be!* I deleted them all and vowed not to tell Taryn that I'd had a message from a creep so as not to invoke shrieks of: *I told you so!*

Dad grabs both my hands and shaking them, looks straight into my eyes.

'Channy, promise me that you won't spend time and energy looking for this man, will you?' he says earnestly. 'This John Smith. Honestly love, it's just not worth it.'

'You said you'd help me look for him when you told me,' I remind him. 'Maybe next summer.'

'I know what I said, and I meant it at the time, but promise me you'll leave it until after A Levels?' His hands are really gripping mine now. 'Please.' To go back to the doctor and the terminal illness analogy, it feels as if Dad's pleading for a little extra time to live.

I don't say anything, just stand in the sunshine, the smell of Shepherd's Pie wafting through the open front door.

It's good to be home. Spending two nights amongst the wind chimes and crystals at Sue and Bob's with Whiny Claire made me long for Lea Crescent, despite the lack of books and the full-length mirror in the field-like living room. I'm still desperate for a sister, and I know that the moment Mum and Dad leave me on my own to go to a gig I'll feel lonely again, but on balance, I'm pretty lucky.

I can put my curiosity about The Sperm Daddy on hold, for now.

'OK,' I assure him. 'I promise.'

Chapter Twelve

'Can't we just slam and go?' I grumble. 'If you'd remembered to post them, that's what the postie would have done. He wouldn't like, ring the bell and sing *Happy Birthday*, would he?'

It's late afternoon on Saturday 26th June. We're hurtling towards Aunty Nicola and Uncle Kevin's house at the posh end of Kingsgate because Mum forgot to post Stacie and Tracie's fifteenth birthday cards. Annoyingly, she's insisting that we knock on the door and show our faces rather than just put them through the letterbox and scoot, my preferred *modus operandi*.

'Absolutely not,' Mum says firmly, dropping two pink rectangles on my lap, one card a picture of a white rabbit with a pink nose, the other, three kittens in a basket, both Mum's choice, *not* mine. 'What if they saw you sneaking up the drive and sneaking back without saying hello? They'd think it was weird.'

'They think I'm well weird anyway,' I point out, sneering at the envelopes, at other drivers, at the smart houses in Kingsgate, at everything. Wedged between the parentals in the front of the Abbamobile, I'm in yet another narky mood because against my better judgement I've agreed to piglet sit tonight, i.e. look after Claire Myers whilst Bjorn At The Beach play a gig, a seventies evening at a Travelodge near Sittingbourne. Sue rang in a panic late last night to say that Claire's childminder had gone down with a bad dose of shingles, and would I like to earn some money sitting in their house watching telly and eating snacks? Faced with a financial crisis (I always need more money) and a Saturday night without any social plans (Taryn's got a stinky summer cold), I agreed, and now the prospect of spending all evening with Whiny Claire is depressing me.

Dad pulls off the main road into The Maltings, a small and exclusive development of modern executive homes with Tudor influenced architecture. I know this not because there are clearly only a handful of identical cream houses clad in brown beams dotted either side of the tree-lined lane, but because when she moved here two years ago, Aunty Nicola used to carry the glossy

126

brochure around in her handbag, showing everyone the room layouts, pointing out close-up shots of the designer mixer taps: *Italian! Marvellous flow! Practically a work of art by the basin!* Yawn.

But despite the exclusivity of the mock-Tudor enclave, this afternoon there's nowhere to park the Abbamobile. The Maltings is bonnet-to-boot packed with transit vans.

'Looks like one of the neighbours is having a bit of a do,' Dad says, backing the van out of the road and parking on the main street.

We clamber out and trudge back to The Maltings, specifically Number Three, or *Tudor Grange* as the name picked out in seashells on the plaque on the five bar gate announces.

From the amount of scurrying up and down the gravel drive, it looks as if the Allen family (*nouveau riche* branch) are the ones having the bit of a do.

'The twins wouldn't have a birthday party without inviting Channy, would they?' Mum throws Dad a dark look we approach the front door. 'I mean, they're cousins.'

Step-cousins, I think. Just because I've put on hold my search for The Sperm Daddy doesn't mean I've been able to put the whole family tree thing out of my mind, especially since I'm still getting Facebook replies (three hundred and forty seven so far) from weirdos. Taryn was right. It was a stupid thing to do.

The door opens before Dad has a chance to grab the black metal gargoyle knocker.

'Mrs Allen didn't mention anything about booking an Abba act,' a snippy-faced woman says, pulling a crumpled piece of paper out of the back pocket of her jeans and scanning it. 'Or is this a cold call on the off-chance of a booking, as if so, we've got more age-appropriate entertainment lined up.'

Did I forget to mention that the parentals are totally Abbafied? They're dropping me off at the Myers' on their way to Sittingbourne, so they're on the doorstep dressed in sequins, platforms, slinky catsuits: the whole hot chilli.

A flushed Aunty Nicola appears in a denim mini-skirt and pink strappy top.

'Oh!' she says, peering behind Snippy Woman's shoulder, sounding surprised, looking embarrassed. 'We weren't expecting you.'

'We've brought the twins' birthday cards,' Mum says, then shoves me in the back so that I'm standing on the step, offering two pink envelopes to two women, neither of whom seem to want to take them. Eventually Snippy Woman stomps off, consulting her list, and I thrust the cards at Aunty Nicola, who has no choice but to take them.

'I'd invite you in,' Aunty N says lamely, 'but we're a bit busy.'

'Really?' Mum's voice drips with sarcasm.

We step aside to let a man carrying a giant hammer and an armful of ropes through the door.

'The twins are having a little party,' Aunty Nicola explains. 'Just a few close friends from school. More of an intimate dinner really.'

The Helium Twins crowd the doorstep, peering over their Mum's freckly-brown shoulder.

'Hello Aunty Sandy! Hello Uncle Trevor!' they trill, leaving me out.

'Happy Birthday, girls!' Dad says to his nieces. He tries to reach over to kiss them, but there's too many people and not enough room and clearly Aunty Nicola isn't going to let any member of my family put even so much as a silver platform toe over the threshold of their crappy Tudor new build. 'I hear you're having a party.'

'It's not *just* a party,' Twin One trills. 'It's a pop-up club! Like, you know, those pop-up clubs and restaurants in London, the one-night only jobbies? We're having one in the garden.'

'We've got a marquee and a top DJ from Margate!'

'And a plunge pool!'

'And sushi! Remember the sushi!'

'And glowy hand stamps, like in real clubs.'

'And bouncers! We've got bouncers!'

'We're calling it: Ministry of Mayhem at The Maltings!'

Their shrill voices get even shriller as they start bobbing around on the doorstep with excitement.

'Hardly an intimate dinner party then,' I mutter, throwing Aunty N what I hope is a knowing look, the sort of look that says: *I know you didn't want to invite me.* 'I didn't see you put anything on Facebook.'

Twin Two gives me a half-smile. I expect it's Trace. She's dressed like her sister: teeny-weeny shorts and a cleavage busting yellow tartan shirt, but Trace is better at pitiful *talking to saddo* faces than Stace.

'We kept it quiet to stop gatecrashers. We did think about inviting you,' she says gravely, 'but we know how much you hate dancing, mixing, you know, having fun. Parties just aren't your thing, are they, Channy?' They both look pityingly at me, as if not liking parties is as terrible as finding out you have an incurable brain tumour.

I feel stabbed through my stomach. Tarty Trace is right, I wouldn't have gone, but I would have liked to have been invited, if only to sneer that I wouldn't been seen dead eating raw fish in a tent in their back garden because I already have a packed social calendar.

'Would you like to come?' Aunty Nicola asks me. She's been standing silent and sheepish. 'I'm sure we could stand a few extra seaweed rolls if necessary, couldn't we, girls?'

That's all I need, a pity invite. The tone of Aunty N's voice leads me in no doubt that she's hoping my answer will be *no*, and the way the Helium Twins are pouting at their mum's outrageous suggestion, they clearly think that inviting me would be like inviting the Grim Reaper to their party (sorry, pop-up club), i.e. the kiss of death.

'I've already got stuff going on tonight,' I say in a tone of voice which I hope gives the impression that I have something *much* more exciting to do than go to their stupid birthday bash.

'Yes, but it's only babysitting,' Mum points out to Aunty Nicola, steam almost blowing from her ears. 'If you'd invited Channy earlier, at least she'd have the option of whether to come or not.'

'Sorree,' one of the twins says without any hint of sorrow in her voice. 'But we'll keep posting photies on Facebook, so you can see what's going on!'

'Claire, get to bed!' I order. 'I promised your mum you'd be in bed by nine and it's now ten. If she comes back and finds you still in your jeggings and stuff, I'll be toast!'

Claire stands in front of me looking defiant behind her thick specs. 'They won't be back until eleven! Just tell me about one more date with Antoine, pleeeeeze!'

She plops down on her chubby knees and pretends to pray in front of me.

'Pretty pleeeeze!'

So far, my evening babysitting Claire Myers has not gone according to plan. I really thought that I would bowl up, the two of us could sprawl on the brown leather sofa watching some cheesy talent-show, and then I could boot her off to bed and settle down with some salty snacks, a bar of chocolate and a film before Sue and Bob came back and pushed a few notes into my hand. Easy money.

I hadn't counted on Claire wanting every detail she could think of about Antoine. It's been like taking part in a real-life version of one of those *How well do you know your fella?* type quizzes you see in magazines: *What is his favourite colour? Who is his favourite band? Does he dress on the left or the right side?*

Clearly as I have no idea about any of these things, haven't seen Antoine since the day at the beach almost two weeks ago, and have never had anything but a one-sided conversation with him (assuming *Merci* counts as a conversation), I've had to make the answers up as I've gone along, which has been totally exhausting. At one point, I said that Antoine's best friend was called Arnaud, then I mentioned he was called Artair, and Claire was down on my inconsistency like a tonne of bricks. In a flash of brilliance influenced by my brush with Stacie and Tracie earlier in the day, I pretended Antoine was bezzies with identical twins, Arnaud *and* Artair. I'm beginning to wish that I had agreed to stay the night as then we could both go to bed and I could plot delicious revenge on the Helium Twins for not inviting me to their poxy pop-up club, something along the lines of the raw fish giving all the guests untreatable intestinal parasites.

'No,' I say firmly, desperate to get Claire out of the way. 'No more French facts! I'm banning the F-word.'

'Does he have any brothers or sisters?' Claire tries. 'What does his dad do?'

'Claire!' I shout. 'He's an only child because his little sister, Giselle, died at birth and his dad is a neurosurgeon specialising in reattaching severed limbs. Now go to bed or I won't bring you the bridesmaid's dress.'

I'd promised Claire that next time I saw her I'd let her try on the pink monstrosity, and she practically peed on the carpet with excitement.

Claire's face shows that she's weighing up which is

more important: getting juicy bits of information about an older girl's sexy foreign fella, or looking like a princess in pink satin. The dress clearly wins as she yells, 'Nighty Night!' and rushes upstairs to bed.

I wait for her to gallop back down again with some new Antoine-related query (I'm amazed she hasn't asked his surname, a shame as I have Depardieu up my sleeve), but after a lot of stomping about above me, it all goes quiet.

I swing my feet on to the sofa, wedge some turquoise satin cushions behind my head, and, trying not to imagine every local teen except me raving it up at The Maltings, switch on the telly and pop open a tube of barbeque Pringles.

Hundreds of channels. Zero to watch.

I dig the book de jour out of my bag: *Girl Interrupted* by Susannah Kaysen; I'm too depressed to read a book about depressed people.

I look at my phone. No texts from anyone and I can't surf the web on my prehistoric pay-as-you go jobby.

My eyes flick restlessly around the room as I decide what to do next. They alight on Bob and Sue's computer set up on a desk in the corner, its green standby-by light flashing on the casing of the dark screen.

I could look at Facebook on Bob's PC, torturing myself

to see what's going on at The Maltings. I'm sure he wouldn't mind me using it. He doesn't seem the sort of man to have weird and possibly illegal things on his hard drive and, anyway, he gave me his password last time I was here. I could just surf away, then cover my tracks by deleting the pages in Bob's browsing history. Sorted!

I roll off the sofa, get up, go over, sit on the swivel chair and press a random keyboard key. The screen bursts into life with a screensaver of the real Abba who, rather alarmingly, seem to be naked and trussed in a strip of silver tinfoil.

I go straight to my Facebook page.

Tracie and Stacie have already started posting snaps of the party.

Humiliatingly, I notice some of the girls from Haine Court are there, girls who aren't at the twins' school but who clearly pass the cute and cool test. They're in their teeny-weeny chavvy pool party gear, boobs out, legs out – Who's that? I peer closer at the screen. At the back of a shot, towering over a group of barely dressed girls, their arms around a variety of semi-naked lads, is Crab.

I'm furious. Even the fact that Crab looks bored doesn't make me feel any better. What's he doing there when I'm stuck here?

To torture myself even further, I look at how many

Facebook friends Stacie and Tracie have now. One thousand and twenty, each! The chances are The Helium Twins don't know any of these 'friends', but it makes them look mega popular, their perfect Facebook lives filled with status updates of parties, new dresses and cool buddies. My status update would be: **Channy Allen** *is piglet sitting*.

I'm just about to log off and cover my tracks when I see a little red 1 next to the message symbol at the top of the page.

I drop down the menu. There's a picture of Herbage Dappledawn, AKA John Smith. Herbage Dappledawn has sent me a message titled: Your Enquiry

My heart doesn't do the whole lurch and hammer routine in the way it did in those first few days after I emailed all those strangers. I'm used to clicking on a message and after I've flicked my eyes over the contents, pressing delete.

I open the message.

Dear Chantelle,

Thank you for your message.

I don't want to get your hopes up too much, but if your mum is Sandra Allen who sang in pubs and clubs around London and Kent as Cher, there's a possibility I may be the man you're looking for.

If you want to start some correspondence, please email me. As I say, it's a long shot, but perhaps worth finding out a little more?

Regards,

John Smith

Chapter Thirteen

I have come to the depressing conclusion that the more you look forward to something (being a bridesmaid, finding out the name of your bio-dad, your first proper kiss with tongues), the more of a let down it is.

Take today for instance.

Whilst not in the same league as Glastonbury or the V Festival, I'd been mega excited when three months ago Taryn and I got tickets for Kestival, a one-day music festival held on the last Saturday in June promoting rock bands with a Kent connection, even if the link is only that the drummer's nan once had a holiday in Margate.

The moment the local radio station announced that this year they'd be sponsoring the event and it would be BIGGER and BETTER than ever (not hard as last year it was a couple of unsigned indie bands and a few totally sad-looking fairground rides), I'd started planning my outfit. I was totally going to rock the look with khaki shorts, red wellies (not because it might rain, but because last year the field was full of cow pats and my toes had moo poo squeezed between them), my favourite Stone the Crows T-Shirt, some seriously dark shades, a straw Stetson, and every festival-goer's accessory of necessity – a bottle of designer mineral water.

I imagined floating around, listening to up and coming bands, perhaps investing in the odd piece of hand-made jewellery from one of the craft stalls, before cramming myself at the front of the stage to see the headline act, a heavy rock group called Death Links, a witty and appropriate anagram of Kentish Lad. Mega thrillingly, their floppy-haired drop-dead totally gorge lead singer, Rob Phelps, went to Haine Court before he was expelled in the sixth form for lighting up a joint in the common room and setting the sprinklers off, *completely* ruining several sets of coursework, including a papier maché sculpture of the O2 Arena in London someone was creating for Art A Level. Rumour has it, the domed roof got so soggy it caved in, looking more like a pancake with cocktail sticks than an iconic music venue. Anyway, in my dreams, just as Rob is coming off the stage he'd clock me looking all-rocked up in my outfit and I'd just say coolly: 'Who needs A Levels anyway?' and shrug in a sort of sullen yet sultry way, at which point he'd tell the bouncers to let me through and I'd end up backstage with him, bonding over the sixth form sprinkler episode before some serious snogging leaning across an amplifier, not caring that I had a guitar fretboard poking me in the back.

But between getting the tickets (actually bright pink wristbands) and today, I have experienced an increasing sense of impending Kestival doom, a feeling which has this morning peaked at a new level of doom: megadoom. This could be for any number of reasons (no boyfriend, more spots, an unexpectedly low mark in English literature because I wrote a stunningly correct answer to an entirely different question), but right now it's because I'm in the back of a silver estate car, the boot crammed with clay sculptures of naked men and women, as Pippa Griffiths crawls the streets around the notorious Northcote Estate: Crab territory.

Crab used to use these streets to practise his skateboard moves, weaving around wheel-less cars resting on bricks, jumping over abandoned sofas and stained mattresses, so the last thing I want is to see him doing a kickflick whilst I'm cruising in a Skoda. Since the fight on our drive a couple of weeks ago, Crab's ignored me and I've ignored him, although it's been totally exhausting continually trying to casually ignore someone who's at the same school and in some of the same classes.

I slump down in my seat and consider breaking the law by unclipping my seat belt and crawling into the footwell.

'Is it this one or the next one?' Taryn's mum asks, peering out of the window. 'I can never remember. All these dreary roads look the same to me.'

'The next one,' Taryn replies. 'Before the Koi Carp shop and after Tattoo You.'

'I had my nose pierced at Tattoo You,' Seren says. 'And this.'

She turns round and sticks her tongue out, a silver ball quivering on its bed of pink muscle.

Seren's mega narked because she'd promised her sixth form friends she'd be driving them down in her dad's car today, the one fatal flaw in her plan being that she didn't anticipate failing her driving test yesterday afternoon (she ran a red light and the instructor had to do an emergency stop with the dual controls), thereby causing a loss of face, a total reorganisation of everyone's travel plans, and a seriously bad mood because she's had to come with us (mere kids!) and her mum (there to sell her sculptures) instead.

'Shut up!' Taryn reaches forward and grabs one of her sister's dark pigtails, tugging it backwards.

In a flash, Seren grabs Taryn's wrist and holds it in a vice-like grip.

'Get off!' Taryn screams flapping her arm around, trying to break free, waving a pointy elbow in my direction. 'Mum! She's hurting me. Stop her!'

'I'll stop this car and throw you both out,' Pippa says, as Seren finally releases Taryn, who can't resist another quick jab in the shoulder before retreating to the safety of the backseat and sticking two fingers up at the back of her sister's head.

Then my megadoom feeling gets even doomier.

'What are we doing here?' I squeak, as Pippa stops the car outside Ramsey House, a ten-storey block of flats studded with satellite dishes, grubby washing and wilting window boxes.

The Snittersleys live in the first flat on the ground floor, right by the rubbish chute, which is always getting blocked and stinking to high heaven.

Crab's looking out of the front window, like some ghostly grim reaper shrouded in net curtains

'I *told* you,' Taryn says, patting another coat of pale pink gloss on her lips with her finger. The curtains twitch and Crab disappears. 'I asked you on Tuesday if you were cool about him coming with us today, and you said *Yeah*.'

'Did I?' I have absolutely no recollection of Taryn mentioning anything about Crab and Kestival. 'Where was I when you asked me?'

'We were going into English and I'd just seen Crab in drama and he'd asked me and I asked you.'

'You did?'

'And I checked you and him were, like, totally over for ever and ever and, like, could I start seeing him, and you said: "Yeah. No probs".'

'You're seeing Crab?' I gasp.

As the dumper rather than the dumpee, I am totally over Crab for ever and ever, but I didn't expect him to make a move on Taryn so quickly, not after he gave me a hard time about Antoine; we only split up three weeks ago today! And I'm gobsmacked that Taryn even considered going out with him, let alone agreed.

'You always said he was a loser with a capital L!' I point out. 'You even gave him the L sign.'

'He's a good-looking loser,' Taryn points out. 'And I didn't, like, just steal him. I did ask you.' She pulls a huffy face. 'God, Channy, you've been well out of it this week. I don't know what's up with you. You're not, like, on drugs or anything are you?'

Seren and Pippa swivel in their seats to stare at me.

'Pale skin; glazed eyes; not quite with it.' Seren ticks off the symptoms of being a druggie. 'Are you sure you're not on something, Channy?'

'No!' I'm stung that Seren is inferring I look like a deranged coke-head when I thought I looked rock-festival cool. 'I haven't even taken a Joy Ride!'

It's not drugs. As if!

It's something much more addictive.

It's Herbage Dappledawn.

Big Daddy Rabbit is taking over my life.

The fact is, since getting John Smith's message last Saturday at Claire's, I've been unable to concentrate on anything else but the man and the message (hence the rubbish English mark). But despite hours of contemplation, sleepless nights and searching on the net for advice, I still haven't a clue what I'm going to do next.

One moment I'm def going to reply, make contact, find the family I've always known exists. The next I think: *You idiot, Channy! This could be some pervy weirdo out to trap a teen, plus you promised Dad you wouldn't.* Then I look at John Smith's message and decide it's far too polite too formal, even a bit boring to be from a net nutter, and anyway, what Warp Head disguises himself

144

as a toy brown rabbit? So then I decide I am going to contact him, even though I told Dad I wouldn't, and the whole: *Shall I? Shan't I? Will I? Won't I?* vicious circle starts again.

As a distraction from stressing about potential DNA matches I even *forced* myself to have a little Antoine fun, running through my favourite fantasy where The Fabulous Frog bounds up the beach steps towards me, and instead of choosing one of his own kind and abandoning me like he did that day on the beach, takes me in his golden, muscled arms and smothers me in sultry snogs. The problem is, just as I'm enjoying a little foreign smooch on the stairs, a giant brown rabbit in denim dungarees and a striped shirt pops up behind the white stone banister and trills: *It's Herbage!* which rather ruins the moment.

The front door opens, and Crab dithers around, patting his jean pockets to check for his phone, and then blowing into his hand and sniffing it. Clearly, he fails his own breath test as he pops some chewing gum in his mouth and begins chomping.

'Sorry!' he opens the passenger side door and leans in. 'Decided to have a last minute Jimmy Riddle. Didn't want you to have to stop so I could have a slash in a lay-by. I brew stacks of pee in the mornings.'

Then he plonks himself next to me, crushing my straw Stetson which is on the seat because Pippa said she couldn't see through the rear-view mirror if I wore it in the back.

'Crab!' I yell, pulling it from under his butt, the sound of straw snapping. 'You've totally ruined my look!'

If I had any slight feelings of lingering jealously over the fact that my ex is now seeing my best friend, they've been well and truly smashed by Crab's running commentary on his urinary system and his demolition of my headwear, not to mention the cloud of something pungent which has accompanied his arrival. Even Taryn, newly loved-up with the loser, clamps a hand over her mouth.

'God, that's toxic!' Seren splutters. 'Have you rolled in fox poo?'

'It's aftershave based on the musk glands of Highland rutting stags,' Crab says proudly, as I wonder whether he's deliberately fiddling around by my thigh or really looking for the seat belt buckle.

The aftershave is totally unnecessary as, unlike Antoine's dark stubble, there's only a tiny bit of gingery-blond fuzz on Crab's upper lip. I don't remember him smelling of anything other than medicated soap when we were together, and feel mega miffed that he's made more of an effort for Taryn than he ever did for me. He's even ditched the football shirt for a clean, white, *ironed* T-shirt.

'You look nice, Taryn,' Crab says, sounding oily. 'I like your dress.'

Seren makes gagging sounds, Pippa raises her eyebrows in the rear-view mirror and Taryn giggles and adjusts her purple and white tie-dyed dress, her newest look being Homespun Hippie complete with purple ribbon tied around her forehead.

This, I think to myself glumly as Pippa does a three-point turn in the road and Crab tries to hold hands with Taryn over my lap, *is going to be a very long day*.

On a scale of one to ten of being peed off and fed up, I am a twelve.

As soon as we get there, it's the wedding all over again: everyone having fun, whilst I'm totally mis and stuck on my tod. It's about two hours since I spoke to another human being, unless: 'I'll have a Red Bull and a cheeseburger, please', to a sweaty man in a white van and blood-stained apron counts.

It's not that I don't know anyone: there are familiar faces from school milling around, the sort of cool, effortless trendy girls that form glossy flocks, but as I'm not in their clique, I can't launch myself on them without either being humiliated or totally blanked. The Helium Twins are here, dressed up to the nines, but I'm blanking them after they blacklisted me from their pop-up party. Seren is being snotty with her sixth-form friends, floating around as if she owns the place, and Taryn has wandered off hand-in-hand with Crab who's continually telling her in a loud voice how wonderful she is. Friendless, I've resorted to hanging around Pippa Griffiths' stall, just for the company, so further underlining what a total saddo I am. Fifteen, at a music festival, and instead of roaming the fields swigging designer water, I'm clutching a trashed Stetson and hanging out with a middle-aged, grey-haired mother who's wearing denim dungarees, a blue top and *no* bra. And I've totally misjudged the footwear situation. The field has been cleared of moo-poo, something which clearly all the cool kids knew in advance, so I'm the only one in sweaty wellies on a boiling hot day, everyone else shuffling around in flip-flops with brightly painted toes and anklets.

'You feeling OK, Channy?' Pippa asks, rearranging her collection of naked figurines into little groups on the trestle table. I wish she wouldn't. It looks like some sort of roman orgy. 'You seem a bit down.'

'I'm OK,' I shrug, picking up a small statue of a man

148

with a seriously large gentleman's sausage. 'Sort of.'

'Is it Taryn and Crab?' Pippa keeps moving the sculptures around as if they're changing partners. 'Taryn assured me she'd checked with you first; that you were OK about him and her.'

'Nah,' I reply, though in truth I am mega miffed that Crab didn't make more of an effort to get me back and has moved on to my bezzie so quickly. 'It's not that.'

'Then is it all this stuff about John Smith? Is that what's worrying you?'

I almost drop the naked man with shock, a potential disaster as Pippa has propped up a large sign that says: Breakages MUST Be Paid For.

'Taryn told me,' she explains. 'She told me you've been looking for him.'

'Not really,' I say, carefully putting down the figurine in case I snap the clay sausage off and wipe out my entire month's allowance. 'I sent some random messages, that sort of thing.'

'And did you hear anything back?' Pippa pushes her hair behind her ears and gazes at me with mother-on-a-mission eyes, the sort of eyes that bore into you with an *I'll know if you're lying* look.

I toss up whether to tell her about Herbage Dappledawn and my contact dilemma. Despite the free-flowing boobs and dodgy dungarees, I really like Pippa and I could do with her advice, but then she might tell Taryn who'd be narked that I hadn't told her first. And what about Mum and Dad? With Dr and Mrs Griffiths being more inclined to read a book or see a play than dance around on stage in next to nothing, the two sets of parents aren't friends. Still, friends or not, there's still the mothers' mafia to consider, and I can't risk Mrs G ringing Mum to tell her what I've been up to.

'Just a couple of false leads,' I say casually, avoiding Pippa's gaze. 'I've stopped looking.'

The conversation peters out, Pippa carries on displaying her porno pottery, and I scope the milling crowd. It's mostly teenagers, some with their parents, a few older sorts carrying cans of beer and smoking skinny ciggies. Lots of very visible tattoos and piercings.

And then I spot him.

Not Daddy Dappledawn.

Antoine. La Grenouille Fabuleuse.

He's standing by the stall next to Pippa's, bent over a table covered in a green cloth, his slim brown fingers lightly touching a tan wrist strap, turning it over, examining it, running a thumb down the smooth-looking leather, a grey messenger bag strung across his body. He's wearing a white T-shirt, which clings to him, hinting at the six-pack underneath. He looks sexy, steamy, unbelievably knee-tremblingly gorgeous.

Not so gorgeous is the rest of the unwashed bunch from the language school; they look like turtles scuttling around, their bulging backpacks hunching their shoulders.

I push my sunnies down from the top of my head, clamp my battered Stetson on and, pretending that I'm looking intently at Pippa's figurines, watch The Fabulous Frog out of the corner of my eye, taking in every detail of this perfect foreign specimen as he pays for the wristband, digging a hand into the front pocket of his faded jeans, fiddling for change.

'Yeow!'

It's Taryn, poking me in the ribs to get my attention.

'I've left Crab watching a band so we can spend some time together,' she says. 'I'm worried you're not really OK about me and him. You seemed a bit angsty in the car.'

'I was just upset over my hat,' I half-lie. 'I'm cool with it, honestly.'

My hackles rise as I watch a French super-fox help Antoine fasten the wide leather bracelet around his wrist. She's an alien with acne, but she's still foreign with long brown limbs and that slightly exotic look that tourists have. And then a thought occurs to me: Perhaps the acned-one isn't exotic to Antoine because she's from the same country as him? Perhaps *I* look as exotic to Antoine as she does to me.

This cheers me up no end.

'Channy!' Taryn nudges me. 'I mean it. If you're not happy with me seeing Crab you've just got to, like, say, and I'll bin him. You come first, you know that, don't you?' She waves a hand in front of my face. 'Seriously, are you OK? You seem a bit dazed. Seren wasn't right about the drugs, was she?'

'Next to us,' I whisper through clenched teeth. 'See the lad with the blue sunnies? *That's* Antoine.'

'That's Antoine?' Taryn shrieks. 'Hot-eeee!'

'Which one is Antoine?'

It's Crab. The smell of burning veggie burgers and soya sausages has obviously drowned out the stink of rutting stag, otherwise I'd have smelt him coming.

Before either of us can answer, Crab pushes his way into the gaggle of foreigners.

'Which one of you is Antoine?' he demands.

'Er . . . moi,' The Fabulous Frog answers with a delicious shrug of his broad shoulders. '*Pourquoi? Que voulez-vous?*'

'Don't you start quoting Abba songs at me, you froggy

152

freak!' Crab yells, his arms hurling around like a windmill in a hurricane. 'I can list every one of them! Alphabetically!'

Oh, no! Surely Crab isn't going to start reciting the titles of all one hundred and eleven Abba songs? He did it once in front of Mum and Dad who thought it was amazing. He never did it again though; I told him if he did, I'd bin him. But now he is binned, there's nothing to stop him.

I brace myself to hear *Angel Eyes* . . .

'I also know that you stole my girlfriend, you thieving snail-muncher!'

Oh. My. God. If only Crab *had* listed the songs. This is worse, much worse. My prediction of Kestival megadoom is coming true!

'Your gurlfriend?' Antoine queries in a knee-tremblingly gorgeous voice, rolling his r's and his u's. The looks, the accent, this lad is the mutts nuts. Sadly I'm too humiliated by what is unfolding in front of me to feel anything but terror. 'Who is your gurlfriend?'

'Her!' Crab points at me. 'The one in the manky hat!'

Forget looking like a crab stick, my face feels so hot I undoubtedly resemble a freshly boiled lobster. The French mob are probably looking at me right now and thinking *Homard!*

'Actually,' Taryn says icily. 'I think you mean your ex-girlfriend. *I'm* your girlfriend now.'

'Oh, get real!' Crab rounds on her. 'Do you really think I *wanted* to go out with you? You called me a loser! You laughed at me! I only asked you out and togged myself up to make Channy jealous and get back with her.'

Taryn looks horrified, then scoots off in floods of tears.

'You idiot!' I scream at Crab, feeling secretly thrilled that he was still angling to get me back, and then mean because he was using my bezzie to do it. 'Now look what you've done!'

Finally grateful I'm wearing wellies, I'm about to kick Crab hard in the shins with my rubber covered toes and follow Taryn, when Antoine says to his group of little foreign friends, '*Il est complètement dingue*,' at which they all snigger and snort, with French accents of course.

I'm pretty good at French, but I don't recognize this as the sort of phrase I might need on a day trip to Calais on the ferry. It also doesn't take a GCSE in French to know that the sniggering frogs are sniggering at us, which is a shame because Crab isn't doing GCSE French, but has obviously realized he's being mocked.

'What did you say?' Crab demands. He turns to me.

'What did that greasy frog say? Did he call me a dingo?'

'I dunno,' I mutter, which for once, is the truth.

'He said, he thinks you are a complete fruit cake,' Acne Girl unhelpfully translates into English with a heavy French accent, giggling. 'A nutter.'

I don't know anything about Acne Girl, but I hate her. If only I could easily translate the phrase: *You sanctimonious spotty cow* into fluent French.

'Does he now?' Crab yells, squaring up to Antoine, bending over him like, well, a giant pink and white crab stick. 'Go on!' he taunts Antoine. 'Say it again, if you dare – garlic breath!'

Antoine tilts his perfect face up at Crab and says slowly, '*Il. Est. Complètement. Dingue,*' before pushing his sunglasses into his springy hair, glancing sideways at me and giving me The Loaded Look he gave me at the beach, at which point The *Entente Cordiale* between our two countries collapses, and World War Three breaks out in a field in Kent.

Chapter Fourteen

Six o'clock.

Death Links will be about to start their set, but instead of looking cute and cool in my cut-off shorts at the front of the mosh pit as I send subliminal messages to Rob Phelps, willing him to notice me whilst hoping he can't see my Brantano wellies, I'm lying on my back, on my bed, in my room, in an empty house, *seething* with embarrassment and humiliation.

I can still remember with butt-clenching clarity the moment Crab pounced on Antoine, grabbing his T-shirt, nutting him on the forehead, a spectacularly unsuccessful move as Crab's nose came off worst and started spurting blood.

Still ringing in my ears is the sound of the deafening crash as both lads staggered, lost their balance, and fell on to Pippa's pottery covered trestle table.

Forever branded on my brain will be the way *everything* collapsed: the table, Antoine, Crab, and the way they tussled on the ground, rolling around on the figurines, *completely* disregarding the sign about breakages.

It was clay carnage. As well as total body disintegration, there were a number of men with their gentleman's sausages snapped off, and several of the lady statues suffered rather brutal boob reductions and amputated limbs.

I screamed at Crab that France had helped us in the war and was this any way to repay them? Antoine's friends started yelling things at Crab in French, which, even without the accompanying hand gestures, I could tell were offensive and unlikely to be on the GCSE French syllabus. Crab got his limbs wedged in the collapsed table legs and thrashed around on the grass like a daddy-long-legs caught in a spider's web, swearing. Pippa stood with her head in her hands, Taryn was nowhere to be seen, and Antoine? Antoine got up, put his vintage Ray-Bans back on, brushed pottery dust from his long brown arms and without giving me any look, let alone a loaded one, coolly sauntered off, followed by his posse of gabbling froggy friends.

With no stock to sell, Crab in disgrace and facing a massive breakages bill from Pippa, Taryn (found hysterical by the veggie burger bar) wanting to murder Crab by strangling him with her headband, me happy to help her, and no one feeling the slightest bit festivalish, Pippa packed the table and the pottery dust into the Skoda, and we all came home in icy silence, except Seren, who not being part of World War Three was allowed to stay and carry on being snottily cool. Taryn sat in the front and I was in the back, trying to keep as far away from Crab and his wodge of bloodied tissue as possible, even though it meant the door handle stuck in my side for the entire journey.

I pick up my moby and dial Taryn's number. Voicemail.

'Um. It's me,' I say. 'Um. Hope you're OK. Ring me.'

Then I stab out a text saying the same thing.

My phone buzzes. *I'm OK. Just need to be alone xx* she's texted back.

But she won't be alone, will she? She'll be in her house on the right side of the roundabout with her parents and little sis Carys, who didn't come with us to Kestival because she didn't want to miss her Stagecoach class as they're doing the musical *Annie*. Pippa will be all motherly despite her naked figurines losing their bits, fussing over her distraught daughter, telling her not to waste any tears over Crab. They'll have something nice to eat, maybe homemade lasagne. Pippa will run Taryn a bath with lots of smelly bubbles, and when Taryn goes to bed, Pippa will come in and tell her that everything will feel better in the morning.

I look up at the stars Taryn painted for me on the black ceiling, listening to the sounds of the house and Lea Crescent: the hum of the fridge-freezer downstairs vibrating; the noise of someone mowing their lawn a few doors away; a group of kids playing football outside; next door's two Chihuahuas yapping in their back garden.

I expect no one out there has any idea I'm up here. Even Mum and Dad, playing at a wedding in Bexley, don't know I'm in my bedroom rather than in a field. I could be being held hostage by a burglar or having a heart attack, and no one would know. And even if they did know, would they care?

I haul myself off the bed, get my laptop from my desk and, pushing three pillows up against the bamboo headboard, slump back down on to the mattress.

I'm fifteen, I think miserably as the laptop whirrs. *This isn't how my life should be on a Saturday night, sitting on my own in my bedroom.*

To torture myself even further, I click on Facebook.

Stacie and Tracie have Facebooked from Kestival.

Stacie's update says: **Stacie Allen** *Thinks Rob Phelps has given her the eye.*

Tracie has commented: *Give it him back sista!*

Tears prick my eyes as I look at the photos they've posted: snaps of glossy girls having fun in the sun. I know I'm feeling sorry for myself, and I know that I shouldn't, as right at this moment, somewhere in the world, kids are scrabbling around on a rubbish tip trying to find something useful to use or sell, or living in a cardboard box under a tunnel. When I came back from exile at Sue and Bob's I was *determined* not to dwell on what might have been, to be grateful for what I've got and the life I lead rather than the life I might have had if The Sperm Daddy had been around. But right now, thinking of those poor kids doesn't help me get things in to perspective; it just makes me even more tearful and gloomy, although perhaps having black walls doesn't help.

I reach under my mattress and pull out a couple of sheets of paper. It's an article I printed off the net about a girl who found out at sixteen the man she thought of as her father, wasn't. Her parents told her that her mum had had an affair and got pregnant, and that her bio dad was a famous journalist who was also married and already had children. After the bombshell, for a while it was all a bit sticky, but eventually everyone bonded: the bio father and the other father and the two wives and their children; now once a month they have a big family Sunday lunch, and every August they go camping together, in Cornwall, a big blended happy family.

That's what I want, except without the tent bit.

I click on Herbage Dappledawn's message and stare at it.

What would be the harm in replying, just finding out a bit more about this man, as long as I'm cautious?

When we were in Year 8, a man who, rather alarmingly, looked exactly like the sort of pervy weirdo I imagined would stalk young girls on the net (starey eyes, bad teeth, sunken cheeks) came to talk to us, telling us how to Stay Safe Online. So, I'm not about to start arranging to meet some tattooed weirdo in a dark alley just because a potential mentalist has written to say he might be my dad. I need more details if I'm to believe this man really could be The Sperm Daddy.

I start typing.

Thank you for your message. Please could you tell me something more about yourself? C

My clicking finger hovers over the keyboard as I

mentally tick off all the things Sunken Cheeks told us to be careful of. There are no personal details such as: *Here's my phone number and address; come round and meet your daughter and the woman you slept with fifteen years ago.* Thanks to the book burqa, Herbage can't see what I look like from my profile pic. I haven't revealed my online banking password or arranged to meet him in a disused warehouse, so what's the harm in sending it? I don't actually have to *do* anything with any information I get, do I? If I don't like what I read or it freaks me out, I can just disappear back into the anonymity of the information superhighway.

I press *send* and get up to go to the loo.

By the time I come back a little red 1 in a bubble is glowing at the top left-hand side of the screen. It's a new message from Herbage Dappledawn.

Dear Channy, (Can I call you that?)

Of course you want to know more about me! Very sensible of you to ask. You read terrible things about strangers on the Internet.

I'm forty-one years old and work for a large American investment bank in the City. My hobbies are reading and rock music, a throwback to my misspent youth in pubs and clubs! Writing this makes it sound as if I'm composing an advert for a lonely hearts column, doesn't it? Perhaps I

should, as I've recently got divorced which has been hard on
my daughter, Hannah, as she's only nine.

Is this enough, for now?

Regards,

John.

I stare at the message, my heart hammering, my hands shaking.

Hannah. I might have a half-sister called Hannah. OK, so we won't need a big tent or table for our family get-togethers, but still, a sister! She's probably right now sitting in her room, miserable and lonely, upset over her parents splitting up, totally unaware that she has an equally miserable and lonely sister.

Whoa! I rein in my racing imagination as a vision of a disapproving Sunken Cheeks pops into my brain. I'm already fast-forwarding to family camping holidays even though there is absolutely nothing in this email that proves Herbage is the right John Smith.

I type back: *I'd really like to see a picture of you. At the moment I think of you as Herbage Dappledawn! C*

Within moments comes Herbage's reply:

I don't put my picture on Facebook because I want to remain anonymous to my work colleagues. I'll try and find one that I can scan and send to you. I must warn you, if you had fantasies that your biological father might look like

George Clooney, you'll be disappointed in me. Hannah says I look like a pug in a pinstriped suit.

Best,

John

Chapter Fifteen

'Last day of school for six weeks?' Dad asks. He knows full well we break up for the summer hols today.

'Uh, huh,' I say through a mouthful of milk and Coco Pops, whilst I try to read *1914* by Aleksandr Solzhenitsyn.

John recommended it to me. To be honest, I'm finding Russian literature a bit like organic muesli: worthy but hard going and difficult to digest. I'd like to ditch it and start on some Marian Keyes, but I'm worried John will ask me what I think of it and question me about the plot and the characters. If he's not to think I'm a total dimwit, I'd better plough on.

'Look, love, I'm sorry we can't go away,' Dad says, opening the dishwasher. 'It's such a busy time for the group what with weddings and festivals and stuff.'

'S'OK,' I shrug, skipping several pages, wondering whether these will be just the pages John refers to.

'I'd suggest we go away at Christmas, but then there's all the Christmas parties.'

'S'not a problem,' I assure him, going back to the pages I've missed, just in case.

'It won't be forever,' Dad promises over the clatter of stacking plates in the overhead cupboard. 'We can't be Frida and Benny when we're old. Maybe another two years, and then we'll start a talent agency, one for lookalike acts. We've got to know quite a few Eltons and Madonnas on the circuit.'

'OK.'

'We could book somewhere next Easter. Spring is always a quiet time for us. How about ten days away at Disneyland in Florida next April?'

I look up from the book. 'Dad!' I can hear the exasperation in my voice. 'I'll have to revise for my GCSEs at Easter. Honestly, it's OK.'

He abandons his plate stacking and comes over and puts his arms around me, kissing the top of my head. 'Channy, your mum and I are really proud of the way you've dealt with all the . . .' he hesitates, '. . . stuff of a few weeks back.'

Stuff. The elephant in the room. The enormous thing that no one talks about but everyone knows exists: finding out about. The Sperm Daddy.

John Smith hasn't once been mentioned since the day I came back from Sue and Bob's, but the subject is always hanging in the air like the stale smell of a cooked kipper.

'We were worried it might affect your schoolwork, you know, derail you a bit,' Dad continues, 'but the amount of time you've been spending in your room studying has proved us wrong! And look at the sort of stuff you're reading now!' He taps the pages of *1914* over my shoulder. 'My clever girl!'

I try not to feel guilty that Dad thinks I've been holed up in my room poring over books, when in reality I've mostly been on the net, emailing John or re-reading his emails, dissecting them line-by-line. We've been in touch pretty much every day for the last four weeks, nothing heavy, no major inquest into him and Mum or what happened fifteen years ago, in fact, it's never been mentioned. I didn't want him as a Facebook friend in case Taryn or the twins saw him and started asking awkward questions, so we just swap light-hearted emails, a few lines about everyday stuff I've done, books I've read, he's read, what we've watched on telly, the plot of *EastEnders* getting ridiculous, etc. I haven't seen a picture of him yet, but he emailed me one of Hannah when she was a baby, a pudgy-faced little thing wrapped in a pink blanket. To be honest, it was a bit disappointing. OK, so she's got a shock of dark hair and a pale face, but she could be anyone's baby; at that age they all look the same with their squashed faces and button noses. You never see a new baby and think: *Wow, that sproglet has a massive hooter!* do you? Anyway, when John can get some more family pictures from his ex-wife, he'll scan them and send me some. It's shocking how Laura (that's the ex) doesn't let him see Hannah very often. Even though she ran off with his best friend (now ex-bezzie, obviously) *she's* the one who's making the divorce really evil, carping on about money and access. He's pretty cut up about it, but he says that whatever the ex does, he'll move heaven and earth to keep in touch with Hannah, which makes me realize that if he had known about me, he'd never have abandoned me to a life of Abba songs and meals for one.

I don't feel guilty that I'm keeping all this from Mum and Dad: what they don't know can't hurt them, but I do feel bad that I've kept it from Taryn. I will tell her, *and* Mum and Dad, but not yet, not until I'm one hundred per cent sure he's the John Smith I'm looking for.

Dad gives me a final squeeze and goes back to the dishwasher. 'And you're fine about us accepting the booking for your school prom? I mean, I know it's almost a year away, but we do get booked up.'

I have to admit that I'm not exactly thrilled that Bjorn At The Beach will be playing at the Year 11 leavers' prom next July, but I can barely think beyond next week, let alone next year. I've got much more important things on my mind.

'It's cool,' I shrug, finishing off the chocolate crispies, dumping the dirty dish in the sink and swiping my book from the table.

'What's cool?' I meet Mum at the door, yawning, still in her fluffy white dressing gown. She shuffles past me and flicks on the kettle.

'Our playing at Haine Court next July,' Dad says, handing her a clean mug with pictures of guinea pigs dressed as Abba on it.

'And you're OK about next Thursday?' she shouts after me.

I spin back and peer round the doorframe.

'What about next Thursday?' I ask, as casually as I can.

'You said you'd spend the day with Claire; we're on a boat on the Thames with some Japanese tourists.' Mum spoons instant coffee into her mug. 'Some lunch cruise thing, a last minute booking. You said it wasn't a problem.'

'I don't remember saying anything!' I protest.

'I did ask you,' Mum points out sharply. 'Bob and Sue

169

are dropping Claire off on their way to London.'

'Well I can't,' I say flatly. 'I've got plans.'

'Oh?' Dad holds a fork and looks at me suspiciously. 'What's come up then?'

'Nothing,' I lie. 'Look, I've got to go or I'll be late for school.'

Mum follows me into the hall. 'Well, if you're up to nothing, you can do nothing with Claire,' she says, cupping her mug. '*And* get paid for it.'

'I'm seeing Taryn,' I mutter. 'We were going to go out. Maybe go to Canterbury.'

'I thought you said Taryn was going to South America with her family?' she reminds me. 'Flying from Gatwick on Sunday.'

Damn! I really must get my brain sorted out. I keep forgetting things or not listening to things because my head is chockablock full of Herbage Dappledawn, which is why I have no choice but to meet him next Thursday.

In all the weeks of emailing, neither of us mentioned meeting. Then, last week, John sent me an email to say he had an appointment near the British Library on the Euston Road in London. The thought of all those books had made him think of me, and did I fancy meeting for a coffee, just for half-an-hour or so, no big deal, just a quick face-to-face after all the emails?

170

I reckon I'm a good judge of character; and I think I would have spotted any signs of John being a nutter in the emails. If there had been even a hint of him asking me about what I was wearing, what I've got up to with my boyfriend or my bra size, I'd have shut down my secret email account and scuttled back to anonymity, but all he seems interested in is what I'm reading and whether I'm happy. And in any case, we're going to meet in Starbucks on one of the busiest roads in the country. One hint of weirdness over a hot chocolate and I'll yell the place down.

'So that's settled then,' Mum says. 'You'll look after Claire.'

Grabbing my schoolbag from the end of the banister, I leave the house and slam the front door behind me.

I'm *this* close to finding out if Herbage Dappledawn is The Sperm Daddy. London is only eighty miles from Broadgate, less than two hours by train. So, whatever the parentals say, whatever Claire Myers thinks and *whatever* it takes, I'm going to be in Starbucks on the Euston Road at twelve-thirty on Thursday 29th July.

Chapter Sixteen

Claire Myers looks as if she might burst as she stands pink-faced and beaming in our sunny hall at nine-thirty on Thursday morning. She's dressed in white footless tights, a pink, bum-skimming T-shirt and silver ballet pumps, from the look of them, *all* box-fresh new. I have a feeling that the thought of spending the day with me might be the best part of the poor kid's summer holiday, and she's dressed up for the occasion. She's even wearing a crystal hairband, the fake diamonds sending arcs of coloured light shooting across her mousy head, although she could be sparking with over-excitement.

'We'll be back around six,' Mum says, kissing me on the cheek. 'If it's any later, I'll let you know. Any problems, just ring. We'll keep checking our mobiles.'

I think she's saying this for Bob and Sue's benefit. She never normally does.

'Take this,' Bjorn Bob says, pressing some money into his daughter's chubby palm. 'Get Channy to take you shopping and buy yourself something nice. And you too.' He hands me a purple twenty-pound note.

And then in a flurry of bags and outfits on coat hangers they're gone, backing out of the drive, Mum and Dad in the Abbamobile, Sue and Bob in the pea-on-wheels, off to London to sing on a boat for a gaggle of unsuspecting sushi lovers.

'Shall we go shopping?' Claire looks eagerly at me through her thick specs smeared with greasy fingerprints. 'We could go to Top Shop. Or what about Primark? This came from Primark.' She holds out the hem of her T-shirt and does a sort of half-curtsey, either that or her knees have suddenly buckled at the thrill of being with me.

'Do I look like the sort of girl who goes to Primark?' I say, pointing at my outfit. I'm in full slutty ballerina mode today: black tutu, grey batwing off the shoulder top, a hint of black bra strap and my trusty red sneakers. Actually, the top did come from Primark, but after twenty-four hours in the garage soaking in a bucket of Persil bio, it's got a good vintage vibe, i.e. it looks faded and is disintegrating. 'This is all *genuine* retro stuff.'

'I think a pink top would go better with the black skirt,' Claire suggests shyly.

My knees buckle and I slump on the bottom of the stairs and burst into tears, burying my head in my hands, sobbing loudly whilst I rub my eyes so much they start watering, beautifully adding to the realism of my fake sobs.

'Don't cry!' Claire gasps, rushing over to sit next to me, a tight fit as the architect of these houses didn't consider two parallel sets of meaty thighs in his staircase planning. 'I didn't mean it about the pink top! You look lovely!'

The poor kid thinks I'm pseudo-sobbing over her fashion advice! As if!

'It's not that,' I say solemnly. 'It's Antoine.'

'It's Antoine!' Claire parrots. She clutches my arm. 'You haven't split up, have you?'

I shake my head and do some more very convincing (if I say so myself) sobbing and moaning.

'So, what is it?' Claire asks softly. 'You can tell me.'

I glance sideways at her with what I hope are red-rimmed pathetic eyes. They'll definitely be black-rimmed as I purposefully put on non-waterproof mascara to complete the *trashed by tears* look.

'I don't know if I can,' I say dramatically, wondering whether despite my usual inability to join in with things, I might consider auditioning for the school play next year. This level of acting talent is wasted if it's only going to be displayed to a twelve-year-old on a staircase; a much wider audience should see it. 'How do I know that you'll keep a secret? How do I know that you won't crumple into a heap of truthfulness at the first sign of parental interrogation?' I glare at Claire.

'I won't!' Claire squeaks. 'Cross my heart and hope to die a painful death, I won't.' She does a series of complicated movements across her boobage, which I think is designed to prove the point she'd rather drink hemlock than squeal on me. Then her chubby chops fall. 'Oh, Channy!' she gasps, digging her fingers even further into my flesh. 'You're not having Antoine's baby, are you?' She looks pointedly at my pudgy stomach. 'You're not – *preggo*?'

'No!' I say, thrown by Claire's assessment of the situation. I pull my gut in and look suspiciously around, as if there might be a bug in the hall or a parent at the door. 'The problem is, Antoine is leaving for France today,' I confess. 'I was supposed to be spending the day with him, but now I have to spend it with you.' I restart the sobbing. 'I can't even say goodbye!' Sob. Sniff. Sob. Sniff.

Claire's face runs through a variety of emotions as she processes this terrible information. Then she says,

'Couldn't you just have told your mum and dad you couldn't see me because you're seeing him?' which of course, had I really been planning to see Antoine rather than The Sperm Daddy, would have been the logical solution.

'They don't approve of him,' I say darkly. 'He's been involved in dodgy dealings.'

'Like what?' Claire's tongue is hanging out. 'Really serious things?'

I contemplate making up the fact that Antoine is wanted in several European countries for drug trafficking, but decide even for me this is stretching it, so I just mutter a non-specific, 'Stuff,' under my breath, and do some more fake sobbing.

For what seems like hours, I sob and sniff whilst Claire clutches my arm, occasionally giving it a sympathetic squeeze. I'm just beginning to wonder how long I can keep this up, whether I'll miss the ten fifty-nine train to London, and if I throw in a dog like howl of pain amongst the sobs it would scare the pants off Claire or speed things up when—

'I know! Why don't you go and see him off and leave me here?'

Bingo! Whiny Claire has finally fallen into the carefully planned trap I hoped she would.

'I don't mind. Not if it's for you and Antoine.'

'I couldn't possibly,' I protest. 'I mean, I've promised your mum and dad that I'd look after you. And I wouldn't be back until, say, four. You'd be on your own for hours.'

'Honestly, I don't mind,' Claire shrugs. 'I could just stay here and watch telly. I do that anyway at Mrs Wallen's.' She snuggles up to my shoulder and makes cow-eyes at me. 'Mum and Dad don't need to know. It could be our secret.'

'I suppose you could try my bridesmaid's dress on and use all my make-up whilst I'm out,' I suggest, feeling wretched that this good natured kid who adores me is so easy to deceive, and that I'm bribing her not with cash, but with pink satin and Maybelline. 'If you *want*.'

'Do I!' Claire looks as if all her Christmases and birthdays have come at once. 'That would be awesome!'

'Come on, then,' I say, un-wedging myself and racing up the stairs to my bedroom, as like an elephant in tap shoes, she gallops breathlessly after me. 'I'll show you where everything is. And I promise I'll be back by four.'

Chapter Seventeen

As I walk across the Euston Road from St Pancras station, I feel as if I my legs might collapse from under me at any minute, depositing me in a quivering heap right in the middle of the pelican crossing. So, I'm both surprised and relieved that I make it to the other side, where I cling to a grey metal railing, hyperventilating, as the lights change and cars, buses, lorries and taxis thunder past me.

Everything in London seems so much louder and faster and bigger than I remember it. I've been here millions of times (slight exaggeration) with the school or for birthday trips, but I've never been on my own, and I've never arranged to meet a strange man inside a coffee shop.

Lying to Claire, running to the station, buying my return ticket, getting on the fast bullet train, my cunning plan had seemed surreal, an exciting adventure straight out of the pages of a novel. But as the train whizzed through the Kent countryside hurtling towards London and Herbage, I began to have second thoughts, and then third and fourth, all the way up to at least a thousand. And now I'm here, I'm scared. Jelly-bowel scared. So scared I could barf over my Hi-Tops.

The fact of the matter is I've spent the last eighty-two minutes on a train, on my own, because I'm going to meet a man I'm ninety-nine per cent sure is my father, but I haven't told a soul what I'm up to, not even my best friend, because if I had told Taryn, I know what she'd say: *You bloody idiot* and make me promise not to go.

And then I think of Claire in my bedroom, and feel ashamed at the thought of how I've deceived her, even though I had no choice. Because of her barrel bod and podgy tum it took me ages to do the dress up, and several times she yelped in pain when I caught her skin in the zip. But when I finally yanked the zip to the top, Claire looked so happy twirling around in the satin and lace, tottering in my silver sandals, the tiara slipping off her mousy hair, it almost made me want to stay and hang out with her. But then she reminded me that at any minute my true love Antoine was heading back to

Frogland, and practically pushed me down the stairs and out of the front door, waving at me from the doorstep, smiling and shouting out, 'Good luck!'

It's not like I have to actually meet this man, I think, taking a deep breath, checking the map I've printed and starting off again. As I'm early I could just hide near Starbucks and watch people going in and out, see what John Smith looks like from a distance, then if I feel scared or weird or freaked I can just turn round and get on the first train home and spend the rest of the day mucking about with Claire. We could go down to the seafront, choose a couple of three-scoop cones from the forty-two flavours of ice cream at Sorcorelli's and take them to watch the boys tombstoning from the pier. Claire would like that, as long as no one bobbed back up with blood pouring from their head, though even that might be quite exciting, especially if one of the cute lifeguards in the yellow and red shorts dived in to rescue them. We could call in at Superdrug on the way back up the high street and play with the make-up, trying not to worry about getting eye infections or cold sores from the germ-infested samples, and then if there was any of Bob's money left, we could buy chips and flirt with the sexy lad behind the counter at The Fish Fryer, the one who twirls the salt and vinegar pots in the air like they're cocktail shakers. Claire would love him; we all do. Taryn even sketches him, but he's already got three babies by three different girlfriends and another one on the way with the woman who works in the kebab shop next door. Perhaps we'll wander down there when I get back. Have chips for tea. Maybe even scampi. Take them to the bandstand and torment the seagulls by holding out a chip and then eating it at the last minute. It's *sooo* funny when that happens, though Mum says that the seagulls are getting more aggressive and one of these days will peck my eyes out for teasing them.

'Channy?'

A man in a grey pinstriped suit, white shirt and pink tie steps out from behind a lamppost, making me jump.

He holds out a hand. 'I'm John. John Smith.'

Since the bombshell at Aunty Julie's wedding, I've read thousands of stories on the Internet about people who finally manage to track down their real parents. They always talk of taking one look at a stranger's face and realising it feels incredibly familiar, that it's basically their own, slightly rearranged. So, I always thought that when I found The Sperm Daddy it would be like looking in a mirror. If this man is the spitting image of me, I'm going to hide in a darkened room for the rest of my life and only venture out with a bag over my head. He's ultimate FatBooth man: short, bloated, triple-chinned, droopy-eyed, skin the colour of the unbaked grey-clay of Pippa Griffiths' figurines, and what looks like a dead ginger guinea pig draped across his head.

As I politely shake his clammy, pudgy mitt, I feel sick to my shoes with disappointment. I so wanted this man to be my father; I was so sure he was my father, but this tub of lard can't be him, can it? I mean, I know you shouldn't judge a book by its cover and all that, but I can tell you that there is no *way* I would pick this particular book by choice. He's a genetic freak from a greasy swamp, a total chubster with a stained tie and seriously weird hair.

'Oh. Hello,' I say, a lump in my throat.

For a moment, we both stare at each other, before I have to look away and examine the pavement in great detail. I hadn't realized just how much chewing gum is ground into the concrete slabs. I'm sure we don't have as many gum gobbets on the streets of Broadgate. Does everyone in London go around spitting in public?

'Look, shall we grab a quick drink?' the man suggests. 'I don't know about you, but I feel a bit nervous and could do with a shot of caffeine.'

'I dunno,' I say, tracing patterns on the pavement with my foot. 'I think maybe this wasn't such a good idea.'

'Oh,' the man says. 'I'm sorry. You're disappointed. I'm obviously not what you expected.'

'I didn't know what to expect,' I lie.

Tears sting the corner of my eyes. The truth of the matter is, I'd dreamt about meeting this man and everything just falling into place, perhaps even throwing my arms around him and feeling that finally I'd come home, that John Smith was the last piece in my DNA jigsaw. I'd even fast-forwarded to Christmas, no longer on my own night after night whilst Mum and Dad sing at Christmas parties and cheesy 'Back to the Seventies' concerts, but sitting with John and Hannah round a tree groaning with lights and baubles, looking at family snaps, basking in the warm glow of belonging, possibly opening fantastic presents such as first editions of classic novels or a silver Tiffany heart book mark. Now I just feel disgusted and gutted, stupid for spinning such a ridiculous fantasy, as ridiculous as really believing that a hot frog like Antoine would even give me a second glance.

Then something occurs to me. How did this man know what I looked like? Neither of us had pictures of each other, but it didn't matter because I had sort of assumed that I would instantly recognise him.

'How could you tell it was me?' I ask.

'You look just like my mother,' the man says.

'Really?' I wipe my eyes with my fists and glance up.

'Oh, Channy, don't cry,' the man says, rearranging the black laptop case strung over his shoulder. 'Look, this was bound to be emotional for both of us. At least come and have a drink and calm down, and then I'll make sure you get on a train home, or go wherever you need to, and we can leave it all, can't we?'

I shuffle about on the pavement.

'I'll throw in a chocolate muffin,' he suggests. 'Or a brownie.'

He might look an odd blob, but actually, he seems really nice. I could do with a drink, some chocolate and the loo, so I nod and we carry on a few steps up the road and go into Starbucks.

'I'm sorry,' I say, blowing my nose on a scratchy napkin John Smith has brought over to the bar by the window with the drinks: a frothy coffee for him, a hot chocolate *and* a chocolate muffin for me. Today *defo* needs maximum chocolate intake. 'I guess I thought I'd look at you and immediately realize you were my dad.'

'Ah,' John sighs. 'I'm afraid that I rather comfort ate when Laura and I divorced. My features have become somewhat obscured by blubber.' He gives a wry smile. 'I go back to an empty flat after a day at work, can't be bothered to cook, so I ring for a pizza, or a Chinese, or an Indian. Sometimes I go mad and choose Thai. If I keep going like this it will be death by dialling!'

'I'm the same,' I admit. 'When Mum and Dad are out I get a kebab or chips.'

'Yes, but I do that *every* night!' John pulls a face, which given that he is so fat looks really funny, like one of those crazy bendy mirrors you see in fairgrounds. 'Seriously, Channy, I really should start going to the gym. The only exercise I get is going up and down the stairs to meet the takeaway man, that and weight-lifting the odd can of lager.'

I smile.

'It's true!' he says, rolling his bloodshot eyes. 'Though of course, I would be my perfect weight if I was at least a foot taller.'

I giggle.

John turns serious. 'It was the reason I didn't send you a photograph of myself. I know how I must look and I feel ashamed.' He sips his coffee, eyes downcast. 'I didn't want to put you off meeting me. I'm sorry if I wasn't entirely straight with you.'

'It's OK. I understand.' I think of my Facebook profile photo. 'You said I look like your mother.' I blow the froth on my hot chocolate and watch people in the street outside: office workers weaving their way through dawdling sweaty tourists; a tramp trudging along with his life on his back and a can of Tenants Extra in his hand. 'That's how you recognized me.'

At the back of my mind, I'm thinking: *She could be my grandmother, my only grandmother*.

Mum's mum, Rita, choked to death on a fish bone (a haddock) when she and Aunty Julie were very young, and they were brought up by my Granddad Bill, a builder, who had a fatal encounter with an electric hedge strimmer when I was five. Nana Allen is OK, but as Dad's mum, she and I are not biologically related, and Dad's dad scarpered the moment the pregnancy test came back positive.

'You're the spitting image of her,' John says. 'She passed away eight years ago.'

'Oh, I'm sorry.' I'm just not lucky with grandparents, am I? They're either not who you think they are, or they peg or leg it before you know them. Taryn still has two sets of grandparents, which isn't only good from a genetic point of view, it means she gets twice as much birthday and Christmas money.

John's bloated features cloud over. 'I wish Mum had lived long enough to see Hannah grow up. Oh, by the way, I've brought some more photos of her.'

He reaches into his jacket, pulls out a brown wallet and grinning from ear to ear, produces a battered dog-eared rectangle. 'Here she is, as a baby.'

It's the picture he emailed me: the standard new baby shot.

Then he ducks under the counter and rummages in his case.

'I'm sorry I couldn't send you any before, but like I said, Laura has all the early family snaps and it took me ages get some.' He hands me a picture. 'This was taken in Dorset, in Mudeford. She's about five there.'

I stare transfixed at the image of a girl in a pink frilly swimming costume standing in front of a yellow and white striped beach hut: dark hair, pale skin, snub nosed, stocky legs, arms folded high across her chest, scowling at the camera, looking as if she's just walked straight into a wall.

'And this was her in the back garden when she was seven.'

A bit older and now dressed in jeans and a black T-shirt, but with the same: *Try it on if you think you're hard enough* glare.

'She looks just like me!' I whisper, shuffling through the photos with sweaty, shaky hands. 'She looks *exactly* like me.'

I move the cups and the nibbled muffin, brush chocolate crumbs on to the floor and put the three snaps side-by-side. If I were in these photos with Hannah, I wouldn't look like a stranger. We'd look like a family at the beach or in the garden. Girls who belong together. Peas in a pod. *Sisters.*

'She's a sweet girl, but like I told you, the divorce has hit her hard. Laura keeps getting new boyfriends, and the poor kid has to put up with a never ending succession of uncles.'

John makes quote marks with his fingers as he says the word *uncles*. I feel desperately sorry for him being separated from his daughter, his ex-wife having loads of boyfriends whilst he spends his nights missing Hannah and stuffing low-rent food into his chops, turning into a mega-chubber. And what's with the hair? It's obviously a toupée, but does he honestly think that having a dead mammal on his head is convincing? It's not so much weird as sad.

'Have you told Hannah about me?' I ask. 'Have you said anything?'

'I told her there was a very slim possibility she had an older sister,' John says. 'I know I shouldn't have jumped the gun,' he holds his hands up, 'but she was in floods of tears one day, so I just mentioned it, told her not to get her hopes up until we'd done a DNA test.' He gives a warm smile. 'She was thrilled.'

He looks at his watch, raises his eyebrows and heaves himself off the stool. 'Sorry, Channy, I have to go. You can keep those photos if you want, but not the baby shot. That's my only copy.' He slides the photo back across the bar and tucks it into his wallet.

'Oh!' I feel disappointed. On the one hand, with my pictures of Hannah I've found out so much more about my family than I hoped to. On the other, I don't seem to have learnt anything new about John Smith, other than he's fat, sweaty, has fake hair and eats too many takeaways. The time has just whizzed by, though to be fair, the first ten minutes were spent with me, on my own, in the loo, trying to pull myself together. I've hardly touched my muffin. 'It's just gone super-quick,' I say, wrapping the muffin in a napkin and dropping it into my bag. No point in wasting good carbs.

'I'm sorry, I did say we only had half an hour.' He flips the flap over his case. 'I've got to get back as Laura is dropping Hannah off. School holidays play havoc with childcare. She's with me this afternoon.'

'It's OK,' I say, tucking the precious photos next to the muffin. 'I've got to get back anyway. I've got a friend staying with me. I promised her I'd be home around four.'

It's just gone one. I could wander around the shops at St Pancras for a bit, maybe buy a little something for Claire (a guilt present!) and then get the two forty-two back to Broadgate.

We leave Starbucks and cross the road, walking slowly as John waddles rather than walks.

'Oh, before I forget, I bought you this.' He digs into his jacket pocket. 'It's nothing much, just something I thought you'd like.'

He hands me a little brown rabbit dressed in denim dungarees and a blue and white striped shirt. It's Herbage Dappledawn. Big Daddy Rabbit.

'Oh my God!' I squeal, and despite my earlier disgust, find myself clutching John's arm. 'He's *so* cute! I love him! Thank you.'

John looks thrilled I'm thrilled. 'Look, I'm running late so I'd better get a taxi,' he says, scanning the thundering traffic. 'Should we meet again, or have I totally put you off?'

'Please,' I say, tucking Herbage in my bag next to the photos and the wrapped muffin. 'I'd love to meet Hannah.'

John stops looking at the traffic and looks at me. His

eyes are droopy and sad: not so much pug as overweight Bassett Hound. 'Look, it's a bit mad, and say no if you think it's a bad idea, but . . .' He stops mid-sentence. 'No. Ignore me. It's too soon.' He flaps his hands about as if he's swatting a wasp. 'Stupid to even have even thought it.'

'Thought what?' I say. 'What's too soon?'

There's a pause and then he says, 'To meet Hannah. I only live about fifteen minutes from here. It just flashed through my mind that you could come and say hello to her, and then I could put you in a taxi back to the station. It might really cheer her up.

Hannah. The girl who could be my sister is only fifteen minutes away from me. Of course I want to meet her!

'Will I still be able to catch a train at two-thirty-ish?' I ask excitedly, as John flags down a taxi. The traffic behind screeches to a stop and motorists blare their horns as the cab pulls to the kerb. 'I really have to get that train.'

'Easily!' he laughs. He leans through the front window. 'Chatterton Road in Finsbury Park,' he says to the driver.

'Wow! Crab would be well impressed,' I say as the taxi swings by a football stadium covered in a gigantic Arsenal crest. 'He's a total Gooner.'

'Crab?' John queries.

'My ex-boyfriend,' I explain, as the black cab negotiates its way through North London, its streets narrowed by parked cars. 'I dumped him and then he started seeing Taryn, just to get me back, but then he dumped Taryn at Kestival, but I'm not back with him. There's this lad called Antoine instead.' I flash John a knowing smile. 'He's French. Very Ooh la la!' I giggle. 'He gave me loads of looks but then there was this fight between him and Crab at Kestival and I haven't seen him since.'

Now we've spent a bit of time together it feels much easier to talk to John. He's more like the man in the emails than the bloated weirdo I met in the street. And maybe knowing me might turn his life around, give him another reason to go to the gym. Maybe between us Hannah and I can get John fit and healthy.

'I thought your boyfriend was called Gordon,' John says. 'Gordon Snittersley.'

'That's his real name,' I reply before frowning. 'How do you know that?' A tiny smidgeon of uneasiness creeps into my mind.

'You told me, in an email,' John laughs. 'Along with loads of other stuff.' He leans towards the glass window separating the driver from his passengers. 'Cabbie, anywhere round here is fine.'

The taxi stops in the middle of the street outside a row of terraced houses, and after some huffing and puffing and me pushing him out from the inside, John manages to stagger on to the pavement and pay the driver.

'I'm just around the corner,' he says, as the taxi chugs away and we walk to the end of the road and turn in to a busy street. 'Laura got the big house in swanky Highgate and I'm up there.' He points to a window above a greengrocer's shop, next door to an Indian takeaway. The window is filthy and the curtains are closed. 'Come on. Hannah will be arriving at any minute.'

Chapter Eighteen

The stench of curry and garlic is overpowering from the moment John opens the front door. He slams a big white button on the wall with his fist, and a single naked bulb dangling from the ceiling on a dusty black wire, lights the gloomy hallway.

'It seems a bit unfair that your ex-wife gets the house and you have to live here,' I say, looking around as we clatter up several sets of steep, bare stairs, stepping over piles of unopened post and takeaway leaflets. Other than the traffic noise outside, the building is eerily silent.

'Oh, it's better inside,' John assures me, drenched in sweat from the walk up. He adjusts the guinea pig, which has slipped to one side, and fiddles around with keys and locks. 'I don't know what it's like round your way, but London house prices are insane. I'd much rather Hannah stayed in the family home: less upsetting for her.'

Finally, we're in.

'Dump your bag,' John instructs, flicking the light on and dropping his case on the threadbare beige carpet. 'Fancy some lunch?'

'Er, no thanks,' I reply, feeling slightly uneasy at how shabby the whole place looks. As an investment banker in the City, I expected John could afford something better than this, divorce or no divorce. There are boxes against the wall and things stuffed in carrier bags, and the whole place smells of food and stale sweat. 'I'll just say hello to Hannah and then I'll be off.'

'No problem,' John says brightly, heading off down the hall. 'Make yourself at home.'

I peer round a half-open door.

It's the living room. After John's lengthy emails about how much he loves literature and all his book recommendations, I'm surprised to see there isn't a single book in evidence, just a black leather sofa; a massive flat-screen television in one corner; a glass coffee table; a printer; piles of paper strewn across the floor; grubby net curtains framed by limp brown curtains; empty foil containers and pizza boxes; a mirror and . . .

My insides jolt with shock: my stomach, my brain, my

lungs, my heart. Is this what it feels like to be in an out-of-control lift hurtling towards the basement whilst touching an electric cable? I feel as if I'm both moving very fast, and yet frozen in time.

Hung around the cream and brown wallpapered walls are pictures of me, all neatly framed behind glass.

One by one, I look at them. There's the snap of me in the bridesmaid's dress with the pugs; one of me on my own but with Crab's bony hand in evidence around my shoulder; some taken randomly in the street or at the beach or mucking about at the shops. Chillingly, everyone but me has been cut out of the shot.

My eyes flick round and round the room. There must be at least twenty photographs of me, not one of Hannah. A couple of candles and some incense sticks and it would be a shrine: a shrine to Chantelle Elizabeth Allen.

'I know you said you didn't want it, but I've made you a ham bap,' John says, coming back into the living room carrying a plate. He's taken his suit jacket off and loosened his tie. 'I'm assuming you're not one of those picky veggie sorts, but if you are, just leave the ham and I'll get you some Dairylea cheese triangles later.'

I feel sick and not just at the thought of the ham bap. Sick and scared. *Very* scared.

'Where did you get these?' I croak, nodding at the

photographs. 'I didn't send them to you.'

'I love that one,' John says, wandering over to the bridesmaid snap and stroking the glass with his bloated mottled fingers. 'You look like a princess in that dress, not all trampy and weird like today.'

'I said, where did you get them?' I whisper. I can hear my voice, thin and wobbly, loaded with fear.

'I'm Facebook friends with your cousins,' John replies casually, wandering from photo to photo. 'Nice looking girls those Allens, if rather tarty.'

My blood freezes in my veins.

The Helium Twins! This psycho blimp must have asked Stacie and Tracie to be his friends, and in their quest to get their Facebook numbers up, they've friended him. They've no idea who he is or why a bloke called John Smith with a picture of furry toy rabbit as his profile wants to be friends with fifteen-year-old girls, but they've added him, and through them he's seen Crab and some of the other photos I've been tagged in and . . .

'You saw my comment about being a pug,' I gasp, the full horror of the situation I've landed myself in hitting me. 'That's why you said you were a pug in a pinstriped suit! That's how you knew Crab was called Gordon Snittersley. I never told you. You've seen it on Facebook! That's how you know what I looked like! I don't look like your mother! You knew my mum's name – and about the Abba tribute group – because of what I've said on Facebook! You don't love books, but you guessed I did from my picture! You've tricked me! You've been my Facebook stalker! You're a man who grooms young girls!'

I can hear my voice rising with terror: shrieking, hysterical. I should have jumped out of the taxi the moment he said he knew Crab's real name. I *never* use Crab's real name. That should have been the clue, my cue to escape.

'You're not The Sperm Daddy, you're some fake-haired psycho kiddie fiddler who's lured me here!' I scream.

'Don't be ridiculous,' John Smith, or whoever he is says calmly. 'You're perfectly safe here. Much safer than roaming around London on your own dressed as a slut.'

He goes to hand me the sandwich, but I hurl the plate back at him and start running, dodging the furniture towards the door. I can body swerve a chair, but I can't avoid the piles of paper littering my path. As I kick them out of the way, they fan across the wooden floor, and I slip and slide over the sheets as if I'm running on ice, finally losing my footing and falling to my knees.

It's only then that I notice what I've slipped on.

Dozens of photos of girls printed on to glossy paper.

I pick one up.

It's a picture of a little dark-haired snub-nosed girl riding a pink Barbie bicycle, glittery streamers dangling from the handlebars. It could have been me. It was, I realize, feeling cold with fear, intended to be my sister, Hannah.

'There is no Hannah, is there?' I say, unable to stop my hands shaking, the paper in front of me fluttering uncontrollably. 'You've looked on the net for pictures that could be my sister and passed them off as your daughter, just to get me up here.'

The man just stands there, impassively, a massive lump of blubbery jelly.

I scramble to my feet, push past him, and scoot into the hall.

'My bag! Where's my bag?' I yell, running up and down like a scalded rat. 'What have you done with it?'

This psychotic blimp must have taken it. I'll have to abandon it. I can get a new iPod and another copy of The Day of The Triffids (my book *de jour*), but I can't get a new life. I need to get out and get away from this creep to find the police, someone, *anyone*.

I scrabble at the front door.

Three locks.

No key.

I'm trapped!

I run through to the back of the house.

A kitchen with bars on the window, a bathroom with a tiny skylight, but no way out.

I try another room: dark, curtains drawn, stinks of BO and old clothes.

Then finally, the last room. Perhaps there's a fire escape or a window I can bang on or—

I burst through the door and skid to a halt.

If I was younger and not being held captive against my will, this would be the most perfect bedroom in the whole world. Painted on one wall is a giant mural of rabbits and bears and hamsters playing amongst trees, sliding down rainbows, frolicking in dappled sunlight. There's a bookcase without books, but filled with dozens of tiny furry critters dressed in outfits, huddled together in groups. The bed is covered in a bunny-patterned duvet, and there's a row of furry animals lined up along the heart-shaped wooden bedhead.

I am standing in Sylvania.

'What do you think?' The Psycho Blimp asks, looming behind me. 'It was meant to be Hannah's room, but it's yours, for now.' He picks up a tiny cream mouse wearing a pink flower-sprigged dress, and lovingly and lightly strokes its head. My stomach turns. 'They all have such perfect families in Sylvania, don't they? Mother, father, brother, sister; such a complete little unit.'

If you'd asked me at any point up until now what I would do if I found myself in a strange flat with a total weirdo who downloads photos of girls who could pass for my sister, and has decorated a room with toys for a daughter who doesn't exist, I would have bet my iPod that I'd scream louder than I did when Taryn and I went on the Oblivion roller coaster at Alton Towers last summer. But when I open my mouth I can't scream: my throat is frozen with fear.

'Please,' I plead, tears starting to fall. 'Please let me go. I promise I won't tell the police or anyone. I've got to get back to Claire. She'll wonder where I am. I *have* to go back today. I have a return ticket!'

The man just stands there, stroking the mouse, caressing it, smoothing its dress, saying nothing.

I lean against a chest of draws, drained, dizzy with terror. My legs give way as my back slides down the wood, my spine bumping over the handles until I'm sitting on the brown carpet, my head on my knees.

'This is your home now, Channy,' The Psycho Blimp says chillingly. 'You belong here. With me.'

Chapter Nineteen

Seven o'clock.

I've spent the last six or so hours lying on the bed in 'my' room, staring at the ceiling, trying to work out what the hell I'm going to do to get myself out of this mess. I've screamed a few times, just things like: *Help! I'm being held hostage by a fat mentalist!* and even hammered on the floor in the hope someone below would hear me, but no one came, not even The Psycho Blimp, who by the sound of the noise coming through the wall from next door seems to have spent the afternoon watching back-to-back episodes of *Come Dine With Me*.

The window is tiny and covered by metal bars, and from what I can remember of the living room, it looks out over the back of some derelict buildings, so little chance of me being seen shouting for help from there. The Psycho Blimp's room must be at the front, the one I saw from the street with the closed curtains.

I clench my fists and try and quell the wave of hysteria that keeps rolling through my body.

I can't believe I've been so stupid as to get myself into this mess. Sometimes you see things on TV or in the papers, stuff like: FACEBOOK MAN LURED AWAY TEEN, or hear stories about a girl going to meet a sixteen-year-old hottie who's been flirting with her on the net, and the hottie turns out to be a sixty-year-old with a video camera and a room of creepy friends. I've always thought those girls must either be one bean short of a chilli, or some microbrained chav from a broken home who was too thick or too desperate to know any better. But now one of those girls is me, a girl with (on reflection) two perfectly nice parents living in a perfectly reasonable house, about to take ten GCSEs. I'm doing Latin, for goodness' sake! Girls who take Latin aren't kidnapped by pervs on Facebook.

Until now.

'Chinese, Indian, pizza or Thai?' The Psycho Blimp stands at the bedroom door, shuffling through a pile of takeaway leaflets as if he's dealing a deck of cards.

I scoot up the bed and clutch the headboard, as if somehow it will protect me from this toupée wearing mentalist. 'Keep away from me, you psycho,' I shoutysob. 'Keep away from me or I'll . . . I'll . . .'

What will I do? What can I do in a locked flat if this warp head turns nasty? Absolutely eff-all. I'm as helpless as a fly caught in a spider's web; all the terrified thrashing around in the world won't change the fact that I'm trapped.

'What do you fancy?'

'I mean it, one move towards me and I'll KILL you!' I scream.

'I think Chinese,' The Psycho Blimp says smacking his lips. 'I'll get a set meal for two, and then if you change your mind, the food's there.'

'How long are you going to keep me here?' I demand. 'You know they'll start looking for me, don't you? *Then* you'll be in mega trouble. You'll be put away for years without takeaways, *and* they'll confiscate your head rug. You'll be banged up and bald!'

'As this is a special occasion, I think we'll go for the luxury meal with crispy duck pancakes,' The Psycho Blimp says, either ignoring me or in a takeaway world of his own. 'And extra prawn balls.'

He seems much more excited at the thought of ethnic food than lunging for my knicker area, which is obviously a good thing, but could simply mean he can only perv on a full stomach.

'Look, I mean it when I said you could let me go and I won't tell the police.' I soften my voice. This angle is worth a try, even though obviously the moment I was free I'd be straight on to the cops. 'I promise.' I make the sort of complicated hand fluttering over the boobage movement Claire did. 'Cross my heart and hope to die.' I'm clearly going to die anyway, so making a false promise is neither here nor there.

The Psycho Blimp moves towards the bed. I scramble underneath the duvet and pull it protectively around me.

'But Channy, what sort of a life would I be letting you out to lead?' he asks, lowering his flabby bulk on the end of the mattress, freaking me out that the bed will become a seesaw and catapult me straight into him. 'When your mum was singing *Does Your Mother Know?* she didn't even know what her own daughter was up to, did she? Your parents were never around, they left you to do your own thing, you said yourself they didn't understand you, didn't know what you were up to half the time, which was feeling miserable, eating meals, alone.'

Hot tears sting my eyes thinking of how once I've been found cut up in a recycling bin, Mum and Dad will find the emails between The Psycho Blimp and me and think that I didn't love them, that I never loved them, which of course I do; it's just at the time I felt lonely, left out, angry.

'Prancing about on stage, legs out, shaking their bottoms. I've seen the videos on YouTube,' The Psycho Blimp says primly. 'That's no example to set an impressionable young girl.' He grinds a hand on the duvet cover as if he's squashing one of the rabbits. 'I had to do this, Channy. I had to save you from those around you, from your own family.'

'I don't need saving!' I yell. 'Well, I didn't, but I do now!'

'Look at you, already on the road to slutdom. Dyed hair, short skirt, *far* too much make-up, *two* boyfriends!' He counts my crimes off on his bloated digits. 'Take those Allen girls. Dressed in next to nothing in photos for the entire world to see. Fourteen and parading in silver swimsuits, bosoms barely covered.'

'They're fifteen and they didn't expect some middle-age Warp Head to be looking at their baps!' I snarl.

'And then there's your other relations,' The Psycho Blimp continues disapprovingly. 'I've seen the so-called wedding photos of those women. Tracie and Stacie posted them. Mrs and Mrs! It's disgusting.' He curls his lips. 'Theodora Dappledawn doesn't leave Herbage and marry Eleanor Bramble, does she?'

'Hedgehogs can't marry rabbits!' I scream. Discussing possible weddings of Sylvanian Family characters has pushed this already surreal situation to a whole new level.

'Your mother never kept in touch with your father, just a name, that's all she had to give you!' The Psycho Blimp says. 'What sort of a woman keeps a father away from his child?'

'Stop it!' I yell putting my hands over my ears. 'You're mental! You're an effing bungalow brain! Nothing up top!'

'You never looked happy in any of the photos,' The Psycho Blimp points out loud enough for me to hear through my palm earmuffs. 'Scowling in every one of them. You weren't happy in your old life, Channy. I can make you happy.'

'You're sick,' I snap. 'Sick and fat with a dead guinea pig on your head!'

'You giggled when I gave you Herbage Dappledawn. I made you laugh in Starbucks. You smiled when you thought Hannah was your sister. *I* make you happy when everyone else makes you sad.'

'That's not true!' I cry, having to take my hands off my ears to wipe my eyes. 'You're making it all up!'

'Am I?' The Psycho Blimp asks.

'Yes!' I yell. 'I love my parents!'

'Pah!' he spits. 'You didn't even tell them you were looking for me, let alone meeting me. *My* daughter would be able to tell me anything.' He sounds so sanctimonious, so smug, I want to hit him, but that would mean leaving the safety of the duvet, and anyway, I'd probably just get a fistful of sweaty blubber.

'Yeah, right, the daughter in your dreams,' I snap back. 'Another figment of your sicko imagination!' I can hear the sneery disbelieving tone in my voice. Winding up a potential perve is probably not the best hostage-escape technique, but I can't help myself. 'News flash! You have no daughter, just a warped brain!'

'I do.' The Psycho Blimp gives a rueful smile. 'I just don't know where she is, but she's out there, somewhere.' He lets out a deep sigh. 'Funny, wasn't it, that I was searching the Internet for Hannah at the same time as you were searching for your father. Fate brought us together. We were meant to be.'

It takes me a moment to process what he's saying.

'So you really do have a daughter?' I let a smidgeon of duvet drop from around my shoulders. 'What happened to her?' I'm thinking that she might be locked in a basement somewhere, forced to wear long dresses with frills at the neck.

The man's face collapses, his pelican pouch of a throat wobbling. 'Laura took her,' he says quietly, his eyes watering. 'I haven't seen her since she was four. She'd be your age now.'

The baby shot, the one he wouldn't let me keep, the one from his wallet. That must really be Hannah.

'And she loved Sylvanian Families?'

The man nods and starts to weep. 'Especially the Dappledawn rabbit family. We had a real rabbit, a little brown thing Hannah called Dapple. It lived in a hutch in the garden, but after she left it got out and a fox ate it, everything but its back legs.'

In amongst this madness, some things are starting to make sense.

'Is that why you put a picture of Herbage Dappledawn on Facebook, to send her a sign?' I ask.

'Yes,' he wipes his eyes on the corner of the duvet. 'There are so many John Smith's out there, I needed something to show her it was me. She's probably called something else by now, her mother will have changed her name, but I'll still be on her birth certificate. Laura can't change that. One day Hannah might find out the truth and start looking for me.'

'So you honestly are called John Smith?' I say.

'Yes,' he sobs and gives a half-smile. 'Boring, isn't it?'

I'm surprised. I thought he was probably called something odd like Ivor Pile, had been horribly bullied at school, and that's why he's turned into a teen-napping psycho. But I was wrong. This man, this creep sobbing on the end of the bed, isn't a kiddie-fiddler or a murderer – he's a lonely bloated weirdo who's missing his daughter, and by looking for The Sperm Daddy, I've somehow become caught up in his fantasy of finding Hannah and bringing her home. Screaming for help hasn't worked. Being sarky hasn't worked. Time to try something else.

'John,' I say gently, leaning towards him. 'You know this can't go on, don't you? I'm not your daughter, I never can be. Just like you miss Hannah, my real family will be missing me, out of their minds with worry.' The reality is, Mum and Dad are probably still on the motorway, unaware their only daughter has been kidnapped.

He keeps crying. If he wasn't a psycho who's lied and tricked his way to get me here before holding me hostage in this wacky indoor woodland, I'd almost feel sorry for him.

'I could help you look for her,' I suggest, though of course I wouldn't. How do I know he wouldn't hold her hostage and feed her takeaways until she got too enormous to try and escape? 'Shall we stop this before it gets any worse?' I slide my hand along the duvet cover, as if I'm reaching out to him, though of course hoping that I won't actually need to touch psycho flesh.

John Smith nods, and I feel weak with relief that finally I seem to be getting through to him.

Then he gets up, wipes his nose across the back of his hand and says brightly, 'How about that Chinese then?'

Chapter Twenty

My cunning plan had been to storm the front door when the crispy duck arrived, pushing the delivery guy out of the way, smashing his prawn crackers and screaming all the way down the stairs and out into the street, lobbing hot prawn balls at The Psycho Blimp if he tried to follow me. Guttingly, when the buzzer went, The Psycho Blimp unlocked all three locks, went out, re-locked the door and stomped downstairs, giving me just enough time to rush around the flat trying to find my bag (no luck), the laptop (ditto), and see whether there is internet or email on the telly (just like at home, I couldn't find the remote) before he came back with the food, none of which I ate last night, but which I'm picking at this morning because despite being angry and scared, I'm also starving.

'Sleep well?' The Psycho Blimp asks, as if I'm a guest,

not a hostage in his scrotty flat. 'Bed comfortable?'

'No and no,' I growl, concentrating on finger-fishing a bit of chicken out of the special egg fried rice.

I'd spent all night fully dressed in case I was wrong about the weirdo and he was a kiddie-fiddler after all, but there is a reason net tutus haven't caught on as nightwear, which is that they're *incredibly* uncomfortable to sleep in. The net kept poking me in places I didn't realize I had, and when I finally got to sleep I had a nightmare about The Psycho Blimp drilling through my brain with a massive Black and Decker. I came round sweaty and tearful with fear, and seeing giant rabbits with tombstone teeth the moment I opened my eyes didn't help my overall mood of terror.

'Well, maybe you can snooze for a few hours whilst I'm at work.' I can hear and smell my kidnapper making coffee, but I daren't look at him in case he's wandering around either starkers, on in a pair of undercrackers with things dangling out. 'I should be back about lunchtime.'

'You work?' I'm taken aback. I'd rather thought The Psycho Blimp spent every day like yesterday: luring young girls to his flat, watching television and eating takeaways. 'Where?'

'I told you,' he says. 'I work for an investment bank in

the City. I'm head of security. I'm just going to pop in and sort out some time off, then I'll come back early and we can spend some quality father-and-daughter time together. How about that?'

'Huh! In your dreams, fat man,' I mutter under my breath.

And then, horror of horrors, stinking of coffee breath, The Psycho Blimp's massive face looms next to mine and like a darting Cobra, his wet lips hit my cheek.

Even though it was the sort of kiss any ageing relative of either sex might give you, body contact with The Psycho Blimp leaves me feeling shocked and contaminated. After scrubbing off nutter spit with a wet tea towel, the moment I'm on my own I tear around the flat like a whippet on speed, sniffing out *anything* that might spring me from my Sylvanian prison. During the long, net-poked night, I formulated a series of escape plans, which at the time seemed sneakily brilliant, but now feel ridiculously optimistic.

Plan A, to recover my bag and my phone and ring 999, I now realize is destined to fail because no one who is head of security is likely to leave a hostage alone with a Nokia and a generous talk plan.

Plan B involved escaping through a window and

running along the rooftops like the chimney sweep in Mary Poppins, but even if I could find an open window, I'm reluctant to put this one into place in case I fall off the roof and land on the street below, paralysed from the neck down, the sort of paralysis that means someone else has to wipe my butt for the rest of my life.

Plan C is safer, to write HELP! in the condensation on a window, preferably The Psycho Blimp's bedroom at the front. I'll have to remember to write it backwards so that people can see it from the outside. How awful if someone looked up and saw PLEH on the window. They think whoever was inside has a pleh! attitude to life and didn't care about anything, especially clean net curtains.

But there's been a new and shocking development: a padlock on The Psycho Blimp's bedroom door. That explains the night drilling! It wasn't the Warp Head drilling through my brain in a dream; he was drilling through wood in reality!

I examine the padlock, a great big brass and silver thing. I expect because of his job he has these things lying around all the time, just like at home, we're never far from a sequin.

I know! I think to myself. *I'll pick the lock!* I've seen Phil Mitchell do it loads of times in *EastEnders*. He goes somewhere, bangs on the door, it doesn't open, so he sticks something in the lock: a paperclip, a credit card, a sledgehammer, and hey presto! The door opens.

I don't have a credit card or a paperclip but . . .

I take out a silver hoop earring, and feeling grief-stricken at what I'm about to do, bend it into a sort of wobbly long pin, ram it into the lock and start twiddling as if my life depended on it, which I suppose it does. Sacrificing such a thing of beauty (it's real silver, a present for my fifteenth birthday from Mum and Dad) is truly heart-breaking, but it has to be done. But after lots of twiddling clockwise, anticlockwise and then up and down so hard my whole body shakes, the lock still hasn't sprung open, and all I'm left with is a sore finger, a headache and a seriously bent piece of silver wire.

I'm obviously not lock-cracking properly, which isn't my fault: it's the fault of the current education system. A year or so ago we had to take Life Skills lessons at school. Designed to teach us about how to open a bank account, write a letter for a job, watch out for loan sharks, etc., what the curriculum failed to address was how to use a bit of wire to spring a lock, something that right now would be far more useful than knowing the difference between simple and compound interest.

Abandoning the lock and feeling truly bereft that I've murdered a perfectly good piece of quality jewellery *for nothing*, I try the next approach, also used by Phil Mitchell in emergencies: smashing the door down. But despite trying to batter it down with my hands (more trying to slap it into submission), a kitchen stool and a drawer from Sylvania, all I manage to do is break is the drawer, not the door.

I try a bit more screaming, trying *Help!* in other languages, but the only thing I can come up with is yelling 'Assistance! Assistance!' and then in desperation, 'S.O.S!' which is a mistake as it reminds me of Mum and Dad singing *S.O.S.*, which starts me crying and then I start singing, 'Where are those happy days, they are so hard to find?' which just makes things a million times worse.

Kidnapped, sobbing and warbling Abba songs to myself. I really have hit an all-time low.

Having established that the boxes and bags in the hall don't contain anything but old newspapers and stinky clothes, the kitchen drawers have nothing that might help (no sharp knives, just some mismatched cutlery, quite a lot of plastic forks and a cheese grater, though I did contemplate grating The Psycho Blimp to death), I then spend quite a lot of time sitting on the floor, staring at the front door, imagining strong-armed police storming through it, tossing a smoke bomb and rescuing

217

me, whereafter obviously I would become a celebrity, appearing in newspapers and magazines, and receive an award for my work helping other teenagers to avoid being kidnapped by weirdos on Facebook.

But when after several hours no muscle-bound storm troopers appear, I wander into the kitchen, pick at some more cold Chinese, wonder if I might get food poisoning, climb on the draining board and try to bend the window bars with my hands, then give up and eat another cold battered king prawn, which is actually delicious.

Then I decide on a new plan. Plan D. And this one is going to be a good one.

Armed with a bit of broken drawer I'm going to lie in wait for The Psycho Blimp and ambush him as he comes through the door. I'll overpower him with the element of surprise; one sharp whack with a bit of wood on the side of the head, down he'll go and sweet freedom will be mine!

'Hi, Channy, I'm home!'

Damn! I hurriedly pull my knickers up. I'd waited for hours by the door, and just as I was desperate for a pee and couldn't hold on any longer, The Psycho Blimp comes back, scuppering any chances of a surprise ambush and escape.

I'm now forced into Plan E. I'll order an extra hot curry for tea, something blow-your-socks-off, like a Nuclear Vindaloo, and then when he comes back with it, overpower him, rubbing the burning sauce in his eyes before legging it to freedom. I'll have to find a tap and a sink the moment I get out, just in case I accidently pick my nose with a chilli-juiced finger and get blisters up my beak.

We meet in the hall, just as he's relocking the front door, putting the keys in his trouser pocket. It occurs to me that I might have to fiddle around in his crotch area to get the keys if I'm ever going to get out of this place; a disgusting prospect, but one I'll have to face.

The Psycho Blimp holds up a white plastic bag. 'I bought you a present,' he says, smiling, trying to hand it to me. 'That's why I'm a bit late.'

'I don't want it,' I growl, keeping my arms folded.

'And I bought something for me, well us.'

He pulls a book out of his laptop case, which of course is where the computer will have been all along. I sneer at the cover, a photograph of some truly skanky kids leaning against a brick wall on which has been scrawled: *Stormy Hormones: A Guide to Living with Teenagers* in graffiti-style writing.

'It will help us to get along better,' he announces

brightly, before delving into the plakky carrier and pulling out a box. 'And I thought we could play Monopoly. I'll let you buy Park Lane.'

'Will you let me go home if I win?' I ask weakly.

'I keep telling you, Channy,' The Psycho Blimp smiles. 'You are home.'

Chapter Twenty-One

Imagine you are holed up in a tiny flat at the top of a strange building with a man who is deluding himself that he could be your father, there's no way out, no one to hear you scream, you've been wearing the same clothes and haven't dared strip off to have a wash for three days (at least I think it's Sunday afternoon, I'm struggling to keep track of time) and your mouth feels like it's lined with felt, you'd think you'd be jelly-bowel scared, right?

Wrong.

I was bricking it at first, totally petro, but now I'm not scared, just mind-numbingly bored. Bored. Bored. Bored. Bored. Bored. So bored without a book to read, I've even starting playing with the critters in my room, making up stories. I used to do this as a kid, though I have to admit that back then Mrs Bramble the hedgehog never had an extra-marital affair with Mr Furbanks the squirrel, resulting in a strange hybrid love-child who can climb trees and has prickles down his back, the plot of my latest story. It's sort of a woodland soap opera: Hollyoaks with toy mammals.

Occasionally The Psycho Blimp will wander in and say, 'It's nice to see you playing,' at which point I hurl the closest Sylvanian creature at him and he retreats, muttering about consulting THE book.

The *Stormy Hormones* book is driving me almost as mental as he is. I've tried *everything* to convince him that I'm a million miles from what he wanted, i.e. a cute little daughter who plays with toys and bursts with love at the mere sight of him, but whatever I do, he just calmly refers to the self-help guide and reads out their advice.

Thrown a stompy-footed hissy fit? Chapter Two: *Moody Madams and Masters* assures him that this stroppy phase will pass, but only when I'm twenty.

Refused to speak to him? Chapter Four: *The Silent Scream* says it's normal for a fifteen year-old to behave this way. In fact, it is TO BE EXPECTED.

Rebuffed another takeaway? Chapter Seven: *Eating with The Enemy* has alerted him to anorexia or bulimia, though not surprisingly, it doesn't cover being held hostage by a madman as a possible reason for totally losing your appetite and occasionally anxiety-retching into the loo.

He even tried to claim that I wasn't being held captive against my will, he was simply following the advice in Chapter Eleven: *When All Else Fails*, grounding me for being stroppy and uncooperative and damaging the bedroom drawer.

One of weirdest things about being here is that I'm finding it hard to envisage what's going on without me; I feel *totally* disconnected from my previous life. Are Mum and Dad going frantic with worry or will they just assume I'm having a teenage strop and will be back with my tail between my legs once I've run out of money? What's happening in *EastEnders* and *Corrie*? Has Claire Myers forgotten I exist now she has the bridesmaid's dress? Is Antoine still playing volleyball semi-naked on the beach? Has anyone told Taryn in Patagonia I'm missing?

Through the paper-thin walls in the other room, I can hear The Psycho Blimp watching TV. After his attempts to play board games with me were met with derision and I refused to watch *Nanny McPhee* with him, he's spent most of the time slumped on the sofa staring at the TV, or slumped on the sofa staring at his laptop, or just slumped on the sofa reading THE book, occasionally scratching his bits and the dead guinea pig. I did contemplate rushing at him to try and gain control of the laptop, a sort of computer coup, but then I fretted that I wouldn't be able to get on the internet, find the mail programme, put in the password and type an email saying I've been kidnapped and am being held above a greengrocer's shop near Arsenal's football ground before he overpowered me with flab. And my plan to kill him with curry has come to nothing. Every time he comes back in with food I realize his bulk is so massive, attacking him would be like trying to climb Mount Everest wearing flip-flops and a summer dress: impossible without dying in the process.

A wave of megadoom descends again. What the heck am I going to do? I could be in here for years! I'd miss my GCSEs, so scuppering any chances of A Levels or a degree, and come out with zero qualifications other than enough knowledge to take a PhD in Sylvanian Families, not something most employers (other than people who run toy shops) are looking for. Maybe I'll point this out to The Psycho Blimp. If he really wants to be a pukka father, he won't stop me doing exams. In my experience, parents bang on about exams *all* the time.

There's something else about being held captive that's worrying me. I hope I'm not going to be held hostage for longer than a week as I'm due on soon, and there is no way am I asking that freak to go the chemist for me. I'll just have to sit on the loo for days, or make something out of toilet paper and kitchen roll like they did on *Blue Peter*, although obviously they didn't make emergency sanitary supplies. That would be of no interest at all to boys, and put entire families off their tea.

Then, just as I'm stressing over how many pieces of kitchen roll I might need, I hear, '*Police in Kent have travelled to Chantilly, near Paris, to question a sixteen-year-old French language student over the disappearance of fifteen-year-old Chantelle Allen who's been missing from her Broadgate-on-Sea home since Thursday morning.*'

Despite Claire's promise of rather dying than tell the parentals about Antoine, she's obviously told them all about him. I'm off that bed and into the living room at warp speed, just in time to see the picture of me impersonating a raspberry gateau fill the screen. Only weeks ago I was fretting that Stacie and Tracie's Facebook friends would clock me looking a frocked fright. Now the whole country can see me not on a little computer, but in wide-screen high definition. I look shocking stretched to about forty inches, and the erupting poo-bags look well weird, like I have black fungus creeping up my chest. The picture doesn't even look like me!

It might be the most up-to-date shot, but people are going to be on the lookout for a real life loo-roll holder with ringlets and a crown, not an edgy teen in a crumpled tutu.

'Chantelle left to meet her French boyfriend on Thursday morning, but failed to return home. *Sky* sources say that Chantelle, known locally as Channy, had been seeing her boyfriend for some time, but was upset that he was going back to his home in France without her. Earlier today, her parents who are part of the highly successful Bjorn At The Beach Abba tribute act, made an emotional plea for her safe return.'

The screen cuts to Mum and Dad sitting at a table in front of the Kent police logo of a rearing horse. It looks as if it's kicking Dad in the head.

'Channy,' Dad says solemnly, staring straight into the camera, his arm around Mum who's sobbing, 'we just want you to know that we love you and that we want you home, whatever you've done, wherever you are, whoever you're with. We just need to know you're safe.'

Tears prick my eyes, and then Dad ruins the moment by saying, 'Just ring ring, why don't you give me a call?'

OMG! Dad can't even give a press conference without slipping an Abba lyric in. I also can't help but notice that both Mum and Dad have the group's website plastered across the front of their black T-shirts in silver glittery letters. I wonder how many sympathy bookings they'll get from my disappearance? They do say that all publicity is good publicity, and appearing on national television weeping over a kidnapped child is about as good as it gets, unless of course I die, when the demand for Bjorn At The Beach pity gigs will rocket.

Then Mum looks up. It breaks my heart to see her looking such a fright, her dark hair greasy and hanging like limp curtains, shadows under her eyes, no sign of any lip-gloss. Once she sees this footage, she'll be broken hearted too. She looks trashed, as if she's had one too many rum and cokes.

'Channy,' Mum gasps. 'I just want to say I'm sorry. If I could turn back time . . .'

The she breaks down again, and the footage cuts to the *Sky* studio.

I despair. Firstly, Dad recites an Abba lyric. Now Mum has popped in a Cher song. What is *wrong* with my parents?

'*Friends of Chantelle have also appealed for her to get in touch,*' the newsreader says. '*Our reporter, Michelle Mayle, is in Broadgate. Michelle, what do we know about Chantelle Allen?*'

A glossy bobbed blonde in a white shirt and pearl

studs nods earnestly as kids on bikes circle next to her, waving at the camera, making rabbit ears behind her head. *'Yes, Mark. I'm here outside Chantelle's house in Lea Crescent, which is in the quiet seaside town of Broadgate-on-Sea. With me are some of Chantelle's friends and family, including her cousins Stacie and Tracie Allen.'*

The Helium Twins appear on the screen dressed in identical pink sparkly tops, pouting and batting their mascara-drenched eyelashes for the cameras. Next to them stands Crab in his Arsenal shirt, a skateboard under his arm, his spots looking shockingly throbby in high def.

Instead of interviewing the Helium Twins, who are clearly gagging to get on screen, Glossy Blonde turns her back on them and thrusts a microphone towards Crab.

'This is Crab Stix. Crab, you used to go out with Chantelle Allen. Is this disappearance out of character for her? Is she the sort of girl to just vanish? Is she a typical troubled teen?'

'Nah.' Crab shakes his head.

'She's never done it before?' Glossy Blonde presses.

'Nah.' Crab shrugs as the twins sneak their heads around the corner of the screen, trying to look both concerned and poutily gorge at the same time.

'You see!' I yell, as Glossy Blonde tries in vain to get Crab to say something other than *Nah.* 'They're looking for me! They're going to find me and then you'll be *toast*!' I've been trying to avoid speaking or interacting in any way with the psycho, but I can't help but point out that he's not going to get away with this for much longer. 'So stick that in your teen book and smoke it!'

'But they're looking for you in France,' The Psycho Blimp calmly points out. 'And you're in North London.'

My stomach plummets. How long will it take them to realize that the whole Antoine thing was made up, that they're on the wrong track and need to start stripping down my laptop to find my Facebook page (always password protected) and the secret hopesandgenes email account I set up to correspond with John Smith.

But just as the reporter decides to give up with the monosyllabic crustacean, Crab grabs the microphone. '*But, like, I don't think she's gone off with that garlic geek,*' he says. '*I think she's gone to find her real father, you know, The Sperm Daddy.*'

Chapter Twenty-Two

Sunday turned into Monday, and then Monday into Tuesday.

Shortly after Crab's bombshell, I dropped off the twenty-four hour rolling news channel and was replaced by an item about the annual spud hurling festival in Dorset. Instead of pictures of my cousins posing outside my house and Dad spouting Abba lyrics, the screen was filled with shots of men dressed in wellies tossing potatoes at an old tree stump. It was all very depressing, especially as to cheer myself up (not to mention pass the time) I'd concocted a little fantasy that Rob Phelps from Death Links would be asked to make a sexy solemn-eyed appeal for my safe return, and then when I was rescued (by hunky cops), after a shower, a change of clothes and some artfully applied make-up, I'd appear on TV with Rob, breathlessly thanking him, after which the fantasy pretty much followed the same path as the one that involved him taking me backstage at Kestival for a serious snog fest.

Clearly, Andy Warhol was right. I've had my fifteen minutes of fame.

The Psycho Blimp didn't go to work.

I sat in my room playing with the Sylvanian Families who by now were fighting amongst themselves, resulting in Otto Hazelnut the dormouse going to woodland prison (under my bed) for unprovoked head-butting of one of the Hamilton Hamster family at a music festival. Occasionally the buzzer would go, The Psycho Blimp would shuffle along the hall, the door would be unlocked, locked, unlocked and locked again, and a takeaway for two would appear.

Just like tonight.

The buzzer goes and the door lock routine begins, after which I can hear feet stomping down the stairs to collect food. It's pizza. I heard him ordering over the phone: a Meat Feast with extra pepperoni, BBQ ribs and garlic mushrooms for him, a Hawaiian for me which he'll end up eating. I've given up with my plan to ambush him on the way back in or grab his mobile, as instead of escaping to freedom, I think I'm more likely to be crushed behind the door or squashed by his weight. And the thought of gasping my last breath with my nose pressed up against The Psycho Blimp's sweaty flesh puts me off any heroics. Plus, I'm too tired. I'm still pretty sure that he isn't going to do anything pervy to me, but the thought of him coming into my room to look at me when I'm sleeping is so creepy, it stops me doing anything more than just having the odd light and fitful snooze.

It was only after the mass riot between the dormice and hamsters ended – Slick Slydale the fox threatening to eat them all unless they broke it up and went back to their nests (different shelves on the bookcase) – that I realize The Psycho Blimp hasn't come back.

There's been no crashing up the stairs, the smell of cooked cheese and garlic preceding him; no rattling of locks and the sound of his wheezy breath as he walks along the hall. He hasn't put his head around the door to announce that the food has arrived, smacking his lips as he tells me he's about to eat.

I start to freak.

What if he never comes back?

What if he's just gone and left me here alone, locked up to die surrounded by toys?

What if the pizza delivery guy has murdered him, mugged him for his wallet?

What if he's had a heart attack on the stairs and is right now dead under a mound of pineapple chunks and pepperoni?

What if we're both eventually found, just skeletons, lice eating away at our flesh, bluebottles buzzing over our bodies?

My mind is running away with itself, and it's running to a *seriously* dark place.

I leave the bedroom and go into the hall.

Somewhere in the distance, I can hear muffled shouts and thuds, and then the sound of a herd of elephants clattering up the stairs. I break into a cold sweat as for one terrible moment I think that I've been wrong about The Psycho Blimp, that he *is* a kiddie-fiddler after all, and that he's invited his friends around for a pizza and perve party.

'Chantelle! Chantelle! Are you in the there?' A gruff male voice calls out. 'It's the police!'

'Help!' I yell, banging on the door. 'I'm locked in here. He's got the keys in his trouser pockets!'

There's more shouting and clattering down and up stairs, and then after what seems like hours, but is probably only a few minutes, there's the sound of locks being rattled and bolts sliding free.

When I was first held hostage I imagined the police

battering the door down, storming the flat, smoke bombs exploding and deep voices shouting: *Go! Go! Go!* as a hunky man in uniform scooped me up in strong arms and raced with me to freedom, whilst in another room, men with batons fought a furious man versus blubber battle with The Psycho Blimp.

But all that happens is that the front door opens and a rather old looking policeman wearing glasses peers at me and says, 'Hello, Chantelle!'

Chapter Twenty-Three

'Mum! Dad!'

My parents hurtle into the cramped room at the police station in London as I collapse in their arms, sobbing.

I've been waiting for them here, on a bed, with a very nice policewoman called Gloria, who's assured me that even though I haven't had a shower or a bath for six days, I don't smell rank, something I don't believe given the amount of sweating with fear I've done recently.

I thought I was totally fine when they popped me in a car and drove me here, in fact, my first emotion was one of mega disappointment that the police car was an unmarked green thing rather than something with pulsating blue lights and blaring sirens, and instead of being driven at high speed through the streets, the policeman drove like my dad, i.e. he stuck to the

235

speed limit, stopped at red lights and even got stuck in a traffic jam.

But when I arrived, I started shaking and my teeth began chattering even though it's not cold, so Gloria called for a doctor, a good looking man with blonde hair and white teeth, whose expert diagnosis was that I was suffering from delayed shock. Doctor Dreamy stuck me in a wheelchair and brought me into this room which turns out to be a cell (!) because it was the only place with a bed, and once I'd laid down for a bit, covered with lots of blankets and had a cup of hot chocolate, I felt *much* better. Actually, I think Doctor Dreamy's diagnosis is wrong: I don't think I'm shaky from shock, I think I'm shaky from hunger. I could really eat that Hawaiian pizza right now.

For a few moments, no one does anything except sob buckets as we cling to each other.

Then Gloria trots off saying she'll organize more drinks, and the three of us sit in a row on the cell bed, Mum on one side of me, Dad on the other, all of us wiping away tears and snorting back snot.

'Did you drive up the M2?' is the first thing I say, which is such a weird thing to come out with if you've been held captive by a psycho for six days, and this is the first time you've seen your heartbroken parents.

Discussing routes is the sort of thing that middle-aged rellies do when they meet up. Uncle Kevin and Dad can spend hours talking about whether it's best to go through the Blackwall Tunnel or via the City if they're going to London. Perhaps shock has aged my brain.

'Kent Police brought us,' Dad says. 'Blue-light taxi all the way. Sirens, lights, the full monty. They've been marvellous from start to finish, haven't they, Sandy?'

'Marvellous,' Mum echoes. 'Marvellous.'

It doesn't seem fair that the parents of the hostage had all the transport fun.

'I can't believe my little girl's safe,' Mum sobs, hugging me again before fishing in her bag and getting out a wad of white tissues. She blows her nose on one and hands Dad and me the others. 'Are you sure you're OK?'

'I'm fine,' I assure her. 'Stinky and starving, but fine.'

'The sooner they charge him, the better,' Dad growls, jumping off the bed and pacing the floor, before realizing that you can't do much pacing in a cell designed for one, but filled with three people, a lidless steel toilet and a narrow bed. 'I'm not a violent man, but I could wring that monster's bloody neck.'

'He's not a monster.' I'm surprised to hear myself defend him. 'Don't call him that.'

Dad stares at me as if I've just said I'm going to become

a nun and take a vow of chastity and silence.

'He's just a sad lonely man who missed his real daughter.' I'm trying to explain, but I don't really understand myself. 'It was just something that got out of hand. For both of us.'

'Oh my God!' Mum screams. 'She's got Stockholm syndrome!'

'Huh?' How typical of Abba-obsessed Mum to bring something Swedish into all this.

'It's when hostages take pity on their kidnappers,' Dad explains. 'When they make friends with them.'

I can't say that once I was trapped in the flat I ever felt friendly towards John Smith, but when I was led out into the street wrapped in a blanket (just as well, as the slutty ballerina get-up hasn't faired too well after being worn for twenty four hours a day for six days), I saw him handcuffed, his arms yanked behind his back, waiting beside a police van like some vast frightened whale stranded on a beach, the dead guinea pig toupée lying on the ground, twitching in the breeze as if it might scurry off down the road at any moment. He looked at me and mouthed: *Sorry*. I looked at him, bloated, bald and emotionally beaten, and felt gut-wrenchingly sad at the way his life has turned out. Perhaps if his wife hadn't taken his daughter away, kept her from him, things might have been different; perhaps he wouldn't have turned into an obese psycho who kidnaps young girls via Facebook. Or perhaps he always was a nutter, which is why Laura left and took Hannah with her, disappearing off the face of the earth.

'Did he, er . . .' Mum looks uneasy. I know what she's trying to ask.

'He didn't touch me,' I assure her. 'He just wanted to play Monopoly and eat takeaways. I spent all my time playing Sylvanian Families. He wasn't as bad as people will make out. Honestly.'

'Wasn't as bad! Wasn't as bad!!' Dad explodes. 'He tricked you and locked you up! He wouldn't let you use your phone to ring us! How the hell can you defend him, Channy?'

I swing my legs, watching them move backwards and forwards over the edge of the bed. 'I dunno,' I shrug. 'It's complicated.' I want to change the subject. I don't want to think about him. 'How's Claire?'

Throughout my kidnap ordeal, I've felt terrible about deceiving her, about using her. At the time I really thought I had no choice but to meet John Smith, however I did it. Now I realize I did, and I'm truly sorry I dragged her into this mess.

'Worried sick about you,' Dad says. 'We all were. I

doubt Sue and Bob will let you look after her again.'

Poor Claire. She'll be back at Mrs Wallen's, troughing away, slowly expanding into a female version of The Psycho Blimp.

'How did they know where I was?' I ask. 'DNA? My moby signal? Security cameras? An infra-red tracking helicopter?' I watch crime programmes. I know how high-tech detective work can be these days.

'After the appeal on the telly, a taxi driver came forward to say he'd dropped you off in Chatterton Road,' Dad explains. 'The police started making enquiries in the area, and several takeaway places on Blackstock Road said a man had started ordering meals for two when he'd spent years ordering meals for one. The police checked him out, found he was called John Smith and hadn't been at work since you went missing, and, well, there you were and here you are.'

Not so high-tech then. John Smith was caught by his addiction to takeaways.

'I'm sorry.' I start sobbing again. I'm so tired I can't sit up. I curl up on the bit of the bed Dad has left. It feels warm against my cheek. 'Really sorry.'

'You're sorry!' Mum wails, stroking my head. 'This is all my fault. If I hadn't—'

'Sandy!' Dad interjects. His voice has a steely warning

tone. 'Not now. Maybe later. Channy's tired and the police still need a statement from her.'

'But it *is* all my fault!' Mum cries as Gloria comes in with three steaming cream plastic cups, puts them on the floor and beetles out again. 'I'm to blame for all of this, Trevor! Our daughter could have been murdered or raped and *I'd* be to blame!'

'No, you wouldn't!' I assure her. 'You didn't arrange to meet a mentalist on the Euston Road. I did. Anyway, it doesn't matter any more. It's over. Finito. End of. I'm never going to look for John Smith ever again. I didn't really want another dad anyway. I was just curious.' I close my eyes and feel myself drifting off.

'It *is* my fault because you were never going to find your biological father, however long you looked!' Mum's voice rises to a shriek, blowing any chance of a quick kip. 'He doesn't exist!'

How weird. Is she saying I was the result of some sort of Immaculate Conception, the product of a virgin birth? This rather blows the sex education I've been given out of the window. Then I realize what she's getting at.

'You mean – he's dead?'

Bummer! All this time I've been looking for him on Facebook and he's pegged it. OMG! Did he die young from some terrible hereditary disease? Am I going to inherit it? Did he need a new kidney? Heart? Liver? What?

'I don't know whether he's dead or alive,' Mum admits. 'I don't know what he looks like or his name. I just picked the name John Smith because it was the most common name I could think of.'

'Why?' I ask.

'Because for fifteen years I kept a secret, not just from you, but from your dad. A guilty secret.'

I don't feel sleepy now. I'm bolt upright on the bed, my eyes locked on Mum's stricken face.

'I didn't have a boyfriend called John Smith during The Blip,' she admits. 'I pretended I did because I didn't want your dad to know the truth.'

'Which is?'

Mum's face is ashen under the harsh fluorescent light. She bites her lip and scrunches her eyes up as if she's in pain. 'I had a drunken one night stand in a pub car park with a man who came to see my Cher act. It was dark. I think it was a Mercedes because I could feel the emblem on the car's bonnet in my back . . .'

'OK! Enough!' I stop her. This is waaay too much info. It's bad enough thinking your parents do the deed without having to face up to the fact your Mum had sex with a total stranger, outside, whilst off her head on alcohol. It's all too much. Only moments ago, I was thinking she might be a modern day Virgin Mary!

I rub my eyes with my palms. Perhaps I'm so tired I'm hallucinating and this is all just a dream. Maybe I'll wake up and The Psycho Blimp will be standing at the end of my bed, waving his selection of takeaway leaflets, suggesting a chicken biryani.

I look across at Dad. He's leaning against the wall, staring into his plastic cup, swirling it in circles, first clockwise, then anticlockwise. I can see on his face this isn't some dodgy dream.

'Your Aunty Julie and I came up with the John Smith story,' Mum continues. 'That's the story I told your dad and Julie told Omar the dodgy Greek. To get back at her in their bitter divorce, Omar told some of the family. I was dreading you finding out, asking more questions and your dad realizing I'd lied. I've lived with the worry every day of my life since it happened.'

'And when you did find out and I told you his name, the name your mum gave me, she told me the whole truth,' Dad says. 'As you can imagine, there was one hell of a row that I'd been kept in the dark for fifteen years. I didn't think we had secrets from each other.'

'Which is why you stayed at the Myers' for a few days.'

Mum wipes her eyes. 'So we could sort things out, decide what to tell you.'

'And then we decided not to tell you anything, at least for now,' Dad jumps in. 'Which, as it turns out, was a mistake.'

'We just wanted to protect you,' Mum says, twisting a damp tissue in her hands. 'We didn't want to hurt you any more than you already had been. It would all have been too much too soon, more information than we thought you could take, what with exams coming up . . .'

'So you were so sozzled you know nothing about this man, other than he might have driven a Mercedes fifteen years ago?' I say. 'That's everything you know?'

A flash of panic sweeps across Mum's face.

'Mum?' I grab her hand. 'What is it? What's so terrible about this man that you couldn't tell me the truth?' I'm thinking murderer, paedophile, a Chris de Burgh impersonator.

Mum and Dad exchange glances and Dad nods. She blows air between her teeth and squeezes my hand. 'I don't know what this man looked like or his name, but even though I was pickled, I remembered what he said he did for a living.'

'Which was?' I'm on the edge of the bed, my hearing

heightened like a bat on a night flight. 'Come on, Mum, you have to tell me!'

She takes a deep breath and whispers, 'He said he was a drug dealer.'

Chapter Twenty-Four

Waking up this morning (or rather this afternoon, it's three o'clock!) in my own bed, wearing a nightie instead of a tutu and surrounded by books rather than tiny woodland creatures, the last few days seem like a weird dream. And then I sniff myself and the stale smell of John Smith's flat reminds me that it wasn't a dream, and that really even if I was asleep under the spray, I should have had a shower last night.

It took ages to get out of the police station. I'd had a statement to make and questions to answer and it all seemed very creepy knowing John Smith was doing the same thing, in another room, just along the corridor. Weirdly, I kept worrying that he wouldn't be allowed his wig back, that on top of everything he'd feel humiliated because he was hairless.

I stretch my legs to the bottom of the bed and mull

everything over in my head: looking for my bio dad; being held hostage; finding out The Sperm Daddy is a nameless drug dealer with a Mercedes. But like I told Mum and Dad last night, it's all over. I can honestly say that even if right now a bird flew in and dropped The Sperm Daddy's real name and address on to my bed, I wouldn't look at it. Well, maybe I might look at it, but I wouldn't do anything with it. I don't need to know whose DNA I'm carrying, and if I need a new kidney, I'll just have to hope that by then medical science will have moved on to grow them in test tubes or on the back of mice or something.

Of course, if a bird did try to fly in the window he'd knock himself out on the glass: the window is shut and the curtains are drawn.

I get out of bed and pad over to the window. I expect the drive is full of people, reporters trying to get a scoop on my kidnap. I wouldn't mind a bit of celebrity attention, but not when I've just woken up and without the benefit of serious grooming. Don't want to be snapped by the paps looking rank.

I peer through a gap in the curtains. Nothing. The drive is completely empty except for the Abbamobile and Aunty Nicola's silver Jeep.

Bit of a shame about the lack of press attention, but

never mind. I'm looking forward to a few days of being pampered, cosseted by my family who are clearly thrilled that I've returned safe and well. Now will be the time to raise a few things I might not have got away with before, like substantially increasing my allowance and letting me have Kurt the rat. Perhaps we can have a trip to Pets At Home later and choose one complete with cage and accessories. I'll spend the summer wandering around Lea Crescent with Kurt on my shoulder, freaking everyone.

But before rat shopping, a shower.

On the landing, I can hear raised voices downstairs in the kitchen. It sounds like Aunty Nicola and Mum are arguing, going at it hammer and tongs.

I creep down a few stairs and leaning over the banister, listen.

'Nicola, the fact remains that if your daughters hadn't been so stupid as to make friends with someone they didn't know, a man in his forties with a thing about young girls, Chantelle wouldn't have been put through all this.' Mum sounds highly strung. There's lots of banging of crockery and slamming of cupboard doors. 'Because of them, this monster knew what my daughter looked like, who she was friends with, what she'd been up to!'

'Can I remind you, *Sandra*,' Aunty Nicola's voice drips

with sarcasm, 'that it was *your* daughter who went looking for this pervert behind your back. Stacie and Tracie wouldn't have been so dumb as to trot off to London to meet a stranger and not tell anyone.'

'They were dumb enough to pose in their underwear on Facebook!' Mum shouts. 'You didn't know about *that*.'

'They were in *designer* bikinis, and unlike Channy, they didn't lie!' a smug sounding Aunty Nicola points out. 'Though of course given your background, it's not surprising. Like mother like daughter!'

'How dare you!' Mum snaps back.

'How dare you deceive Trevor all these years!' Aunty N shouts. 'John Smith?' I can almost hear her spit with contempt. 'You picked a name out of a hat and a man out of the audience!'

So much for a cosy family reunion. I might not raise the subject of a pet rat straightaway.

Amidst more vicious accusations, including one that Mum is far too old to still impersonate Frida, something that will wound her deeply, I go downstairs and put my head around the living-room door. Sitting side-by-side on the green velour sofa, dressed in identical denim shorts and cleavage-busting white sleeveless shirts are Stacie and Tracie, their faces as hard as granite.

'Hello,' I say, waiting for them to squeal with delight that I'm home, tell me how terrified they were that I was going to end up tossed in the Thames, and promise to invite me to *all* their pop-up parties for the rest of their lives.

But there's no warm welcome. Neither of them speak nor look at me.

How odd. Perhaps they haven't noticed me come in, either that, or they've taken some weird twins-only vow of silence.

'Hello!' I say, raising my voice, and just to make sure my entrance isn't going to go unnoticed again, wave.

Both of them slowly twist their skinny necks to glare at me, their eyes blazing, as if they've been taken over by some evil force.

'You. Have. Ruined. Our. Lives,' one twin says, robotically.

'Trashed. Our. Dreams,' her sister adds in the same sinister voice.

Seriously, am I dreaming? Is this a horror nightmare where Stacie and Tracie have turned into staccato speaking zombies? Has the shock of my kidnap twisted their brains? Are they suffering from a form of post-traumatic stress?

Hang on a minute; shouldn't *I* be the one with the

post-traumatic stress?

'Excuse me?' I say sarcastically. '*I* was the one locked up by a loony. What's eating you?'

They sneer at me as if they've just discovered they've brought dog muck into the house on the soles of their bronze-leather gladiator sandals, either that or I really do smell rank from a distance. I should have showered before meeting guests.

'We were spotted,' Twin One explains, 'by a man who has discovered *all* the top calendar girls and page three models.'

'He saw us on *Sky News* and thought we could be the next glamour twins,' Twin Two says, tossing her hair. 'He wanted to brand us StaceTrace: like the Olsens, but prettier, less grungy.'

'There was talk of a recording contract,' Twin Two sniffs. 'Cover versions of Rhianna songs.'

'And underwear work!' Twin One, squeaks. '*Promotions!*'

Damn! It's happened again! *I* was the one who was kidnapped, and just as with Mum and Dad and the police car, my cousins have had all the fun and even the promise of some money. I can see it now: StaceTrace calendars; StaceTrace stationery; StaceTrace T-shirts, even their own range of StaceTrace bras. I'd rather go braless and wobble around showing nipple through my T-shirts than wear a cousin-branded bap-pack.

'But now our chance of fame is over before it's even started, and it's ALL *your* fault!' Twin Two jabs a threatening finger at me.

'What's it got to do with me?' I ask, wondering if I can risk going into the kitchen for a custard cream. I can't hear any more arguing, but that could be because right now Mum and Aunty Nicola have their hands around each other's throats.

'Dad put his foot down,' Twin Two snaps. 'Says we're too young to do that sort of modelling. Told the guy he was a dirty old man for trying to get fifteen-year-olds to pose in bras, even though they'd have been tasteful bras, wouldn't they, Trace?'

'I still don't see what any of this has to do with me,' I grumble. 'He's your dad, not mine. And because of me you were nearly famous.'

Both twins glare daggers at me. 'It's your fault because of your Facebook fiasco!' Tracie yells, as it occurs to me how quickly someone can turn from pretty to ugly when they're angry. 'Dad's going to police our emails and monitor the chat rooms, *and* he's made us unfriend most of our Facebook friends!'

'He's set our privacy settings to the top level; we're

not allowed to be friends with anyone he hasn't met.' Stacie looks close to collapse. 'He stood behind me this morning and we went through all one thousand one hundred and sixty two friends and now I'm down to . . .' she starts to hyperventilate, 'seventy five! It's social suicide!'

Tracie leans forward and shoots evils at me. 'Mum and Dad had a terrible row about it because Mum wanted us to do the modelling, but Dad didn't, and now they're not speaking to each other. You've ruined everyone's lives and it's not even as if you're proper family!'

Aunty Nicola puts her head round the door.

'Channy!' she says stiffly, a fake smile pasted on to her face. 'Glad to be home?'

Chapter Twenty-Five

Downstairs, the front doorbell (capable of playing up to ten different record-your-own ringtones) shrieks out *Voulez-Vous*. Again.

Over the last seventy-two hours, there's been a steady stream of people swinging by Lea Crescent to see how I am, though guttingly, no one has thought to bring me chocolate, or even a bunch of wilty flowers in cellophane from the local Shell garage.

I listen as the front door opens and Mum and Dad greet the latest visitor.

It's ironic, really. I used to sit in this house feeling lonely, and now it's turned into party central I wish they'd all bog off and leave me alone. I need a closing bell, like the one in Uncle Kevin's home bar. The moment someone annoyed me or arrived sans gift, I'd ring it. Because it doesn't matter who's sat politely in the living room as Mum forces tea and Mr Kipling cakes on them – Aunty Nicola and the glacially unfriendly Helium Twins; Crab, who thinks he's saved my life by mentioning The Sperm Daddy on *Sky News*, so putting the police off the Antoine lead; Aunty Julie but not New Aunty Ros because she had to take Puglicious Kylie to be mated with a stud dog called Pugster Jack the Lad and it was now or never; Nana Allen, clearly frosty with Mum and taking sides with Aunty Nicola; the Crawfords from over the road, who complained the news crews blocked their drive when they were hoping to take the motor home to Eastbourne for the week, and even Gaia Taylor, just because she's a gossipy, nosy cow – the visit always follows the same course.

First, it's lots of hugs and gushing sentiments along the lines of they're glad I'm back, everyone's been worried sick, they saw me on the telly, blah blah blah.

Then they'll look at me slightly oddly and say in an embarrassed low voice with lots of nodding and sly glances towards my lady bits: *He didn't DO anything to you, did he, Channy?* at which point I vigorously shake my head, pull a face and confess I spent six days playing with a vast collection of Sylvanian Families and eating takeaways, whereupon their mood changes entirely and they look disapproving, angry even, and give me a lecture on how idiotic I was to do what I did, and how I could have ended up missing *forever* or damaged *for life*, which of course is true. I don't need people to tell me what a complete microbrain I've been; I'm painfully aware of what I've done and the possible consequences. So to avoid any more embarrassing conversations over a boob-like cherry bakewell, I've taken myself to bed, and I'm going to stay here for as long as possible with the curtains drawn, at least until Taryn comes back from Patagonia to cheer me up.

Because there's nothing to get up for now. Absolutely nothing at all.

People who've escaped death usually say that it's given them a new perspective on life, that they're going to live every day as if it's their last, seize the day, follow their dream, sell the family house and spend a year travelling around Australia studying wombats.

Not me.

Lying in the dark, I've come to the depressing conclusion that my life post-kidnapping is considerably worse than before it, because pre-kidnapping, I was *already* following my dream. There was an exciting chance that The Sperm Daddy was a booky-boho type, part of a big noisy family, a dynasty of writers and journalists who would warmly welcome me into their world and include Antoine (!) and me in their family lunches and camping trips. Despite Mum and Dad being more in to Abba than Austen, everyone would get on, seamlessly blending into each others' lives like the smug-faced families who pop up in magazine articles about how to have a friendly divorce.

But now, post-kidnapping, the dream is over. This warm glow of romance and inter-family happiness is never going to happen because my real father is a nameless drug dealer, Antoine thinks I'm a teenage fantasist, and everyone despises me for being such a fool.

I hear several sets of footsteps coming up the stairs towards my room.

Quickly I arrange my face and body into a deep-sleep pose.

As the door opens, I smell something odd. Not horrid odd, just different odd, like the smell of the joss sticks Pippa Griffiths sometimes lights in the shed that she uses as her studio. The incense sticks have names like *Heavenly Dawn* and *Enchanted Sunset*, and smell sort of musky and exotic, but when Taryn and I took one to her bedroom, stuffed it in a lump of Blu-Tack and lit it, we obviously hadn't rammed it in the sticky mound securely enough as it fell over and scorched the cream carpet, leaving a rather nasty-looking long brown streak like a dog had rubbed its bum on the ground. Anyway, right now there's that same sort of mysterious whiff, but without the penk of burning wool and nylon.

'Channy? Are you awake?' Mum whispers.

I carry on lying stock-still, my eyes clamped tightly shut, snoring slightly.

I don't think I usually snore – I'm sure Taryn would have thrown a pillow at me during sleepovers if I'd been a night-grunter – but I've perfected this delicate snore as a way of repelling visitors by audibly demonstrating that I'm asleep, and like Greta Garbo, I want to be alone.

'I'm sorry,' Mum whispers.

Since I got home, she's done nothing but apologize. I think it's about time she stopped beating herself up over getting drunk, getting pregnant by a nameless drug dealer and lying about it for fifteen years. Actually when you list it out like that, I can see why she's mega guilty. Mum and Dad even cancelled today's booking, a Saturday wedding in Whitstable. Having seen Mum weep live on *Sky News*, the bride and groom were very understanding, and Dad arranged for a friend of his who's an Elton John impersonator to fill the booking.

'She's fast asleep. I thought seeing you might cheer her up,' Mum says.

I wonder who this visitor is? I'd like to open one eye

and take a peek, but it might be someone I don't want to see, like Slow Jo.

At the thought of being confronted by my dodgy distant rellie, I up the snoring level. I sound like a truffle pig with a heavy cold. *Very* convincing.

'After the initial euphoria of her release, she's been *very* depressed.' It's Dad's voice, a whisper thick with worry. 'We want her to take the police up on their offer of arranging counselling, but she refuses.'

I shudder inside. Gloria, the lovely policewoman, drove up from London on Thursday to bring me back my bag (147 missed calls on my mobile), and to tell me that John Smith has pleaded guilty to every charge they've put to him: abduction; false imprisonment; perverting the course of justice; deception; obesity (not really, I'm making that one up). This means that I won't have to go to court to testify against him, my statement will do, a mega relief. Because despite what he did to me and even though I know he was wrong and should never have done what he did, I still feel sorry for him, and I was starting to worry that I'd stand in court and plead with the judge to be lenient on account of the fact that he was sad and lonely and missing his family.

Anyway, Gloria sat on the sofa next to me, took my hand (which I thought was a tad over-familiar) and said solemnly, 'Is there anything you want to ask me?'

The first thing that sprang to mind was: 'What's happened in *EastEnders*, *Coronation Street* and *Hollyoaks* whilst I was away?' at which point Gloria suggested that I might like counselling, though I'm not sure whether this is to help me get over being kidnapped, or to wean me off a serious soap addiction. Anyway, I refused. I'm fine, though I don't think I can ever look at another Sylvanian critter ever again without wanting to retch. Herbage was still in my bag along with half a mouldy chocolate muffin and the unused return train ticket. The photographs of the imaginary Hannah were gone: evidence I suppose. I wonder who she really is and whether she'll ever know how she was used?

'I – er . . . understand,' a deep, sexy, FRENCH voice whispers back. 'It is no problem.'

I stop snoring. I stop breathing.

'It was good of you to come,' Mum says. 'And after all Channy put you through. Thank you, Antoine. We appreciate it.'

ANTOINE!

That was the mysterious musky smell – a gorgeous foreigner oozing exotic testosterone. The Fabulous Frog isn't back in Chantilly, he's here, in my bedroom, next to me, and I've been wheezing and snorting. This really completes my pug persona, doesn't it? And have I been dribbling out of the corner of my mouth? Is there a damp patch on the pillow? Can he see drool in the dark?

OMG! OMG! What the heck do I do now?

I speedily run through my relatively limited options.

Option One: Immediately leap up proclaiming I'm fine, therefore exposing this fabulous foreign specimen to my Hello Kitty nightie, a flash of big period panties, serious squid-hair and knock-em dead at twenty paces parrot breath. It would be like some freak from the deep emerging from under the duvet.

Option Two: Wait until Antoine has left the room and in the few moments between him leaving and the front door opening (about ten seconds max, maybe fifteen if the front-door catch sticks as it sometimes does in warm weather), get up, pee, floss teeth, brush teeth, swill mouthwash, get dressed in appropriately casual yet super stylish individualistic outfit, apply entire contents of make-up bag, stick a copy of something by Simone de Beauvoir under my arm and saunter downstairs casually saying: *Oh! Hello!* as if it's every day a French Love God swings by.

Option Three: Given that Antoine has been extensively questioned by the police through no fault of his own and will have been told of the torrid affair we've been having, so secretive even *he* didn't know about it, pretend to stay fast asleep and let Antoine head back to Chantilly with tales of nutty English people, never to set eyes on me again.

I decide on Option Three. In other words, I may have the object of my dreams in my bedroom, but I'm going to hide under the duvet and pretend to be in the land of nod, but without the accompanying sound effects.

'Please give my good wishes to Chantelle, Madame et Monsieur Allen.'

Oh, that voice! It's like warm honey dripping through soft air. He pronounces my name, *Shon-tal*. And Madame et Monsieur Allen! It makes my parents sound like characters out of an arty black and white film with subtitles, rather than seventies wannabes with a disco habit.

I feel light-headed with lust.

Actually, no, I feel light-headed because I've been holding my breath.

And then something *terrible* happens.

I let out an enormous gasp and start gulping for air. Clearly, my involuntary breathing reflex (GCSE biology!) has kicked in. I'm gasping for breath like a fish out of water. Or possibly having a panic attack.

'You're awake!' Mum says before, *quelle horreur!* she

goes to the window and opens the curtains, flooding the room with unflatteringly harsh sunlight. 'Look who's here to see you! It's Antoine! He's back in England!'

Through squinty eyes, I can see Mum flittering around the room like Tinkerbell, pulling back this, smoothing that. Clearly, Antoine's accent is having the same effect on her as it is on me, which given that she's my mother and he's my (pretend) boyfriend is well out of order.

'I'll go and put the kettle on and get some Mr Kipling's,' Mum trills, pushing Dad out of the room. 'Perhaps a nice plate of French Fancies.'

This. Is. Just. T.E.R.R.I.B.L.E!

The house rule is: no boys in the bedroom, but in reality I was absolutely safe with Crab; I'd have belted him if he'd tried anything on (witness the cotton wool in the bra episode). But Mum's chosen this moment to break the rule when I'm not only in my bedroom, but actually *in bed*, wearing practically nothing, looking rank, trying to get my parrot-cage breath back, whilst next to me stands gorgeously Gallic Antoine, smouldering in a blindingly white T-shirt and cut off khaki's, his bronzed hands resting on his snaky hips.

I suddenly freak that lying on my side on my pillows is making me look particularly pug-like, all squish-faced, so I shuffle up the bed and prop myself against the headboard, which also helps quell the heavy breathing.

'I came to see how you were,' Antoine says, looking straight at me with those delicious brown eyes I remember from the day at the beach, the blue-framed sunnies pushed back through his dark curls. He's not giving me a loaded look of lust or love, just one that says I'm also a *complètement dingue*, or whatever it was he called Crab at Kestival. It's disappointing, but I can hardly blame him.

'Spiffing,' I say brightly, wondering whether it's delayed shock or lack of oxygen that has me using such a strange word, further underlining my *dingue* status.

'You want a spliff?' Antoine queries, his eyes widening.

Not surprisingly, I expect spiffing isn't a word they teach the students at the Broadgate Language Academy, though Antoine seems to have no trouble recognising something phonetically similar. I hope Mum and Dad aren't earwigging on the stairs.

'No! No!' I say. 'I meant, I'm good. Thanks.'

There's a brief silence and I feel I need to fill it, so I say, 'Did you see me on television?'

'*Non*,' Antoine replies, shaking his head so his curls quiver. 'The polis – um, they gathered me for questions.'

I feel a flood of relief that this gorgeous foreign

264

specimen hasn't seen me encased in pink satin accessorised with black plastic dog poo bags.

'Um, they showed me a photograph of you. In a pink *et noir* – um, black, dress. Wiv hounds?'

There's lots of sweeping of hands and a clenched fist, which I think is supposed to be me wearing a long dress holding a dog lead. It's like playing charades.

'You looked . . .' he searches for the right word.

'Minging?' I suggest.

'*Très chaud*,' he grins as I wonder whether he means *hot* hot, or sweaty hot.

He flashes a coy smile. 'I understand we were lurvverrs!'

Now I really am *très chaud* as my face burns, not just at the way I spun a story about Antoine, but at the sexy way he says luuurvers: all deep u's and rolling r's. I pull the duvet right over my chest and neck to avoid him seeing the beety-red skin flush I sometimes get when I'm embarrassed.

'Yes, about that,' I mutter. 'I'm sorry.'

'*Pourquoi?*' Antoine says, raising a dark eyebrow. 'Why me for ze lie?'

I bristle at the word lie. Fantasy sounds so much better. Even with a seriously sexy French accent, lie sounds a horrid word. Like slug. Slug would be a disgusting word even said with a French accent: *sluuurg*. Oh, yuk. It sounds like a slowly moving jelly-turd covered in slime.

'Shon-tal?'

I can't believe I'm thinking about slugs when I've got Antoine in my room. I'm sick. I must be. Where was I before I got distracted? Oh, yes. Antoine wants to know why I chose him for my foreign fantasy.

In my head I'm saying: *Because absolutely every bit of you is drop-dead gorge, even down to your feet, and you're waaay more exciting than any of the lads round here.*

'Dunno,' I shrug. 'I just did. I'm sorry.'

And then Antoine sits on the end of my bed. Actually, he lies across the end, his long, bronzed legs dangling over the edge, propping his body up on his elbows, twisting his neck to look at me. I am *so* tempted to get out of bed to get my phone so that I can take a picture I can show Taryn when she comes back, but I can't risk Antoine seeing my dodgy nightie and slightly hairy knees. I bet French minxes don't have hairy knees and cartoon nightwear, or if they do, they're so damn gorgeous no one notices or cares.

'You owe me,' he says.

Oh. My. God! He wants compensation for being falsely accused and arrested on suspicion of being my boyfriend.

In between learning English, being arrested and playing semi-naked volleyball, he's obviously been watching one of those *Where's there's blame there's a claim* type adverts, and thinks he can get mega bucks out of me. If despite the kidnapping Mum is still sticking to her guns and making me pay for the bridesmaid's silver trotters, she's *defo* going to bill me for any Antoine-related compensation. I'm going to be practically bankrupt before I go to university. Can I even afford to go to uni now? I'd already been a bit worried about living expenses and tuition fees. I hadn't counted on a debt of compensation to a hot frog.

'Will you help me learn more English?'

Good heavens! I wasn't expecting that. I'd been bracing myself to hear a six-figure sum.

Antoine is still looking at me, a slight smile creeping across his pillow-lipped mouth. 'I am good on ze spoken word, but not so good on ze writing. When I am at my home, could I email you, in English, Shon-tal, and you correct me?'

Even if a fire broke out in the room I doubt I could scramble out of bed, my legs are so jellified.

'I suppose it's the least I can do,' I say, trying to appear ultra-cool, almost impossible when your entire body is on fire, not just because of lust, but because it's a warm

August day and being wrapped up tightly in a twelve-tog duvet is like sitting in a sauna. This gives me something else to worry about: the smell of sweat.

Then Antoine uncurls his body, leans right over me and picks a pen off my bedside table.

'Please, will you write your email address on here?' He sticks a long golden limb under my nose.

I can barely write for shaking. I have to actually hold his arm with one hand whilst scribbling with the other. I wish my nails looked better.

'I go back to Chantilly tomorrow, but I will write,' he says. 'And you? You will write back?' His puppy brown eyes are locked on mine and there is absolutely no doubt in my mind that he is giving me not just The Look, but a Loaded Look, a gaze which is full of lust and longing because that is exactly how I'm feeling.

Then still leaning over he gently kisses me with soft cool lips.

And all I can think is: WOW!

Chapter Twenty-Six

'This is mental!' I snap at Mum. We're standing in the road outside a modern semi-detached house on a housing estate full of identical semi-detached houses, three miles from Lea Crescent. 'I've told you,' I say sourly. 'I can look after myself.'

It's Saturday, ten days since I was freed, and if I'd thought that my homecoming would be a more modern and female version of the parable of the prodigal son, i.e. much rejoicing, a whole new wardrobe and a fatted calf for tea, I was sadly mistaken. Once the relief had worn off, Mum and Dad went into anger-overdrive at how I lied and what I did, a bit rich coming from a woman whose entire family was built on the mother of all fibs. They won't even let me have Kurt because they say I'm not responsible enough to look after an animal.

I don't think it's helped that every time anyone asks

me why I did what I did, I just shrug and mutter *I dunno*, not because I'm being sullen or awkward, but because I really don't know. It's as if for a brief time I lost both my mind and my common sense, and although I'd like to explain, my headspace is a soupy swirl of random words, words which won't make it out of my brain and through my mouth in a coherent sentence: *EastEnders*. Microwave. Sofa. Silence. Roxy. Table. Roast beef. Donna. They speed through my mind like one of those electronic advertising hoardings at a football stadium, going round and round, driving me mental. If only I could take my brain out of my head and put it somewhere for a few hours, just to give myself some peace.

But I can't and life and Bjorn At The Beach concerts go on, this time a summer spectacular in Gillingham, which means there's the small problemo of what to do with me.

I pleaded, I cried, I promised I'd stay in the house even if it was burning down (extreme I know, suggesting I'd rather be burnt to a human crisp than break a promise, but I was trying to prove a point), but Mum and Dad refused to let me stay home alone, not just because last time I ran away I left a twelve-year-old in a bridesmaid's dress and got kidnapped, but because the police had muttered something about being irresponsible parents and Mum doesn't want social services involved, something she said might happen if they made a spot check on the house and found me on my own. So, with Taryn still away, Aunty Nicola and Mum not speaking and Nana Allen on a body-boarding course at Botany Bay, the only option was to book me in for the day with Mrs Wallen, the childminder.

How humiliating.

'You've proved you can't be trusted,' Mum says snippily, as a group of kids on bikes circle us, sniggering.

We're definitely Exhibit A in Hawthorn Drive, but then it's not everyday at ten in the morning you get a woman dressed up as a member of Abba in your road, a van blasting out Abba, and a hairy man in white silk and sequins singing *Super Trouper* at the top of his voice whilst he waits for us.

'But I've promised you! The whole searching for The Sperm Daddy is over!' I protest. 'And you've met Antoine. He's gone back to Chantilly!'

Even though I'm in a foul mood, I can't help but smile inwardly at Antoine's first email, chockablock with mistakes. OK, so correcting a story about a family going on a caravanning holiday to the countryside, and their dog, Rover, going missing in the woods, isn't the same as having him as a boyfriend, but it's still good. It's still a link to The Fabulous Frog, and that kiss, so steamy my poly-cotton duvet cover nearly burst into flames, will stay with me forever.

'You're going in, even if I have to drag you,' Mum growls.

For a moment, I stand defiantly on the tarmac, wondering whether Mum really would inflict physical violence on me in public, especially given her worry that she could be accused of being a bad parent. Then I look at her towering above me in her silver over-the-knee mega-platform boots, shooting me evils through her glittery false eyelashes, and know for a fact that she would. Being yanked along by a woman who looks like a drag queen would be mortifying.

She stalks up the tiny path and rings the bell, holding me by the wrist, presumably to stop me making a run for it.

In the glass porch, a woman kicks a little tricycle and two pairs of tiny orange and red Crocs out of the way, opens the door, and taking one look at Abba-fied Mum says, 'I'm Angela Wallen. We spoke on the phone. Come in.'

I don't know why, but I'd expected Mrs W to be a total chubster, shoving carbs at her charges just to keep them quiet. But she's like a bird, a tiny sparrow with a peroxide crop and large hoop earrings, neatly dressed in jeans and navy scoop-necked T-shirt.

We follow her in to the house and stand in the narrow hall.

From another room, I can hear the sound of kids screaming.

My heart sinks.

It's the sound I remember from the days I used to go to a childminder, an ear-bleeding screech that vibrates through your entire body and makes you take a mental vow never to have children of your own unless you can guarantee they'll be cute gurgling cherubs rather than screaming banshees.

'Now,' Mrs W says, taking a clipboard and pen from the sideboard. 'I just need to go through a few things and get your signature.'

'Well, we're running late,' Mum points out. 'Channy can tell you anything you need to know.'

The childminder shoots Mum a steely look. Her body might be sparrow-like, but her eyes are as cold and beady as a hawk, the sort of hawk that hovers in the sky before swooping down and ripping the guts out of a cute little field mouse who was minding its own business snuffling for grubs. Actually, looking at Mrs W more closely, she does have a slightly hooked nose. Perhaps she's a hawk reincarnated as a childminder?

'As I'm registered and insured, I do things by the book,' Hawk Woman says icily. 'I need to ask the parent, guardian or carer the questions, *not* the child.' Her blue biro hovers over the clipboard. 'Allergies? Food dislikes? Medication? Local doctor? Bedtime?'

Her questions come thick and fast. Mum does her best to answer them as Mrs Wallen's pen swoops up and down making notes.

I glance at the half-open front door, wondering if despite my promises of being a model daughter from now on I could make a run for it.

'And is Chantelle fully toilet-trained? Does she wet the bed?'

I splutter to show how undignified this is. Even Mrs W must realize not all her questions are appropriate for a fifteen-year-old.

'We should be back around seven,' Mum says. 'Any later and I'll ring you.'

'No problem.' Mrs Wallen's tone is brisk. 'We'll make sure your daughter can't leave the house unaccompanied.'

The door closes, there's the sound of the van leaving the road, and I realize that until Mum and Dad return to rescue me, I'm trapped in a house with a weird hawk-woman who thinks I'm a child who might wet the bed or pee in the corner of the living room. And then I have a flashback to the flat above the greengrocers and John Smith, and every pore in my body opens and gushes sweat.

This spontaneous sweating has been happening a lot over the last few days. When it happened in front of Antoine I thought it was because I was hot with lust, and because I was wrapped up in a duvet. But it's been happening even when I'm not in my bedroom with a gorgeous Frenchman draped across my bed.

The first time was when Gloria rang to tell me that John Smith has been sent to a psychiatric hospital before he's up for sentencing in November. Then it happened when I thought I'd trapped myself in the toilet, but actually, I was turning the lock the wrong way. But the biggest sweats are when I'm trying to decide what to do with Herbage Dappledawn. He's been cowering at the bottom of my bag, covered in general fluff and muffin crumbs. I dumped the crumpled tutu and all the other clothes I was wearing (except the Converse: I'm not *that* mad) in the trash, but weirdly I can't bring myself to throw away the little brown rabbit; to think of its cute head mangled in the refuse cart crusher. But when I've put him in a drawer in my bedroom, he seems to taunt me from behind the wood veneer, reminding me of

Hannah's bedroom, so he's in my bag until I can decide his fate. Every time I look at him or touch him, I sweat. Perhaps I should take-up Gloria's offer of counselling after all. The problem is, I already know my answer when the counsellor asks the billion-dollar question: *Why did you do it, Channy?*

Dunno.

'Come and meet the others,' Mrs W says, opening the door to the living room. She doesn't seem to notice I'm melting like a human ice cream on her laminate strips. 'As it's a Saturday, it's not a full house.'

Two small redheaded boys, about four years old, are throwing Lego at each other, screaming between each launch of a nobbly-topped plastic missile. There are toys everywhere, and by the look of the number of stray limbs and the odd mega-boobed torso strewn on the floor, there's already been a vicious battle between Barbie and Action Man.

'These are the twins, Tyson and Spike,' Mrs W explains, cracking a previously unseen smile. 'There's a toy box in the corner should you want to play with anything.'

'That's well odd, calling your kids dogs' names,' I say, unable to suppress a nervous snigger as I start to seriously wonder if Hawk Woman has cottoned on that, HELLO! I'M FIFTEEN!

'They're my nephews,' Mrs W says, the atmosphere in the room turning sub-arctic. 'My sister's children.'

My body burns with embarrassment, though on the plus side, a high temperature might dry off the sweat.

She jerks her head towards the conservatory at the back of the house. 'Oh, and Claire Myers is through there.'

Claire is sitting on a beige and yellow cane sofa, her head bent, furiously writing in a book perched on her knee. When she sees me, she looks up for the briefest of moments, then continues scribbling, the yellow fluffy chick on the end of her pen bopping around.

'Hey!' I say, closing the door behind me. Standing sweating amongst the pot plants, I feel as if I'm in a jungle. 'You OK?'

Claire ignores me, and hunching further over her book, protecting her words with a crooked arm, carries on writing at warp speed, the chick headbanging.

'I'm sorry about what happened,' I try. 'I wanted to come and see you, but I've been a bit down and in bed, and your mum and dad are angry with me . . .'

'I'm not talking to you,' Claire mutters, cutting my pathetic excuses short. 'Go away.'

If the choice is between the conservatory with a hostile Claire, or the living room with Tyson and Spike the Barbie mutilators, I'll stay here, whether Claire wants me to or not.

'Well you are!' I trill, trying to make a joke. 'You've just talked to me by saying you're not talking to me.'

Previously shy Claire doesn't look up, but flicks a rather unexpected and graphic single finger in my direction.

'Claire! Please! Just let me explain!' I have absolutely no idea what I'm going to say that will make things better for either of us.

'Why should I believe anything that you tell me, *ever* again?' Claire slams the pink furry cover of her book shut and snaps closed a silver heart-shaped padlock, tucking the key in her bra. It must be her diary. 'You lied about *everything*, about your fake boyfriend, about where you were going, even about what you were wearing.'

I'll plead guilty to the first two charges, but, 'What I was wearing?' I think that's piling the guilt on a little *too* thickly.

'Your top.' Claire is clearly mad about my wardrobe. 'You said it was vintage and it wasn't. I saw it in Primark the other day. Racks and racks of them.'

I don't actually remember lying about my top, probably because I was too busy concocting lies about my fantasy fella. I also notice that Claire's wearing the exact same top, but in pale pink rather than grey. Squeezed into matching pink leggings, she looks like a giant condom.

'Honestly, Claire, I'm really sorry.' I sit on a chair opposite her. Her bottom lip is quivering and she keeps pushing her glasses up and down her nose, a nano-second away from blubbing. 'I was a complete idiot to do what I did.'

'I was scared!' Claire says, sniffing. 'Petrified.'

Poor kid. She had been *really* worried. Once she knew I wasn't with The Fabulous Frog, she must have imagined all sorts of terrible things being done to me.

'I know, but I was fine in the end, wasn't I?' I reach across to try and pat her knee or hand or whatever bit of her comes to me first.

'Not for you!' Claire snaps, shrinking away. 'For me! I thought I was going to die.'

'You?' I'm confused. *I* was the one holed up with a psycho blimp in a grotty flat whilst Claire was left swanning around in a bridesmaid's dress in a reasonable house with full access to all manner of salty snacks, biscuits and DVDs, and yet she thought *she* was going to die?

'After you'd gone and I been in the dress for a bit, I was bored so I ate a couple of tubes of Pringles, some chocolate Hobnobs, three cherry bakewells and a fig roll, and then I got bloated and the dress got tighter and tighter and I couldn't unzip it!' Her voice rises with hysteria as she remembers being imprisoned in pink satin. 'I had to call an ambulance.'

'You dialled 999 to get someone to rescue you from a *dress*?' In all the post-kidnapping aftermath, no one had mentioned possible death-by-dress.

'I couldn't breathe!' Claire shrieks. 'I didn't know what else to do! It was cutting off the circulation to my arms!'

'You could have gone out into the street, or asked a neighbour,' I say.

'There were boys outside, on bikes,' Claire growls. 'They would have laughed at me, teased me at school or in the street. Called me names like FatBooth Bridesmaid.'

'Oh, Claire!' I say. 'They wouldn't.'

But of course, that's exactly what mean kids would do.

'And then the ambulance people found me on my own and called the police, so I told them all about you and fake Antoine. And then when you didn't come back, it all kicked off.'

In an ideal world I'd like to point out to Claire that Antoine isn't fake, he's very much alive, well and gorgeous, but perhaps now isn't the time to try and justify what I did.

'No wonder you were freaked,' I say. 'It must have been terrible, the police talking to you.'

Claire stares at her diary, drumming her stubby bitten nails on the pink sparkly fur. 'It was a bit exciting actually,' she says, a brighter note in her voice. 'I was on the news on *BBC Breakfast*, just in the background.'

A woman with the same hawk-like expression as Mrs W comes into the living room. The red-haired boys throw themselves as her, and then start throwing Lego at each other.

'That's Mrs Wallen's sister,' Claire explains. 'She minds us if Mrs Wallen has to go to the shops.'

Claire stops watching the family reunion and turns to me.

'I was worried about you too,' she whispers. 'I thought you might be dead.'

'At one point I thought I might be,' I say. 'It was such a stupid thing to do.'

And then I start sweating, and in a new and shocking development, my body begins shaking so violently, despite regular dental check-ups and as much flossing as

I can be bothered to do when I'm tired or in a rush, my teeth feel as if they might fall out of my gums. This shake-and-sweat combo is horrific, much worse than the wobbly-legged sweaty feeling you sometimes get when you stagger off a swoopy loopy fairground ride feeling sick.

'Channy!' Claire gets up and rushes over to me. 'What's wrong? Are you ill? Shall I get Mrs Wallen?'

'I'll – b – b – be fine,' I stutter, wrapping my arms around my body as if somehow this will keep the shakes from getting entirely out of control and prevent my limbs from flying off in all directions around the conservatory. 'It – will – b – b – be over in a m – m – moment.'

Claire crouches at my knees, holding them, until eventually the shaking subsides to more of a gentle twitch.

'Is it delayed shock?' she asks. 'When I saw a dog run over after school, I went home and didn't start shaking until I got into bed. It was like I'd swallowed a mobile phone on vibrate.'

'Probably,' I say, smiling at Claire and her moby analogy. She's a good kid, really. I wish people weren't so mean to her. I wish I hadn't gone off and left her pigging out on Pringles. We'd have had so much more fun going to the beach, roaming around town, disagreeing over whether black is cooler than pink.

'You should talk to someone,' Claire says, letting go of my knees. She tries to sit cross-legged on the floor in front of me, but her thighs are too large, so after a bit of bum shuffling, she just sits back on her haunches. 'You could talk to a doctor or some phone helpline. There must be one for kids who've been kidnapped.'

'They want me to have counselling,' I admit. 'To talk to a professional.'

'So?' Claire asks. 'Why don't you?'

'I can't,' I say. 'I don't want to re-live it. I just want to forget it.'

'You could try talking to me,' Claire suggests. 'You could stop whenever you wanted, whenever it got too much.'

I shake my head. 'You wouldn't understand,' I say condescendingly. 'No one would.'

'Try me,' Claire says, pushing her glasses up her nose. 'Tell me why you ran off with that weirdo.'

I'm about to give her the same shrug-and-dunno combo I've given all the others, even myself. Then I hear the sound of the twins playing with each other and gaze at Mrs W and her sister standing talking, a mug cupped in their hands as they watch the boys. Mrs Wallen looks older than her sis, but other than a few wrinkles and different hair, not only do they look alike with the same hawk-hooked nose, they stand in the same way: right hip jutting out, left shoulder dropped.

I pull my knees up to my chin and hug my legs, gazing at the two women as they nod and natter. *That will be like Taryn and her sisters in years to come*, I think to myself; women bound together by decades of shared history, not all of it rainbows and puppies, some of it dark and bleak, but stuff they'll have gone through together, always there for one another. There might be rows and disagreements, times they hate each other, but they can't deny their DNA, their place in the family tree. I'll never have that sense of belonging, not just because of Dad and the Unknown Sperm Daddy, but because there's only me. When Mum and Dad have gone to the big Abba gig in the sky, there'll be no one to reminisce with, to laugh over our parents looking like crazy drag queens in their stage get-up, or to share a shudder over the time I went missing with a lonely fat weirdo.

A huge tidal wave of emotion rips through my body.

'He told me about Hannah!' I blurt out. 'If he hadn't mentioned Hannah I'd never have gone with him.'

'Hannah?' Claire queries. 'Who's Hannah?'

Tears start to fall. As fast as I try to wipe them away, twice as many spring from my eyes. I give up and let them bounce off my cheeks and drip down my nose and chin; hot stinging fat tears.

'His daughter. I thought she was my sister, well, half-sister. I've always wanted a sister. I used to pretend to have a sister, Donna, but then she disappeared. Everyone I know has a brother or sister, is part of a little gang of DNA: Taryn; the hateful Helium Twins; Mum; Sophie and Rosie on *Corrie*; Roxy and Ronnie on *EastEnders*. It was never just about finding my bio dad; it was about finding a family, about big lunches and holidays, about not sitting on my own with a takeaway or something heated up in the microwave whilst Mum and Dad pranced about in silk and sequins. I did it because I was lonely. I did it because I wanted to fit in with a family! I wanted to belong somewhere!'

Mrs Wallen and her sister are staring at me, but they don't come in to see why I'm hysterical in the conservatory.

I angrily draw my fist across my nose, wiping snot from one body part to another. 'You wouldn't understand. No one would. Not some poxy counsellor who'd listen to me and be all patronizing about making the most of what I've got and then go back to her neat little family. Mum has a sister, Dad has a brother . . .'

'I have no one,' Claire butts in. 'You're not the only

one who feels lonely, Channy.'

I look down at Claire through damp eyes.

'I don't have any brothers or sisters. I've hardly any friends. I'm left on my own whilst Mum and Dad are out with the group.' Claire flicks her head at the kids in the other room. 'They don't count. I'm always the oldest one here by yonks, left to do my own thing.' She bites her lip and looks away from me, fidgeting with her fingers. 'I used to daydream that you and I were sisters, cos your mum and my dad went out for a bit.'

Given that the parental dating merry-go-round happened before everyone got married, I'm not sure that the genetics actually work out, but I giggle through my tears. 'Crab thought your dad was my dad too! Did you know that my dad and your mum also went out together?'

'No!' Claire gasps. 'Like, no offence to your dad, but I can't imagine them doing it.' She grimaces and shakes her head.

'Claire!' I take a cushion from behind me and throw it at her. 'Don't be gross! It was just a date! *Dirty Dancing* or something.'

'That's what they told you,' she mocks, flinging the cushion back at me.

'So,' I say, clutching it to my chest. 'Who do you talk to when you're feeling minging?'

Claire scoots backwards on her butt across the tiled floor, gets her diary off the sofa, then shuffles forward again. 'I write it all down in here,' she says, stroking the pink fur. 'Everything. And then when I've written it down, sometimes it feels better.'

'And when it doesn't?' I ask. 'What then?'

'I eat.'

'You could talk to me, instead,' I say. 'We've got pretty similar lives. We're almost sisters.'

'Instead of sisters or half-sisters or stepsisters, we could invent a whole new category: Sort of Sisters,' Claire giggles. 'Like SOS!'

'Don't you start quoting Abba songs at me!' I give a mock growl, using the cushion as a missile again. 'It's the ruddy Swedes that got us into this mess in the first place.'

'Everyone behave themselves?' Mum asks as she stands in the hall at just gone seven o'clock.

I think she's expecting Mrs Wallen to say that I've gone berserk with the toy box, or pinched the thighs of strange children.

'Chantelle and Claire spent all day gossiping in the back, didn't you?' Mrs W says. 'They were no bother. Claire left about twenty minutes ago. Gave them all chicken nuggets and chips for tea. Oh, and pizza for lunch.'

'I'll give you a call about future dates,' Mum says as we're ushered out.

'Hang on,' I say, pausing in the porch. 'I've left something behind.'

I dart back into the living room, rummage in my bag and pick out Herbage Dappledawn. Looking at him lying in my palm, face up, ears pricked, I wait for my pores to open, for the stress sweats to start, but my armpits remain Dove-deodorant dry. Herbage looks how I remembered him before I met John Smith: cute, friendly, innocent. I'm glad that I didn't throw him out; I now know where he belongs.

'*Au revoir* Herbage,' I whisper, tossing him in the toy box in the corner to take his chances with Barbie and Action Man. 'Take care.'

Mum and Mrs Wallen are at the living room door, a strange look on their faces.

'Channy?' Mum queries. 'You OK?'

'I'm done,' I smile at Mum, linking her arm. 'Let's go home.'

288

Chapter Twenty-Seven

'Do it again, Crab! But higher this time! And faster!'

'Stop encouraging him, Claire,' I say, as Crab prepares to attempt another daring skateboard move which will either end in Claire Myers looking even more adoringly at him, or us all sitting in the local A&E whilst the medics patch Crab up.

'But he's sooo good,' Claire gushes, watching the group of boys at the bandstand do their skateboard tricks.

It's the same old skate-rat crowd as last summer: Snorbs, Tubs, Bucket and the others. Even the girls are the same, except instead of me looking on adoringly, it's Claire giving Crab the cow eyes and I'm in the Taryn role, only there as support for Claire, constantly pointing out that we'd have more fun watching buff boys tombstoning from the pier.

After ten days or so of being all stern about keeping me in, Mum and Dad and Sue and Bob agreed Claire and I could hang out together, so she's bumped into Crab at my usual haunts: the chippy; the clock tower; the end of the pier, and now it's *Crab this* and *Crab that* and *Do it again, Crab!* and Crab being a lad is enjoying the attention, even if it's from a twelve-year-old in white shorts and a pink Justin Beiber T-shirt.

My phone rings. I look at the screen and my stomach leaps with joy. I've been waiting for this call all summer. No, it's not Antoine; moby calls to and from France are mega expensive so we have to rely on emailing and messaging, which we've been doing A LOT ; -)

'Taryn!' I screech. 'Where are you?'

'Channy! I'm outside yours!' she squeals. 'I thought I'd go round and surprise you, but you're out. Where are you?'

'At the bandstand.'

'Who with?'

'Claire Myers, you know Sue and Bob's daughter?'

'The piglet in the training bra?'

'Don't say that!' I turn my back on Claire and lower my voice. 'She's OK. I've been hanging out with her since I got kidnapped.'

'Yeah, right. What's that noise in the background?'

290

'Crab's just fallen off his skateboard. Snorbs is laughing at him.'

'You're at the bandstand with Crab and Claire and Snorbs?' I can hear the disbelief in Taryn's voice. 'Chan, what the hell has been going on whilst I've been away?'

I giggle. 'You don't know the half of it, you really don't. I wasn't joking about the kidnapping thing. A psycho really did kidnap me. It was on the news and everything! Get your butt down here ASAP and I'll tell you about it.'

'That was Taryn,' I say, closing my phone, grinning at the sound of my bezzie's voice back on Kent soil. 'She's just got back from Patagonia. She's on her way down now.'

I might be thrilled that Taryn's back, but Claire's face clouds over at the news. I can tell she's wondering if now my bezzie's home, she'll be dumped.

Someone else doesn't look thrilled that Taryn's back.

'Is she still mad at me?' Crab asks, nervously fiddling with the hem of his black and orange Tony Hawk T-shirt. 'She was pretty pissed off with me before she went.'

'Why would she be mad at you?' Claire asks, wide-eyed. She's still in that loved-up stage of thinking that Crab is an angel on earth, incapable of doing anything wrong.

'He went out with Taryn and it ended pretty badly,' I explain.

'I'm sworn off women until after my GCSEs, unless they're *seriously* cute.' He flashes a smile at Claire who flushes crimson, and in a fluster, goes to watch Tubs and Bucket perfecting synchronised kickflicks.

'Crab, don't encourage her, she's only twelve,' I say, watching her pretending to watch the others whilst giving furtive sidelong glances in Crab's direction. 'You're sixteen in March.'

'Can I help it if chicks find me irresistible?' he smirks, balancing on his skateboard on one foot. 'Except you, of course.'

'Crab, I'm serious!' I push the edge of his skateboard with my foot and he rolls slowly away. 'She's obviously got the serious tweenage hots for you. I don't want her messed with.'

'OK, I'll tell her to back off,' he says, scooting back. 'That she's just a silly kid.'

'No!' I cry. 'Don't do that. Don't crush her.'

'But you said . . .'

'I just meant be friendly but not too friendly. Nice but not too nice.'

'My dad's right,' Crab mutters, flicking the end of his

skateboard with his foot and catching it with his hand. 'Women are aliens.'

It's about twenty minutes since Taryn's call, and we're still at the bandstand. Claire has gone to the loo to reapply more make-up, even though I've told her that at twelve, less is definitely more if she doesn't want to look like some weird child-tart mutant, when Taryn rings again.

'I'm walking along the seafront,' she hisses into her phone. 'I want you to see if you can spot me.'

'Why?' I ask.

'For Christ's sake, just do it!' she orders.

'Hang on.'

I move away from the bandstand and walk a few paces around the corner. As it's a sunny Bank Holiday Monday at the end of August, the promenade is packed with day-trippers, so it's difficult to pick anyone out of the milling crowd. There's just lots of lobster red shoulders and strappy tops, men in T-shirts, dripping ice creams and some weirdo wearing a black hat and a brightly coloured blanket, even though it's seventy-five degrees *at least*. The weirdo is scurrying along, looking furtively over his shoulder as if he's being hunted.

And then I realize the weirdo is Taryn.

'I can see you,' I say. 'What's wrong? And what's with the blanket get-up?'

'I'm channelling my inner South American woman. Someone is following me,' she whispers. 'There was this bloke hanging around the end of your road, then when I left, he left. He was lurking by the cash point whilst I got twenty quid out. Do you think it's the psycho who kidnapped you?'

I start walking towards her. 'He didn't just grab me off the street,' I assure her. 'Well, not in the way you're thinking.'

And then we're face to face. She throws her arms around me, engulfing me in scratchy blanket, her hat tipping off and rolling along the pavement.

'Seriously, Chan, some bloke was following me,' she says as she retrieves her hat from under tourists' feet and we head back to the bandstand. 'Some middle-aged perve who has a thing about girls.' I don't like to point out that wrapped in a blanket, Taryn doesn't look like the sort of girl a perve would follow.

'You OK?' Crab asks Taryn as he sees us approach.

'Taryn thinks she was followed from Lea Crescent,' I explain. 'By a nutter.'

'I *know* I was followed,' she snaps. 'I'm not making it up.'

'You don't think it was your guy?' Crab asks. 'Psycho Smith?'

Taryn flashes me a quizzical look.

'I'll explain in a mo,' I say, 'but it's not him. He's in a secure psycho unit.' I'm banking on Gloria telling me if he'd absconded.

Claire appears from behind the hedge where the loos are hidden. She's completely ignored my make-up advice and has gone for the more is more effect.

'Humph.' She nods at Taryn, her over-made up eyes flashing with jealously behind her glasses.

'Taryn's been followed by a strange man,' I say. 'She's a bit freaked.'

Snorbs, Bucket and Tubs, as well as a few other skate rats now surround us as Taryn recounts her tale of being stalked.

'There's a man hiding in the bushes by the loos,' Claire shrugs. 'I saw him climb in the hedge. His bum was still sticking out when I left.'

Quick as a flash, the lads dart from the bandstand and swarm round the hedge, followed by me, Taryn and Claire. We arrive just in time to see Crab and Snorbs dragging the man out before throwing him on the ground face down, as Tubs (so named because he is) sits on him. The perve squeaks and starts bucking his body,

295

so Crab piles on top of Tubs and Bucket flings himself on Crab, and I can't help but think that the man at the bottom of the pile will now be squashed flat like a hedgehog under a car's tyre.

Someone must have seen the fracas and alerted the police, as two cops are running over the grass towards us.

'What's going on?' one of them asks.

'I was being followed,' Taryn says.

'And this man was in the bushes,' Claire explains, pink with excitement. 'Crab pulled him out.' She smiles adoringly at Crab who doesn't notice because he's deep within in a human sandwich.

The policemen tell the teenage vigilantes to get off their victim, who they help to his feet. By now there's a major crowd watching the action.

'*That's* the man who was following me!' Taryn says accusingly.

'I wasn't following you,' the man gasps, trying to get his breath back, brushing grass from his clothes. 'I was following . . .' he bites his lip. 'Her.'

He looks at me. 'I'm so sorry,' he says. 'I didn't mean it to be like this.'

'Is this the psycho perve?' Crab growls. 'The one who locked you up?'

I can hear a murmur of: 'That's that girl! The one that was kidnapped!' ripple round the crowd.

'No!' the man cries. 'It's nothing like that. I'm no pervert.'

'I think you'd better accompany us to the station, Sir,' one of the policemen says, holding on to the man by his arm. 'Explain to us who you are and what you're doing stalking young girls at the beach.'

The man doesn't need to explain who he is or what he's doing here to me. From the moment the cops dragged him to his feet and I saw his face, I knew who he was.

'My name's Pete Jefferson. I think Chantelle Allen could be my daughter.'

Chapter Twenty-Eight

'Well, here we are again,' Mum says bitterly, as we sit around a fake wood table stained with coffee rings in the local police station. Dad was mowing the lawn and Mum was pruning roses when I rang them in a panic, so they came straight here in their grubby gardening clothes, a million miles from Abba-esque sequins and silk.

'It's not my fault!' I point out. '*I* didn't go looking for him. *He* found me!'

Mum purses her mouth and pulls her neck in. She looks like she has two chins and no lips, surprisingly pugish.

'I expect it's another nutter,' Dad says, patting my hand sympathetically. 'I always thought a few weirdos would crawl out of the woodwork because of the publicity. It's just something we'll have to put up with until the fuss dies down.'

'He's not a nutter,' I croak, my throat and chest tight with anxiety. 'I know he isn't.'

Mum snorts with contempt. 'Well you thought the last one was the real deal and look how *that* turned out!' Her voice is thick with sarcasm. 'And you still maintained he wasn't a nutter, even when he got sent to a top nutter hospital for major nutters who've done nutty things. So I think we can safely say your nutter judgement isn't to be trusted, *Chantelle*.'

Chantelle. Not Channy. She's angry with me that her past has caught up with her on the seafront. I don't blame her. Suppose fifteen years from now I'm happily married with a family and Crab pops back into my life? That would be well embarrassing, although of course, unlike Mum, I haven't slept with Crab, had a baby with him, and even if I had (gross!), at least I know his name, where he lives, even stuff about his nan. This is just the drug dealer with the Mercedes. No wonder she's in a state.

But this time I know the man in the bushes at the bandstand is who he says he thinks he is. I expect Mum and Dad will demand a DNA test or something, but I don't need a bit of paper to tell me that he's the real deal. Everything about him screams The Sperm Daddy; he looks as if he's walked in to a wall: flat-faced and pug-nosed.

The door opens. A policeman ruddy-faced from broken veins comes in.

'Now, you're aware of what this man is alleging, aren't you?' he asks.

The three of us nod.

'So, it's entirely up to you whether you want to speak to him, but as we can't charge Mr Jefferson, we'll have to release him.'

'Are you telling me there's no law to say that it's illegal to stalk young girls?' Mum snaps. 'That you'll just turf him out to harass my daughter again?' She narrows her eyes. 'You do realize this is Chantelle Allen, the girl who was kidnapped by a nutter, don't you? A girl who attracts nutters like iron filings to a magnet?'

Thanks, Mum! I think to myself. I have visions of walking along the street and random nutters just slamming into me and clinging to my body.

'Mr Jefferson has assured us that if you don't want to see him, if it will upset you, he'll leave you alone,' the copper says.

'You're aware that this man is a drug dealer, aren't you?' Mum hisses venomously. 'Let him go and he'll be pushing cocaine and heroin and speedy things on vulnerable young kids. Is that what you want?'

'That's not the information we have, Mrs Allen,' the

policeman says crisply. 'So, do you want to see him or not?' He's getting impatient.

'We don't.' Mum gets up and slings her bag across her shoulder. 'Let's go.'

'Sandy?' Dad stays seated. 'This is Channy's decision, not ours. We made a decision on her behalf long ago. Now it's her turn to decide what she wants to do.'

Mum's wide-eyed, still and trembling, like a rabbit that's seen a dog.

'Do you want to meet this man?' Dad asks me. 'Even though you know you might get hurt again?'

I examine my fingernails in forensic detail, giving myself time to think, avoiding Dad's concerned gaze and Mum's terrified glare.

When I left the flat on Blackstock Road, I had absolutely no intention of tracking down The Sperm Daddy: I was totally done with being a DNA detective. But that was before I'd clapped eyes on Pete Jefferson, and now I've seen him, I don't want my only memory of my biological father to be a struggle on the seafront with Crab, Bucket and Tubs bouncing on his back.

I look up from my nails. 'I'm sorry, Dad,' I say. 'I'm really sorry. You'll always be my real dad, nothing will ever change that, but I do want to meet him.'

Opposite us, Pete Jefferson sits on the edge of his chair, fidgeting, nervously wringing his hands. He's small, barrel-bodied, thick-necked, neatly dressed in beige chinos and a pink polo shirt with a Ralph Lauren logo, his short dark hair greying at the temples. To be honest he looks well boring; I expected him to be swathed in bling, have a gold tooth and four mobiles constantly ringing. He's more like an accountant than a drug dealer.

'I feel as if I'm at a job interview,' he says, his voice quivering as he gives a nervy laugh. 'Or on a first date.'

There's an uncomfortable silence accompanied by Pete Jefferson pulling weird facial expressions, which I hope are because he's nervous, not because he's got Tourettes or anything.

'Can I just say that I'm sorry?' He looks full of remorse. 'I was just curious. I never meant to cause any upset. You weren't supposed to see me.' He gives a wry smile. 'I wouldn't make a very good undercover detective, would I?' There's more nervous laughing and shuffling on his chair. 'Sorry. I've ruined your Bank Holiday Monday, haven't I?'

Dad puffs his chest out and looks grave. 'Can I ask why you think you might be related to *my* daughter?' he asks.

Very proprietorial: my daughter.

'Well,' Pete says, gurning again, 'I didn't know of course, I mean, I never thought, I never even considered, but then I saw you on the telly, and then I knew, that at least it was a possibility.'

'I don't look anything like I did in that wedding photo,' I say. 'I had ringlets and a tiara.' I tug my hair and look down at my denim mini skirt, not new, but cut down from something I found in Oxfam for two pounds. I don't regret trashing the tutu, but I do miss it. 'I looked minging.'

'No, not you, Chantelle,' Pete points out. 'I meant your mother.' He looks across at Mum who's now got three chins her neck is wound in so far. 'It was her I recognized.'

'Me?' Mum sneers. I notice she's avoiding Pete's eyes, as if she can't believe she ever slept with this man. Actually, looking at Mum and looking at him, I can't believe it either.

'I was watching *Sky News* and I saw the appeal come up. I thought I recognized you, but I couldn't be certain, and then you said: 'If I could turn back time', and I knew for sure you were Cher from the car park, the woman who snapped the emblem off the bonnet of my dad's Mercedes. He went mental; I'd borrowed it without telling him.'

Wow! It has to be him. Who else would know about Cher from the car park except him and, well, Cher.

'But I looked terrible on TV!' Mum says indignantly. 'I hadn't slept for days. I was wrecked!'

'You looked like that when I met you fifteen years ago,' Pete points out ungallantly. 'Well, you did after several rum and cokes, which is what you were drinking when I met you after your act. I was driving so I was just on coke.'

I'm not sure if he's referring to the drink or the drug.

'You were brilliant as Cher, by the way. Really convincing.'

Dad turns to Mum. 'Do you recognize this man?' he asks her.

She stays silent, but Pete states the obvious, which is, 'I don't think you were in a fit state to remember anything about that night.'

'I remember that you said you were a drug dealer,' Mum hisses across the table. 'I remember that much.'

'A drug dealer?' Pete Jefferson's face is a picture. And then he dissolves into peals of laughter. 'I'm a pharmacist!' he says, wiping tears from his eyes. 'I was doing some locum work at Boots in Margate. I work in London now, in Battersea. I must have just said it to be funny.' He sees our faces. 'Which obviously, it wasn't.'

For fifteen years Mum's been under the impression my biological father is a man who sold heroin rather than Nurofen. I don't know whether to laugh or cry.

'And when I thought about the dates, it seemed to fit, though of course I realize that Chantelle might have a number of potential fathers.'

'I beg your pardon?' Mum snarls. 'What are you implying?'

He's implying that my mother is a car-park slag, that he was just one of her many rum and coke fuelled Cher conquests.

'I mean, I assumed that I wasn't the only one you, er, you know.'

'You *were* the only one!' Mum shrieks. 'I don't just go around bending backwards over car bonnets with strangers! It was a one-off. You are *definitely* Channy's father!'

Good heavens! One minute Mum is determined that this man isn't my father, now she's determined that he *is*.

'I think it seems likely that you *are* involved,' Dad says. He's been sitting back, quietly observing everything. It must be so hard for him to watch this man spring into my life. 'The question is, what is it you want from us now?'

'I didn't come here looking for Chantelle because I

wanted a daughter,' Pete says earnestly. 'I came because I was curious.' He looks across the table at me. 'I'm sure you are too. Is there anything you want to know about me?'

'Do you have both your kidneys?' I ask. 'And a fully functioning liver?'

Mum kicks me sideways under the table and Dad groans.

'Do you already have children?' I brace myself to hear that Pete doesn't want a new daughter because he's got several already.

'Er, no,' Pete replies. 'And yes, I have both my kidneys, two lungs, one heart and so on.' Not surprisingly he looks a bit puzzled at having to recite a shopping list of organs.

'Are you married?'

'No, but I will be on the last Saturday in July next year.' He smiles at the thought. 'We're planning the wedding now.'

'And have you told your fiancée about this?' Mum asks crisply. 'About Chantelle?'

We're both obviously thinking the same thing: we'd be less than thrilled to find out our future husband has the sort of past Pete Jefferson has: a teenage daughter popping up, the result of a drunken one night stand on a car bonnet with a pub singer.

'Carlos is fine about it. He wanted to come with me today, but he had to work.'

'Carlos?' the three of us query in unison.

'My fiancé,' Pete explains. 'He's a make-up artist for Giorgio Armani in Harvey Nichols. Well, they call them International Face designers, but it amounts to the same thing.'

'You're gay?' I gasp. In all the fantasizing about my father, the wondering whether it was Barry Bristow or Sir Algernon, the hoping that he would be a writer but finding out he was a drug dealer, the dreams of having a string of brothers and sisters to go on holiday with, never once did it occur to me that my biological father might be like Aunty Julie and bat for the other team.

'Is that a problem?' Pete sounds prickly.

'No, it's just . . . unexpected,' I say, 'given that . . .' I nod towards Mum.

Pete looks sheepish. 'It was the night in the car park that made my mind up,' he explains. 'After Cher, I knew for sure I was gay.'

'I turned you gay?' Mum squeaks.

'No!' Pete says quickly. He hangs his head and starts wringing his hands. Under the bright lights I notice there's sweat glistening on his bald patch. 'Look, this doesn't reflect any better on me than it does on you. I came to see your Cher act at a time when I was confused, when I was trying to be someone I wasn't. I slept with you to prove to myself that I could be with a woman when deep down I knew that wasn't for me. Being with you made me realize I had to be true to my own biological make-up. I'm sorry you got caught in the crossfire of my confusion.'

For the first time this afternoon, Mum smiles. She slides a hand across the table towards Pete who's looking anxious, tearful even. 'And you got caught up in how I was feeling about my marriage at the time; I was angry and drunk, I led you on, used you just as much as you used me. We were both young, foolish and didn't know what we wanted.'

'I did afterwards,' Pete says.

'Me too,' Mum says, kissing Dad on the cheek and taking his hand.

'What about me?' I ask.

Chapter Twenty-Nine

A dark-haired woman stands in front of me, swaying slightly, champagne fizzing in the tall glass flute she's clutching.

'So let me get this straight,' she slurs. 'It's your dad who has just married my second cousin Carlos?'

'No,' I say, watching as, dressed in matching sharp black suits, silver grey waistcoats and pink rose buttonholes, Pete and Carlos work the room. There's lots of laughter and hugging, backs are slapped and hands are shaken, everyone delighted for the happy couple. Carlos is a good-looking Brazilian: small and stocky like Pete, but younger and more outgoing with a wide white smile, a giggly laugh and a stubbly beard. They met four years ago when Carlos asked the pharmacist's advice about athlete's foot, and they bonded over the fungicide cream Pete recommended.

'So you're not Pete's daughter?'

'Pete's my father.' I step back to avoid champagne stains on my bridesmaid's dress. It's strapless, just above the knee, with waterfall layers of gunmetal-grey silk chiffon, as close to being a tutu as you can get without actually being a tutu; it looks fabulous with the silver glittery trainers I'm wearing, a present from Mum and Dad.

This is the second time I've worn the dress; it's already had an outing to our school prom at the end of June, but this time I've made a pink sash to coordinate with the other bridesmaid's dress. Oh, and my make-up is *fabulous*, one of the perks of having a stepfather who's an international face designer at Harvey Nicks.

I went to the prom with Crab, not because we're going out, but because with Antoine in France I hadn't a date, he didn't want a date, and we're still good friends. He looked pretty cool in a tux: those acne antibiotics are powerful stuff. Taryn took Snorbs, Simon Norbert; they've been seeing each other since Christmas. She made her own dress: long, red, strapless, split to the thigh. She abandoned her South American look in January and is now channelling her inner Jessica Rabbit. No wonder Snorbs looked as if he might burst with lust.

It was a great night. Several of us went in a stretch

hummer, Bjorn At The Beach went down a storm, and no one teased me about my father wearing bollock-revealing tight white trousers, in fact, everyone thought it was much cooler to have parents who are rock stars rather than your standard accountant/teacher/banker type.

'That's what I said,' the woman presses. 'Pete's your dad.'

'No, he's not, he's my father. *Trevor's* my dad.'

The DNA test we took last October confirmed that the likelihood of Pete being my biological father is 99.999%, which I think we can take as proof that he is. But just as Dad told me ages ago, a father isn't necessarily a dad. I've already got a brilliant dad, and as far as I can tell, Pete's never wanted to be one, which suits us all just fine. I can't imagine him ever having kids in his life, children who might mess up his and Carlos' perfect flat in Fulham, or wreck their plans for weekends away at boutique hotels in Cornwall. It's still early days and we're not amazingly close, but now I've found him I don't want to lose him; he's a very nice man who devours books faster than I do and didn't get stressed when I suggested wearing Converse trainers with my bridesmaid's dress. And whilst I tried to appear aloofly cool when Pete asked me to be a bridesmaid, underneath my glacial exterior, I was thrilled.

The woman's eyes boggle. 'So who's Trevor?' she asks.

'Him!' I yell above the cheers, as Bjorn At The Beach take to the stage. 'Benny!'

Bjorn At The Beach playing at Pete and Carlos's stylish London wedding was Mum and Dad's wedding present to the happy couple. It wasn't quite what I envisaged during my dreams of everyone getting on together, and looking at some of Pete and Carlos' friends prancing around to *Dancing Queen* it occurs to me that this wasn't the sort of camping I had in mind either, but in its own way, this strange mix of people works.

But some things never change: I don't feel as bone-crushingly lonely as I once did, but I'll never be fan of big parties and I'll never ever dance to Abba in public.

I slip out of the reception and stand on the terrace of the swish hotel, leaning on the railing that runs its length. In front of me, the river Thames flows past, sightseeing cruises bobbing by, tourists staring at the huge wheel of the London Eye next to me, cameras poised, capturing the dramatic London skyline. It feels magical, as if I'm part of a film set.

Across the river, to my right, Big Ben strikes six.

From behind me comes the sound of a door sliding open and closed. Even with the door closed, I can still hear Bjorn at the Beach playing *Voulez-Vous*.

'There you are!' Claire Myers gasps, rustling towards me, clickity-clicking her heels on the stone terrace. 'I was worried where you'd got to. You OK?'

'I'm fine,' I assure her. 'You know parties aren't my thing.'

I turn to roll my eyes at her. She was beyond excited when Carlos (who she adores) asked her to be a bridesmaid, but not so thrilled when I told her she'd have to wear grey to match the colour I'd chosen. So after a few heated arguments, Taryn cut down the pink dress I wore at Aunty Julie's wedding, ripped out the layers of white petticoats and added a grey sash. I've got a pink sash made from the remnants.

'You look great by the way,' I tell Claire. She does. She's lost some weight, even without the silver sandals is much taller, and Carlos has shown her how to make-up her eyes for special occasions so that they look big and smoky behind her glasses. She's turning into a very pretty and bright thirteen-year-old.

'What time shall I pick the girls up tomorrow?' she asks.

'About ten,' I say. 'I cleaned the cage yesterday.'

Concerned they'd get left with looking after a mammal when I left home for uni, Mum and Dad agreed that I could have a pet if Claire and I took shared ownership of it. Claire refused to look after a black rat called Kurt, and I felt I couldn't bond with a cream hamster called Beiber, so thinking one might feel lonely we've ended up with two brown gerbils, Sugar and Spice. Sometimes they fight viciously, practically killing each other over a sunflower seed, but within seconds, they're snuggled up together again. Tomorrow is Claire's turn to have the girls for a week.

'You sure you're OK?' Claire asks, nudging me.

'Sort of,' I say, looking out across the river. Somewhere in this sprawling city is the flat above the greengrocers. 'Do you know it was a year ago yesterday that John Smith kidnapped me? It feels like a lifetime ago.'

'Do you ever think about him?' Claire asks, leaning on the railing next to me, propped up by her elbows. 'About how he's getting on?'

'Every day,' I admit.

Last November John Smith was sentenced to ten years in prison. Gloria came to the house to tell me. I hope he's getting help inside, not just so he doesn't do it again, but so that he's not as lonely and confused when he comes out as when he went in, otherwise, what was the point of any of it? And I still hope he and Hannah find each other, not now, but when Hannah is grown up and able to cope with what her father did in his attempt to find her. Gloria said he's written me a letter to say he's sorry. I haven't read it. I don't need to. I already know how sorry he is.

'I bet you wish you could turn back time,' Claire says. 'You must regret what happened?'

I look down at the water rushing past, the strong currents of the Thames pulling bits of wood and bottles and rubbish along with it. This time last year I was holed up with John Smith and his Sylvanian Families, terrified, there because I was lonely, vulnerable, searching not just for my biological father, but for some sense of belonging, of fitting into the jigsaw of life. Since that day I've found Pete Jefferson; got to know him and giggly Carlos; discovered friends like Crab and Taryn are a better bet than Facebook fakes like Stacie and Tracie; turned sixteen; done ten GCSEs; become closer to Mum and Dad because the guilty secret is no longer hanging over our family like the sword of Damocles; decided I'm going to do psychology at university to learn more about how people tick; acquired two gerbils and a pair of silver sneakers. But best of all I've discovered that I have a sort of sister, someone whose life has been running parallel to mine all along. It just took what happened to make me realize.

'No, Claire,' I say. '*Je ne regrette rien.*'

'You want to dance?'

Claire and I swivel round to see Crab standing behind us. He's wearing the tux he wore to the school prom and he's supposed to be here to help with the band, but in true Crab style, he's been snaffling food from the buffet, this time quails eggs and peppered beef rather than sausage rolls and crisps.

'I don't dance!' I say to Crab. 'Remember?'

'I meant Claire, not you!' he laughs before grabbing Claire's hand. The two of them head off as *I Have a Dream* starts playing. Inside, everyone will either be slow dancing or swaying to the music.

So here I am, at a wedding, on my own. *Again.* Any moment now some well-meaning rellie will come out and try and persuade me to come inside and join in the fun, as if jigging about with a group of people three times my age and whom I hardly know counts as fun.

I finger the leather bracelet on my right wrist Antoine sent me at Easter to wish me good luck for my exams, the bracelet he bought at Kestival a year ago. It's darker now, slightly softer and greasy from wear.

To be honest, I don't know where I am with him. We've been Skyping and stuff loads, but he's never mentioned coming back to England and I can't exactly invite myself to France. I feel sort of in lurve-limbo. There's no one in Broadgate I remotely fancy compared to him, but for all I know, he could be snogging French minxes *droit*, *gauche* et *au centre* all summer. How depressing!

The music gets louder as the door behind me opens.

Here we go. One of the persuasion posse.

'I am not dancing!' I say over my shoulder.

'Not even with me?'

I spin round and there, standing on the terrace in the fading evening sun, is Antoine. He's taller than last summer, but even more gorgeous in the flesh than I remembered, with his springy dark curls and olive skin against a crisp white shirt. Behind him I can see Claire and Crab peering out of the window, giggling.

'Did you know about this?' I mouth to Claire who nods.

'Forget them,' Antoine says, pulling me towards him. He doesn't smell of aftershave or soap, he smells of musky sexy foreign fella. 'How about that dance?'

'I don't dance!' I protest as he wraps his arms around me. 'Not in public!'

'Then out here,' Antoine says. 'Privately.'

'I'd be useless!' I protest. 'Honestly!'

Antoine kisses me gently on the lips. 'Then let me teach you how,' he whispers into my ear.

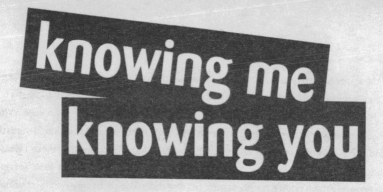

knowing me knowing you

Helen Bailey

Knowing Me, Knowing You raises important questions about identity and contains a positive message about the role of adoptive parents ... If you had been Channy, would you have wanted to track down your biological father?

I have thought a great deal about this since writing the book and I'm still undecided as to what I would do. I'd like to think that if I had lovely adoptive parents I wouldn't look for my bio-dad, but curiosity is a powerful emotion. Remember the saying: curiosity killed the cat? Channy's curiosity about her background could easily have ended in tragedy.

Channy's predicament sends out a warning shot on the dangers of over – sharing on facebook. Is her experience based on a real-life experience you know of?

The Facebook element of the story developed after looking at my goddaughter's Facebook page. Someone had posted a group photo, so, as an experiment, I picked a random name tagged in the photo and followed the links. I was horrified at how much information I could get about the girl I chose, a complete stranger to me. I saw photos of her at school, larking about on her bed with friends in scanty underwear, and at a family wedding (hence the wedding scene in the book). Girls, please make your Facebook security settings as tight as possible! I am just an author doing research. Next time, whoever looks at your information may not have such an innocent motive. You have been warned!

It's such a funny book, but with a fundamentally powerful message. Do you think humour is a good device when writing about issues?

I think humour can help to make all types of difficult subjects easier to handle. When I worked in marketing I used to have to write press releases that included statistics and quite boring corporate information. I became known for making these releases fun whilst still including the correct information. People started to look forward to receiving them but most importantly, reading them. I hope that my writing continues to tackle difficult issues but in an accessible and enjoyable way.

Did your parents ever do anything horribly embarrassing to your teenage self?

I think there were probably times when just the fact that they breathed was embarrassing, but I was very lucky, either they weren't that embarrassing or I wasn't easily embarrassed.

On a lighter note ... Are you an Abba fan? If so ... name your favourite five Abba tracks?

Is anyone not an Abba fan? As a teenager I was a die-hard rock fan, proving that you can love both AC/DC and Abba. In no particular order my five top Abba tunes are: *Dancing Queen; Voulez Vous; Mamma Mia; Does Your Mother Know* and *Eagle*.

Do you know the lyrics to every Abba song?

No – but there was a time when I knew the lyrics to almost all Beatles songs!

 Follow Helenbaileybooks

Hodder
Children's
Books

www.hodderchildrens.co.uk

About the Author

Helen Bailey was born and brought up in Ponteland, Newcastle-upon-Tyne. Barely into her teens, Helen invested her pocket money in a copy of *The Writers' and Artists' Yearbook* and spent the next few years sending short stories and poems to anyone she could think of. Much to her surprise, she sometimes found herself in print. After a degree in science, Helen worked in the media and ran a successful London-based character licensing agency working on internationally renowned properties such as Snoopy, Dirty Dancing, Dilbert and Felicity Wishes. She lives in Highgate, north London and is the author of a number of short stories, young novels and picture books.

www.helenbaileybooks.com

From the best-selling author of the Electra Brown series

RUNNING IN HEELS

From riches ... to bitches.

Daisy Davenport has it all — stunning looks, a spectacular house, a seriously gorgeous boyfriend.

But when her father is sent to jail for corruption, Daisy's life is shattered. Forced to move into rooms above a kebab shop, she and her family have to readjust — fast.

And if life isn't hard enough already, Daisy's new school is a world away from her old one. And the school bully is going to make sure she remembers it ...

As hilarious as ever!

RUNNING IN HEELS

Helen Bailey

www.helenbaileybooks.com

www.hodderchildrens.co.uk

DARK
HEART
RISING

ENTER A WORLD WHERE ONE ENCHANTING
HEROINE MUST DECIDE BETWEEN TWO
DANGEROUSLY ENTICING CHOICES.

Not alive. Not dead. Somewhere in between
lie the Beautiful Dead.

A stunning series that will leave you restless.

Books 1-4
OUT NOW